PHILIP SWAN

WAARTER CATASTROPHE
"A Zoodunnit Murder Mystery"

CHAPTER 1- MONDAY 1 AUGUST (AM)

"It's not a sight you see very often, a young lion lying dead on the floor of a zoo café." said Ariana opening the Channel Roar Breakfast News programme.

Ariana is a pure-bred Peruvian Alpaca and renowned for her husky voice, beautiful face, perfect smile and lightly tanned curvy features.

As a result, she has an army of animal admirers across not only the UK but also around the world.

More importantly, for Channel Roar, she also commanded extremely high animal television viewing figures for the breakfast news show.

Ariana stared straight into the camera, deciding not to flash her smile,

"At Hearts River Zoo last night, Barnsley, the son of the famous lion couple Oscar and Poppy, was found dead in the zoo's café. Some of you may find the next picture shocking so please turn away now."

This was an old ploy that was guaranteed to ensure that everyone, whatever they were doing, stopped what they were doing to watch what was about to be shown on the television screen.

A picture filled the television screens showing Barnsley on the café floor with a bottle of water sticking out of his mouth.

Ariana was perched on the edge of her news desk and dressed in an immaculate Pranda black silk trouser suit.

"Last night Barnsley was hosting a launch party of his new project WAAR, Wild Animals Alcoholic Reform, in the Hearts River Zoo café. He was found dead by one of the zoo animals around 9.00. Although the circumstances surrounding Barnsley's death remains a mystery, it is believed he was choked to death with a bottle of water. We will keep you updated on the search for his killer."

Ariana changed from looking solemn, flashed her perfect teeth and in a more upbeat tone carried on.

"Other news today Prime Minister David Cormorant is today…"

At this point all the animals in Hearts River Zoo who had been watching their television sets turned them off.

They looked at each other in stunned silence.

There was an uneasy atmosphere around the enclosures.

The mysterious death was affecting everyone as they all knew Barnsley.

Also, there was now the possibility that a killer was living in their zoo and that it could be any one of them.

Their happy life at the zoo had now been ended abruptly by this horrific event.

If Barnsley had been murdered, they knew normality would not return until his killer or killers had been caught.

The zoo manager Andy Cousins arrived as usual around 7.30 to open the zoo for the day. He enjoyed arriving early as it gave him the opportunity to wander around looking at all the animals without anyone else being around.

At 7.45 the café manager Karen Chambers arrived at the zoo.

After she had entered the café and found Barnsley dead on the floor a large scream was heard echoing around the zoo. She had rushed to find Iain Moore the lion zookeeper. She then told him that there was a dead lion on her café floor.

Iain couldn't believe the news and at first thought she was joking and when he realised that she wasn't he rushed to Andy's office to tell him the news.

They picked up some tranquilizer guns in case Barnsley was still alive or in case the other lions had escaped as well and were roaming loose.

They then ran to the café collecting other quizzical looking zookeepers on their way.

They arrived to find Karen in a very shocked state.

They entered cautiously and went over to the body of the lion and checked to make sure it was dead.

Andy then used his mobile phone to call the zoo's

vet Doctor Mike, as he was known to both the zoo's staff and the zoo's animals. He was eating his breakfast when his mobile phone rang. After hearing the news, he rushed over to the zoo.

He went immediately to the café and met up with Andy and some of the other zookeepers outside. He was then given an update.

He went inside and checked that Barnsley was dead and then came out looking very shaken.

He arranged for the body to be transported to his surgery so he could immediately undertake an autopsy to determine the cause of death.

He needed to quickly determine the cause of death. It looked to him like it was choking accident with the water bottle.

Also, he was concerned that there might be something dangerous in the water bottle.

He was concerned that a wild and dangerous animal that didn't live in the zoo could have been responsible. If so it might still be roaming loose around the zoo and he would need to alert the zookeepers. Depending on what animal it was local support agencies might need to be alerted as quickly as possible to try and capture whatever it was.

He was still puzzled as how the water bottle fitted in with the death.

After consultations with Doctor Mike, Andy had decided to close the zoo for the day. They needed time to fully investigate what had happened the previous night.

Andy was extremely worried as not only did he have a dead lion to deal with but also, he needed to find out how it had escaped in the first place.

Animal escapes were a major breach of all the Health and Safety rules for the zoo. He knew that investigators in suits would soon be crawling around for ages like flies around fresh elephant dung.

The human press started arriving after Andy contacted the local radio stations asking them to announce that the zoo was going to be closed for the day due to the death of one of the lions.

After interviewing Andy, Karen, and some of the keepers they took loads of pictures and then left quickly to hit their deadlines.

Andy had deliberately not mentioned that they suspected it had died from choking on a bottle of water.

Unfortunately, this piece of information had been leaked by the zookeepers when the press questioned them.

The zookeepers had spent the day trying to think of humorous puns that the newspaper headlines might use to report the death and the best headline they could come up with was "Water CATastrophe at Zoo."

The animal world's press had received an anonymous tip off late on Sunday night. Animal newspaper reporters and animal television news crews had arrived very early on Monday morning.

They had talked to some of the zoo's animals and had taken loads of pictures.

They had made sure that they left before Andy arrived to open the zoo.

The animal press had come with a similar headline "WAARter CATastrophe" that incorporated the name of Barnsley's launch venture.

The zookeepers undertook a thorough investigation of the zoo and its surrounds.

They couldn't find anything amiss at the lion's enclosure to indicate how the lion had managed to escape. They were scratching their heads as to how it could have happened.

Andy requested that the zookeepers undertake a full investigation as well of all the other enclosures to make sure they were safe, secure and that their occupants couldn't escape.

By mid- afternoon everything had been fully checked by the zookeepers and like the lion enclosure they had not found anything amiss during their checks.

When they finished all their checking, they all took the opportunity to leave early to make the most of what was left of a nice warm sunny day.

The zoo animals were all nervous as they knew that later that evening Oscar had called a meeting for them all to attend. He was convinced Barnsley had been murdered and wanted the killer caught. They were not looking forward to the meeting.

CHAPTER 2- MONDAY 1 AUGUST (PM)

The previous evening outside the café where Barnsley's body still lay Oscar had amassed nearly all the zoo animals for a meeting.

He had told them that they must attend a meeting he was arranging for Monday evening at 8.00 in the seal house to discuss Barnsley's murder and agree how to capture his killer.

There was an uneasy nervousness around the seal house as the zoo animals started arriving for the meeting.

None of them were speaking and they were all in place and sitting quietly by 7.50.

There were bright pink flamingos sitting next to zebras and rhinos sitting with camels.

Even the apes, who were usually the most mischievous, were all sitting quietly in their seats.

They all knew there was a time for mucking about and this was not it.

The room fell silent as Oscar entered closely followed by his wife Poppy.

Poppy was still looking very upset and red eyed from the previous night's shocking event. She was dressed in a long black dress.

Oscar was dressed in a black polo shirt and black jeans.

He slowly made his way to the front stage looking left to right to stare at as many of the animals as he could.

He reached the front and turned around to face all the animals.

They were all staring at him wondering what he was about to say.

He stared at them all and made them all feel very uncomfortable before he started the meeting.

He taped the microphone in front of him to make sure it was working.

He looked at Poppy who nodded that she was ready.

"A heinous crime was committed last night in the grounds of our lovely zoo. I believe my son Barnsley was murdered in Aussie's café last night between 8.15 and just after 9.00."

He paused, wanting the full effects of his statement to be digested by all the animals.

"We must have justice done. We cannot have animals killing each other in our zoo. We must find my son's killer quickly and only then will peace and harmony return to our lovely zoo. Everyone must again feel safe lying in their beds at night."

He looked and saw there was a general nodding by all the animals in agreement.

They all wanted to get back to normality as quickly as was possible.

"Before I start does anyone want to confess now that they killed Barnsley?"

There was silence whilst everyone looked around nervously.

"In that case I only want someone from this zoo to investigate his murder. I demand that one of you agrees to take on the responsibility of investigating this heinous crime, uncovering the murderer" pausing "or murderers" pausing for this to hit home before carrying on "and to bring them to justice. Is there anyone here prepared to take on this responsibility for not only Poppy, and me but also the rest of the zoo?"

Slowly all the eyes turned to look at a grey-haired elderly moose dressed in a red Canadian Mountie style tunic and black trousers who had stood up slowly from his chair.

His nickname was Mountie, and no one knew what his real name was.

He had constantly mentioned what a great detective he thought he would have been.

He had appeared in a few long-forgotten episodes of Due South a Canadian crime comedy/drama television series.

He had started putting on red Canadian Mountie tunics during the filming and had always thought how much smarter he looked in the uniform than the star of the show Constable Benton Fraser.

He had mentioned this to brother after the filming stopped and was overjoyed when his brother presented him with his first red tunic as a Christmas present. Then every subsequent Christmas his brother shipped over another new one from Canada where he lived.

It was a staple part of his regular out of zoo hours dress attire.

He liked his nickname and was comfortable with everyone calling him by it.

Everyone knew that he loved his detective novels.

He had briefly courted fame by appearing on Mastermind with his specialist subjects being first Agatha Christine then Arthur Conan Doyle and in the semifinals Edgar Allen Poe. He was extremely upset when he was beaten by a Shetland sheepdog whose specialist subject was the popular soap opera called Emmerdale. This had the same weekly storyline as the human version, but from a farm animals' perspective and with the farm animals being the lead actors. He was so upset that he never watched the show again.

Mountie was looking very thoughtful and didn't look at anybody as he slowly walked up to where Oscar was standing on the stage.

He then turned to face everyone and began to slowly spoke in his Canadian accent.

"Oscar it will be a real honor for me to investigate the possible murder of Barnsley."

He then put on a very stern face.

"I will though expect complete co-operation

from all of you."

Pausing to stare around at the animals' reactions.

"You can be sure I will leave no stone unturned in the pursuit of my investigation".

"Well, he better be careful manhandling my stone "said Bruce, a scorpion, rather too loudly to Jerry, a Cobra, whom he was sitting next to.

Suddenly they realised that all the eyes in the seal house were now looking at them.

"Err, Sorry" said Bruce who had gone as bright red as a scorpion can be with embarrassment.

Mountie coughed loudly over the microphone regaining everyone's attention.

"In addition, though I would like a volunteer to help me with this investigation. I envisage that it could turn out to be a very complex case and I would appreciate some support."

Everyone started to look around nervously hoping that someone would volunteer.

"I don't mind helping out as I have always fancied being a bit of a detective" announced Charlton with his Geordie accent.

Charlton, a football loving zebra, was wearing a red Manchester United AFC (Animal Football Club) football shirt and sporting a matching red colored mane gelled into a Mohican hairstyle had got up from his seat.

Some of the audience started talking loudly.
Others sat back relieved as this meant Oscar would not have to press gang one of them to take

on this responsibility.

The Mountie and Charlton investigation team was duly born that minute.

Oscar stepped up to the microphone and stared hard at everyone present.

"I would like to thank you both on behalf of everyone here for agreeing to undertake this murder investigation. I expect FULL cooperation from everyone present or else you will have me to answer to."

Everyone sat nodding their heads in agreement, not relishing the thought of having to answer for their actions to Oscar. It was normally a very unpleasant experience as Oscar was head animal and ran the zoo.

As there was nothing else to say he gave Poppy a big hug and they both walked out together not looking at any of the other animals on their way out.

Everyone got up from their seats and trudged back to their various enclosures discussing the events of the meeting.

Mountie and Charlton stayed behind.

"Thanks a lot for offering to help me," said Mountie.

Charlton joined him on the stage.

"That's okay, as I said I have always wanted to be a bit of a detective and things have been a bit quiet around here anyway."

"You can say that again. We do need to meet

urgently to work out a plan of action."
"How about tomorrow morning, I'm usually up early."
"Fine, I'm also a morning person shall we meet at my hut around 6.15?"
"That sounds perfect; I'll look forward to seeing you in the morning."
Mountie was looking very thoughtful.
"Okay but you do realize the full implications of this investigation. We are going to be tracking down a lion killer in our zoo. We don't know who or whom they are. You never know they could even be a fellow zebra are you sure you still want to be involved?"
He pondered over what Mountie had just said for a minute.
"I'm still game if you are."
Mountie started to smile.
"I'm still game as well; I'll see you in the morning bright and early."
Charlton nodded and turned and started to walk home.
Mountie sat in his chair looking intently at the water in the seal demonstration pool. Lots of thoughts were spinning in his head and he was looking forward to getting started in the morning and also the prospect of working with Charlton. He was glad to be working with someone who had volunteered rather than a pressganged helper.

CHAPTER 3 – TUESDAY 2 AUGUST (AM)

Hearts River Zoo is in the Hearts River Hall estate on the outskirts of Hearts River town. The estate is set in 250 acres of rolling English countryside. The Hall had been the stately residence for generations of the Packer family.

The first Lord Packer had made his fortune shipping various supplies around the world.

It had been built to his own specifications in the 1700's.

Due to his extensive worldwide travels it was an eclectic mix of Greek, Egyptian, Tudor, and Gothic architectural designs. It was resplendent with an array of fancy domes and turrets with weird statues adorning them.

The last Packer to reside at the hall had been Sir David, a celebrity naturalist.

He had specialized in producing and starring in some very popular and funny marine television documentaries.

He had been a very active member of Greenpeace. His face was on several of their posters, one of which had been positioned in pride of place behind his work desk at the Hall.

Unfortunately, whilst making a documentary in North Australia he had accidentally been stung by a deadly sea wasp box jellyfish. Despite various attempts to save him he had died very quickly afterwards.

Whilst alive he had been passionately pursuing setting up a zoo on his estate.

Plans and designs for its construction had been completed and planning permission had been granted by the local authorities without any objections.

He was single when he died and in his will were strict instructions for a set of trustees to complete the construction of Hearts River Zoo and undertake its daily management.

The nominated trustees were all fellow naturalists who had relished the task of completing the building of the zoo and they loved running it.

They had converted the Hall into a visitor centre commemorating the work of Sir David. It also covered the lives and times of the previous Packer family members that had lived there as well.

One room was set aside for the memory of Sir David and contained a large screen that was constantly playing his famous documentaries.

Sir David had built a great relationship with the local schools in town and had loved visiting the children to tell them about his escapades around the world.

He had stipulated in his will that classes from the local schools should each be allocated an animal enclosure for the new zoo. They had to come up with a design for their enclosure that would then built for them.

At 6.15 Charlton grabbed a slice of toast and added some strawberry jam
He was wearing a pair of blue jeans and a red Manchester United AFC football shirt. It was his favourite Number 8 shirt resplendent with the name of his favourite Manchester AFC player "KEANGAROO" emblazoned in large white letters on the back of it.

The animals also loved football and had their own football leagues.
The top league games were played at night when it was easier for the animals to travel around to play or watch. The games were televised, and all the teams were well supported.

Being a Manchester United AFC supporter was a constant bone of contention not only with his Geordie born family but also with the other zebras in his enclosure who were all mad Newcastle United AFC football fans.
Charlton had the misfortune to have been born in Manchester Zoo on the day that Manchester United had beaten Newcastle United in the human FA Cup final.
A human joker on a local phone-in radio show had suggested that Manchester United might like to sponsor him.
The football team had thought this was a great idea and had named him Charlton after their

great footballing hero Sir Bobby.

The sponsorship was met with much amusement by the national press.

Pictures of Charlton in a Manchester United top had been splashed across the front pages of all the national papers and he had become a national celebrity for a short while.

When he was six, he had been moved to Newcastle Zoo with his mother and whilst there he had acquired his now familiar Geordie accent. Unfortunately, the move came too late to quell his love of Manchester United AFC despite fervent attempts from everyone in his family, every zebra at Newcastle Zoo and everyone in his current enclosure.

He left and walked to where Mountie lived.

As he approached his enclosure a big smile appeared on his face as it always did whenever he saw Mountie's hut.

The hut had been designed by a student in the lower 6 form of Hearts River Upper School. Unfortunately for Mountie, he had just returned from a Heli-skiing holiday in Canada.

The replica Canadian Mountain hut that graced Mountie's enclosure had been built using Canadian spruce trees that had been laid length ways on top of each other with a similar designed roof. The hut had a wooden door in the front and a window on each side.

Unfortunately, the young designer wanted the

enclosure to stand out and he had specified that a thirty-foot set of antlers be erected on the roof.
Mountie hated them intensely.
Much to his disgust they were regularly used either at Christmas or other times to have horrendous flashing lights hang from them.

Charlton knocked on the door and entered to find Mountie putting on his red tunic.
He beckoned Charlton over to the table.
On it was a notepad with some writing on it and a Monte Skunk ink pen.

The Monte Skunk pen was the brainchild of Monte, an American skunk who had got fed up with unreliable pens.
He had started successfully making upmarket reliable black and white coloured ink pens with the end modelled on his large tail.
The pens could be ordered with a selection of aromas, although aroma a la skunk was not on the options list.

Also on the table was a large gold coloured cafeteria and the aroma of freshly ground Peruvian coffee filled the hut.
Charlton knew Mountie only drank Peruvian coffee.
He hadn't discovered if the rumour was true that Mountie acquired his love for Peruvian ground coffee after dating the glamorous Channel Roar news presenter Ariana. He knew their paths had

crossed once at a zoo in France.

Mountie though liked to keep everyone guessing. It was true that he had dated her but wanted to avoid the inevitable questions about why he had stopped dating such a charismatic and gorgeous looking famous female animal. There had been a lot of Peruvian coffee that had flowed under the bridge since then.

Charlton had known Mountie for a couple of years, but this was the first time he had been invited into his hut.

He sat down next to the table and looked around the hut, which was quite small.

Mountie lived quite happily by himself.

On one wall was a framed Due South poster that had been signed by the cast following one of the episodes that he had appeared in. It was one of his most prized possessions as it reminded him of some happy times he had spent on the television sets.

Charlton continued looking around and saw that taking prime position on a side table was a Bang and Elephant stereo system above which were shelves full of CD's, records, and tapes.

Bang and Elephant produced high quality bespoke musical equipment.

Kristen had been a music loving elephant living happily in the Serengeti.

Unfortunately, during his capture a gun had gone off "bang" and had affected his hearing.

When he arrived at Windsor Safari Park, he realised that to continue with his love of music he would need a bespoke music system building and couldn't get hold of one.

Living at the park was a kangaroo called Adrian who was an electronics wizard and was able to build a bespoke music system for him.

Seeing a gap in the market Kristen set up the company and named it after his capture episode. Adrian made all the bespoke musical equipment that was ordered whilst Kristen managed the sales.

"Like your music, do you?"

"It's my main passion. I have the complete set of concertos by Moozart and Beetlehoven."

Mountie finished the last button on his tunic.

"Not really my cup of tea, more a punk man myself give me the Sex Pythons any day,"

He started stroking his mane that was always gelled into a striking Mohican when the zoo was shut.

He noticed the scowl on Mounties face and decided it was best to change the subject.

"Did you see Ariana on Channel Roar News this morning, they covered Barnsley's murder,".

He started looking round the hut trying unsuccessfully to locate a television set.

Mountie came and sat down in front of his notes.

"Alas Charlton I no longer have a television set. Two years ago, I turned on my set to find myself watching a tall mad man with a moustache trying to mount the head of my Uncle Eric on the wall of his hotel. What's more he broke one of his beloved antlers that he was so proud of."

Mountie was looking solemn.

"The final straw was that people were laughing at this and so I decided to ditch the television in protest. What made it even worse was that I didn't know that Uncle Eric was dead. Although I must admit it did explain the lack of Christmas card that year"

Charlton looked at his watch.

"Looks like the zoo will be opening soon. Where are you suggesting we start our investigation when the zoo closes tonight?"

Mountie looked down at his note pad.

"Tonight, I believe we need to investigate the scene of the crime, then speak to Aussie who runs the café. Then we need to visit Oscar and Poppy which I am not looking forward to."

"Me neither"

A loud siren went off in the hut.

The siren is to alert everyone that the zoo is opening shortly, or someone is coming on site and to revert to being seen as a zoo animal.

"Ah that means it is opening time and we will reconvene here at 6.30 this evening."

Mountie closed his notebook."

"And remember everything we discuss about this investigation is confidential and for our ears only, alright?".

Charlton nodded his head in agreement.

He headed out the door and made his way slowly back home.

He started to wonder how the investigation might pan out.

He was not looking forward to the prospect of interviewing Oscar and Poppy later as the reality of what he had agreed to do began to sink in. It was about to get serious.

CHAPTER 4- TUESDAY 2 AUGUST (PM)

The zoo had been very busy during the day.
The news about the suspicious death of a lion had not put visitors off instead it had encouraged more visitors to come.
Some visitors had even complained about the absence of the dead lion in the café.
The café staff had been constantly asked where the dead lion had been found.
By lunchtime one of them had drawn a white chalk outline of a dead lion in the middle of the café floor much to the amusement of the visitors.
Although following a complaint Andy Cousins visited the café and demanded its removal.

Andy always locked up around 6.00 pm handing over the zoo's security to two security guards at the main gate house.
Every night the guards thought they were keeping watch of the zoo via various closed-circuit television cameras positioned around the zoo.
What they didn't know about was a gorilla called Lemming.
He was a whizz with all things electrical and had tampered with the closed-circuit television camera system. As a result, the security guards bank of screens each night replayed the same

piece of film showing a quiet trouble-free zoo.

This allowed the zoo animals to roam around and do as they please undetected.

Lemming had also laid warning sensors around the outside of the main zoo complex in case the guards ever decided to go for a stroll, which they never did, or if any zoo staff returned unexpectedly during the night. If someone did try to enter an alarm would go off in all the enclosures warning them to electronically switch their enclosures back from their luxury pads to look like their normal daytime zoo animal enclosures.

During the day the zoo's café "Out of Africa" catered for the visitors.

It was a large circular building covered in bamboo canes trying to make it look like a jungle hut with a fake straw roof. It had bright yellow doors covered with tigers, lions, and elephant stencils.

Inside the walls were covered with pictures of all the zoo animals and on a large desk there were two computers set up to promote the zoo's activities and its website.

At night the café was run by a large orangutan called Aussie who served hot food, soft and alcoholic drinks from 6.30 through to 1.00 every night.

During these hours the two computers were switched over to the WWW (World Wildlife

Web) for use by the animals to surf the net, download films/music/games and more importantly keep in touch with their families all over the world.

Due to the popularity of animal orientated tablets and laptops Aussie had also acquired a Wi-Fi hotspot to give them web access when the café was shut.

Aussie grew up in Sydney Zoo and had acquired a very broad Australian accent, a love of Australian lager and barbeque food which he sometimes served at the cafe.

Apart from running the café he was responsible for maintaining and running the two computers and the Wi-Fi in the café for the animals' use.

He had first started to become interested in computers whilst his stay at Silicon Valley Zoo. One morning he had overheard an engineer commenting that the programming of the zoo's computer looked like it had been done by a monkey.

Aussie took this as a compliment that a fellow ape could program computers but also as a challenge as he did not want to be outsmarted by a monkey. He decided to take up programming through a correspondence course and had picked it up very quickly.

So much so, that in the evening he had started moonlighting as a computer programmer at a local software company.

Much to his surprise his lack of English and strange looking appearance had done nothing to slow his career progress at the firm.

The only time he had been challenged by a fellow programmer about his funny language he had somehow muttered the word "Klingon" and this magically increased his social standing in the company dramatically.

Unfortunately, he had moved from Silicon Valley to England, and it had really upset him.

He just completed designing the Apepod music player. "So easy an ape could use it" would have been his marketing strap line.

After his move to England, he thought it would never see the light of day because some of the designs had been left behind due to the speediness of his zoo transfer.

He was extremely upset to hear that an ape called Lee, at his previous zoo, had copied his designs and had set up a firm called APELEE. He had made millions selling his Apepod music player machine and Aussie hadn't make a penny. They were now also making multimedia devices and mobile phones.

As such all the zoo animals were banned by Aussie from using any APELEE device.

At 6.30 pm Charlton knocked on the door of Mountie's hut and entered when he was invited him to come inside.

"So where do you fancy starting first then?" said

Charlton keenly to Mountie.

Charlton was feeling really pleased with himself as he had gone via the zoo shop on his way there. He had acquired himself a lurid lime green notebook with a picture of a Cobra and a Hearts River Zoo logo on the front and a matching lurid lime green ballpoint pen with an adder twirling around its case.

He was raring to go and a bit put out to find Mountie was just sitting in his chair half-dressed reading his leather-bound notepad and scratching his head.

"Shouldn't we be up and at them?" said Charlton standing impatiently.

"There's plenty of time."

Mountie looked up at Charlton, smiled and then resumed looking at his notebook.

Charlton decided to sit back down and wait.

Another 5 minutes of silence passed by before Mountie rose and put on a white shirt and his red Tunic.

"I think we ought to start by seeing Aussie at the scene of the crime".

"That sounds like a great place to start."

Charlton got up pleased that they were finally about to start the investigation.

They left and walked slowly over to the café.

Charlton got the impression that Mountie had a lot on his mind and didn't want to talk so he kept quiet on the walk over.

They reached the café and stopped outside.

Mountie suggested that they start by having a look around and spent 15 minutes looking to see if they could find any clues.

Mountie kept bending down, poking at things, and then scratching his head.

"I doubt if you will find anything useful here now. We have had three coach loads of kids visit today and you know how they usually trash the café area leaving cans and food everywhere".

Charlton started looking expectantly at the café entrance door.

Mountie ignored Charlton and carried on looking at the ground outside the café.

Charlton stood back as he considered it a waste of time and waited patiently for him to finish.

Suddenly Mountie stopped behind a bush adjacent to one of the café's windows.

"That's a bit odd" he said from behind the bush.

Charlton moved behind the bush to see what he was referring to.

Mountie pointed to a small green bottle on the floor.

"Looks like it's a bottle of Glen Pig Ditch whisky that only animals drink."

"Ah fresh from the Sties in Skye" Charlton recited their advert whilst trying to put on a scotch accent.

"And that is where it should have stayed "said Mountie under his breath.

He hated this commercially produced blended whisky and often wondered what this brand was blended with by looking at the colour.

"Do you think it is important" said Charlton staring blankly at the bottle.

"Well, WAAR was all about alcohol and the position of this bottle suggests that its owner could have been hiding behind this bush watching the cafe, although we can't tell whether it is recent or not" said Mountie staring at the bottle "On a positive note though it does look like it hasn't been disturbed by the kids today".

"If it was recent then the bottle's owner may have seen what happened when Barnsley got murdered" Charlton said excitedly.

"Or the bottle's owner might be our killer" said Mountie in a surprisingly calm voice.

He carefully bent down and picked up the bottle with a handkerchief and placed it carefully in his tunic pocket.

"I think we will keep this safe until we determine whether it is evidence or not. Do not mention this to anyone."

"Trust me I won't"

"OK Let's go in and see Aussie."

Mountie was still brushing some dirt from the knee area of his trousers as they entered.

"Evening Gent's" said the Australian voice of Aussie.

He was the only one in the café and was cleaning a table with a dishcloth.

He was dressed in a pair of black Levis jeans and a

black T shirt with white writing that read "Born to be a Wild Animal".

"I wasn't sure whether to open or not. I am beginning to wish I hadn't as you are my only customers so far, this evening."

He moved back to the bar and stood behind the beer taps.

"Would you two like some drinks, on the house of course?"

"Thanks, but we have a lot to cover tonight," said Mountie.

Charlton was upset as he was about to order his favourite Newcastle Brown Ale.

Mountie went over to the desk and saw both computers were switched on.

They both had the same screen saver of Aussie swinging on a vine from one side of the screen to the other singing the Men at Work song "Down under".

Mountie was visibly appalled by the tackiness of the screen saver.

Charlton started to laugh upon seeing it.

"Do you have any problems with the computers?" Mountie shouted to Aussie.

"The main problem is stopping them chimp's searching for porn, those nature programs have a lot to answer for."

Aussie joined them by the computers.

"Attenborough as a search engine request has now been blocked. Rory the chimp was in here searching "Attenborough" and came across film of two chimps having sex. Only for him to then realise that the chimps were in fact his parents. Then seeing the date of the film, it dawned on him that he had may well have been the result of this on-screen amorous encounter. He was so shocked he fell off his stool and broke his arm" said Aussie smiling as he remembered the shocked expression on Rory face.

"I have now programmed the computers to set off an alarm when certain key words are typed in and it results in much embarrassment by the guilty users. Although some of the chimps now use the Wi-Fi facility so as much as I try, I can't stop them watching or downloading whatever they want on their tablets especially Rory."

Mountie sat down at a chair in front of one of the computers and put his notepad and pen down beside it.

Aussie and Charlton both pulled up chairs and sat in them.

Mountie opened his notebook and turned to Aussie.

"How did you get on with Barnsley?"

Aussie leant back in his chair before replying.

"I had been getting on very well with him. The WAAR project was excellent for him. He designed and built his own WAAR website. He had finally found something he could properly focus on and make a success of."

Charlton and Mountie nodded their heads in agreement.

"You both remember how Oscar let rip after Jasper the Guinea pig found him in a drunken stupor in the zoo manager's office minutes before he arrived for work."

"I think everyone inside and outside the zoo heard what Oscar said to him after that" said Charlton smiling.

" I did feel that he was hoping that by giving up the booze and successfully launching his WAAR project that Oscar might finally give him the respect and admiration that he so longed for from him."

Mountie wrote something in his notebook.

"What was your involvement with him and the website?"

Aussie climbed out of his chair and went towards the bar,

"You sure you two don't want a drink?" he said pulling a can of Toucan lager from the fridge.

Mountie shook his head in a "That is a no for both of us" sort of way.

He returned and sat back down and opened his can of lager.

"About two months ago he came in and asked me whether there were any websites aimed at helping other alcoholic zoo animals. I started to do some searches for him which was quite funny as my computer alarms for inappropriate searches kept going off. We both had a good laugh at that."

Aussie had a smile on his face.

"When we found no other sites, he proudly said that he didn't care that he didn't know how to do it and decided there and then to go ahead and set one up."

"So, what happened then" said Charlton enviously eyeing up the can of lager.

"Well, I registered a site for him. We then discussed the layout of his new site. We then worked closely together and created the website that he had dreamed of. I showed him how to use the other tools on the computer to design and print off posters and leaflets that he then distributed around the zoo."

"Were you close to him?" said Mountie.

"Not that close. Look, Barnsley was just a strange kid who on numerous occasions I had to throw out of here when he got drunk. He had turned the corner and wanted to act as a grown up. He wanted more than anything to finally prove to Oscar that he could start something and follow it all the way through to completion. He learnt a lot on the way, and I think he could have been a good computer programmer if he had put his mind to it. It's just a great shame that he was killed" said Aussie looking a bit upset.

"What did he say about Oscar" continued Mountie.

"He just really wanted Oscar to be proud of him. He appreciated that it was hard on him having to run the zoo whilst constantly having to ignore rude comments and jokes about his dysfunctional son. Whilst Oscar always appeared to swat off the rude comments in a carefree manner, deep down I think he was really upset about him. He was concerned that his actions reflected badly on him and his authority."

"Was he happy living here?" asked Charlton.

"Whilst working on the website he was very happy. Also, he was really pleased as the launch seemed to have cheered everybody up. All the animals found it amusing to go around singing the chorus to Edwin Starr's "War" song whenever they saw Barnsley or if they were just celebrating being drunk."

Aussie started to hum the song until he saw Mountie's face scowling.

Mountie had got fed up hearing the song every night and there was always a loud drunken version sung by the animals leaving Aussie's cafe at closing time.

"Barnsley took it all in stride and with good humour as there was never anything malicious about it." said Aussie taking another sip of lager.

"Do you know if his website or the launch had upset anyone else in the zoo" said Mountie now eyeing the lager and wishing he had taken up Aussie's offer.

"Everyone found Barnsley harmless. Some quite liked the idea of having alcohol support around here, obviously not me as I would go out of business very quickly,"

He paused before continuing.

"Although he did have a run in with Crocket the flamingo though."

"Why was that" said Charlton interrupting Aussie's flow.

He got his question just before Mountie was able to ask the same thing.

"He was very upset when he found out Barnsley had arranged his launch night at the same time as his fashion show. He had a very heated argument with him to get him to move his dates. Afterwards he just stopped pestering Barnsley as he suspected that no one was going to attend the WAAR launch party anyway."

Aussie sipped some of his lager.

"Actually, Crocket ended up really pleased because word of his argument with Barnsley spread around the zoo and increased awareness of his fashion show. He was convinced that Barnsley would turn up at the show. It was rumoured that if he did then Crocket was going to make a spectacle of him by covering him in champagne."

Aussie finished off his lager and started going to the fridge for another one and turned around.

"You sure I can't get you one?"

"Okay, but just the one" said Mountie with a relieved look on his face.

A relieved look also came across Charlton's face.

Aussie returned with three cans of lager and passed them out and started drinking from the last can himself.

"Can you tell us what happened that night." said Mountie taking a drink of lager.

"Well, the zoo shut at 6.00. As it had been a warm day, I decided around 6.30 to go out for a blast on my Harley Davidson Fat Boy."

Aussie was in the local Hells Angel's gang and his uncanny ability to say "Ug" at the right time had elevated him to the lofty position of leader. Also, his physique had become a real draw for the women at the Hells Angels meets and he was seldom seen without a pretty leather clad female biker by his side.

"I got back around 7.15. I opened the café for him at 7.30 as the launch party was starting at 8.00. I left him to set everything up in readiness for it. I also left him with the bottles of water and some soft drinks as they had not been delivered in time."

Aussie sipped his lager.

"I was okay leaving him there as I trusted him. I also suspected no one would be turning up to the event anyway. Last thing I said to him was that I would be back to lock up after the show. You see Crocket had asked me to run the bar there and I had enlisted my drinking buddies George and Willie the camels to help."

"Blimey fancy asking the zoo's three leading piss artists, especially Willie three bellies, to run a bar. I assume it wasn't being run for a profit" laughed Charlton loudly.

Charlton received a stern stare from Mountie and a wry smile from Aussie.

"Excuse Charlton and please continue."

"Well in return for the promise of free beer George and Willie had agreed to help set up the bar whilst I was out on the Harley. After leaving Barnsley in the café, I went to see how they were getting on with setting up the bar and helped them finish. After that I was serving at the bar with them and getting interval drinks orders ready, it was a busy evening."

Aussie paused to drink some lager.

"I did though keep half an eye out for Barnsley. Then at 9.15 Crockett made the announcement that he had been found dead and I rushed over to the café like everyone else. Oscar did let me into the café, and I found him lying dead in front of the food counter. It was a very shocking sight."

Aussie sat back in his chair and closed his eyes.

Mountie turned his head and looked at the computer screen next to him.

"Are we still able to look at the WAAR website?"

Aussie opened his eyes and noisily scrapped his chair over to the computer next to Mountie.

"Sure, you can I haven't closed it down yet in case it was needed as part of the investigation".

Aussie began typing on the computer keyboard and the computer screen changed.

Suddenly Barnsley's cheery face appeared on screen saying "Welcome to WAAR. Are you a wild animal? Do you drink too much alcohol? Do you want to give it up? Then let me help you on your road to a sober reformation."

It was very spooky seeing his face and hearing his voice again.

They all fell silent while they remembered personal memories they each had of Barnsley.

Aussie then started to show them around the WAAR website. There was a feature on Barnsley saying who he was, who his parents were, where he lived and his likes and dislikes.

There was also a large section about the launch party with details of when it was, where to meet and telling viewers that it was free entry, and anyone could either join him at the Aussie's café in person or interactively online.

"Is that all of it?" said Mountie.

"There is a message board, do you want me to see if there are any messages on it?" said Aussie typing away on the computer.

"Yes, please that would be great," said Mountie.

Although he had noticed that Aussie had started typing away already.

They moved closer to see what was on the screen as Aussie carried on typing away.

Then a new screen popped up which showed that the mailbox contained six messages

"Damn the invention of junk emails. There are three messages for ViAgRa, one about a mis-sold pension and one flogging fake Rolex watches, I really must get those spam filters sorted out."

"What about that message?" said Charlton pointing to a message near the bottom of the computer screen?

Aussie clicked on the message and then with a big smile on his face he read out the message in his broad Australian accent.

"Dear Barnsley. I am a Komodo dragon living in Sydney Zoo. I am 42 years old and spend all day drinking beer. Unfortunately, the female Komodo dragons in the zoo have just discovered they can reproduce without me. Any useful tips for getting back in with the Komodo babes would be appreciated. Good luck with the new site. G'day Gus"

"Thanks a lot for that," said Mountie.

He looked at his real Rolex watch to see how they were doing for time.

"Is there anything else you can think of that might help us?"

Mountie started finishing off his lager and Charlton took the hint to drink up as well.

"Not that I can think of" said Aussie scratching his head.

"Well thanks a lot for all your help. We need to be off now and see Oscar and Poppy."

Mountie walked over to the front of the food counter and began staring at the floor.

Aussie came up behind him.

"Yes, down there is where I saw the dead body. Although you won't find anything to help with your investigation as it has been professionally cleaned before the café was allowed to re-open this morning"

He nodded and started to make his way towards the door.

"I suppose I may as well close up unless you two are thinking of coming back later after seeing Oscar" said Aussie walking back behind the bar.

They both shook their heads and left the cafe.

"Are you ready to interview Oscar and Poppy?" said Mountie.

"My only interaction with Oscar is usually when the zebras have done something stupid. So hopefully I might be able to get them some brownie points tonight."

"Well, we know everyone is so pleased that we have taken on the investigation I am expecting we will get a warm welcome."

"Let's hope so."

CHAPTER 5- TUESDAY 2
AUGUST (PM-LATER)

It was still pleasantly warm and sunny at 8.30 when they left the café.

They had another look outside the café to see if they had missed anything from their earlier search but unfortunately couldn't discover anything more untoward.

Mountie looked at his watch and interrupted Charlton who was on the ground searching around the front door.

"I think we have just enough time to see Oscar and Poppy if we go now."

"I'm still not looking forward to this. We have only just started the investigation and haven't really got anything to go on yet."

"On the contrary Charlton. We are now taking notes and building up a picture as to what happened that evening. We now have some valuable insight into Barnsley's activities from Aussie. Don't forget the whisky bottle we found earlier may be relevant so best not to mention it to Oscar just yet."

They started walking towards the lion enclosure, reached the outer fence and looked in.

The lion house was shaped like a large tent.
A student in year 5 of Hearts River Upper School

had been watching a Lawrence of Arabia film and she had suggested that it be shaped in the style of a large Bedouin tent.

The tent design had been made from sheet metal and painted a bright white, which was now not quite so bright and was beginning to look in need of a new coat of paint.

The back of the tent was a glass wall so that visitors could still see the lions when they were in the tent.

Oscar had employed Lemming to fit some electronic sliding curtains that covered the window when the zoo visitors had left.

The tent roof had been designed to slope down at a sufficient angle to allow the lions to lie out on it.

In the centre of the roof there was a tall flagpole with a Hearts River Zoo flag proudly flying from it.

Also, at the suggestion of one of the students there were two large gold-coloured sphinxes positioned looking like they were guarding the entrance to the tent.

They entered the enclosure and walked between the sphinxes and pressed the doorbell button.

They heard a large loud roar come from somewhere inside the tent.

They looked at each other and smiled as they realised in unison that it was the sound of the doorbell.

The door was finally opened, and they were met by Poppy.

Poppy was looking impeccable in a short black Pranda dress that perfectly highlighted her slim figure. She had short blond hair and just the right amount of make-up needed to bring out the best of her attractive face.

Her marriage to Oscar had been somewhat of a coup for her as she had been brought up in Colchester Zoo. Thanks to her mother having great ambitions for her she had taken elocution lessons to hide her broad Essex accent.

She had met Oscar when she arrived at Hearts River Zoo.

Before arriving she already had a crush on him as he regularly featured in television shows and feature films. She even had some posters of him on her bedroom wall whilst at Colchester Zoo.

Oscar's showbiz family roots stretched back to his Great Granddad Leo who had been the first lion to appear in the Metro Goldwyn Mayer studio cinema production logo.

Then his cousin Jackie had taken over and became the first audible roaring lion for the same logo.

"Sorry I took so long to answer. I suspect you have come to see Oscar. Unfortunately, he is out, but he will be back very shortly. Due to the glorious evening weather, we have been having, he's taken to going swimming in the Hearts River most evenings. I'm surprised no one has spotted him and reported him yet."

Poppy stopped talking and just stood there smiling.

Mountie and Charlton just carried on standing there.

Finally, the penny dropped with Poppy.

"Where are my manners? I mustn't keep you waiting on the doorstep, do come inside." said an embarrassed Poppy and ushered them into the tent.

It was the first time they had been in the tent.

Instantly you could tell the relevance of the term "pride of lions", the place was spotlessly clean and clutter free.

Poppy led them into the sitting room where there was a large leather chair with the side pockets carefully filled with remote controls for a Television, DVD and Hi-Fi.

Charlton was jealous as he had seen this chair for sale on television. He knew that it also contained a drinks fridge and a Shiatsu massager.

The home entertainment systems were tastefully hidden behind made to measure dark oak wooden units.

There was one other large chair and a slightly smaller one with a couple of knitting needles and wool deposited in the middle. There was also a large sofa which Poppy directed them to sit down on.

"Would you like some tea or coffee?" said Poppy.

She had started walking towards the kitchen and cocked her head back in the direction of Mountie. "We do have Peruvian coffee which I believe is your favourite.".

"Coffee would be excellent," said Mountie.

He got himself comfortable and got out his notebook and pen.

Charlton decided to follow suit as.

She returned with a large tray containing a large cafeteria of steaming Peruvian coffee, some chocolate biscuits and four mugs.

She removed the knitting from her chair and then sat down.

"I know it is still very soon after Barnsley's death, but do you think you are up to answering some questions? I will understand if you say you are not ready yet" said Mountie leaning back on the sofa.

She took a deep breath and rubbed the corner of her left eye.

"I suppose I am as ready as I will ever be. Any way I want the killer caught quickly before they decide to strike again."

Charlton and Mountie exchanged glances as they hadn't really considered that the killer might strike again. They had both been assuming that this was the only one murder that they were going to have to investigate and not several.

"OK please can you tell us about Barnsley to give us some background information" said Mountie slowly.

"As you might know I was pregnant. Oscar and I were being moved down here from Edinburgh Zoo. I got severe pains, and the zookeeper alerted the nearest vet that we would have to make an emergency visit. The nearest vet was in a town called Barnsley and I ended up giving birth there. The vet turned out to be the Mayor of Barnsley and coincidentally the President of Barnsley District Lions Club. Spotting a brilliant PR opportunity he agreed to waive his charges if the new lion cub could be named Barnsley" said Poppy trying not to cry.

"It's funny how humans can affect our lives so much don't you agree Charlton."

"You can say that again Poppy. If things had been different, I could have been named Shearer and grown up a Newcastle United AFC fan and never known what it was like to follow a team that wins things" said Charlton with a big smile on his face whilst trying to lift the mood.

Whilst the comment appeared to cheer up Poppy, Mountie gave him a stern look.

"Please can you tell us when you first noticed that he had a drinking problem" said Mountie pen perched over the notebook.

She handed them a mug of coffee and motioned to help themselves to the biscuits.

"As you know visitors bring all sorts of things into the zoo especially cans of beer or lager. Instead of using the bins they often get thrown over the fences into our enclosures. Unknown to us Barnsley started to get a taste for it" said Poppy smiling.

She leant back in her chair and took a sip of coffee.

"As a mother I started to spot him walking funnily, falling over and being asleep more during the day. The penny finally dropped when we saw him encouraging the public to throw cans for him to catch, and turned out he was only catching the alcoholic ones."

Mountie took a sip of his coffee.

"So how did Oscar take it?"

"He was really shocked by it. He wanted us to keep quiet about Barnsley's drinking problem. He wouldn't listen to Oscar's pleas, and he took it as his green light to let the world know. Aussie frequently had to ban him from the café. The other animals started complaining to Oscar about his behaviour and about him being rude to them."

"What happened then?" said Charlton.

He was also taking notes but had been struggling to keep up.

Poppy smiled and waited till Charlton was ready before carrying on.

"At first Oscar accepted it and then came that final straw morning when Barnsley couldn't be found. Everyone was out looking for him and the zoo was about to open. At the last-minute Jasper, the guinea pig came by and told Oscar that Barnsley was sprawled out drunk in the zoo manager's office. I am still not sure how he managed to get in as even Jasper had struggled." said Poppy as a smile came over her face.

"Oscar arranged for him to be moved in the nick of time. I think the rest of the zoo heard him being told in no uncertain terms by Oscar what he thought of his drinking."

There was a moment's silence whilst they all took mouthfuls of coffee and bites of the chocolate biscuits.

"What did you think about this new WAAR project and his new internet venture?"

Poppy wiped some biscuit crumbs from the side of her mouth.

"At first, we were both skeptical about it especially as he was working on it at the café. Aussie kept an eye on him to make sure he didn't start drinking again and true to his promise to us he did stop drinking. He really got into it and we noticed a marked improvement in him both personally and with his confidence levels. He couldn't stop telling us what he was doing and what was going to happen next. He loved the computing side as well,"

She had another sip of her coffee.

"Oscar was initially concerned. Whilst he handled the backlash about Barnsley here, he didn't want the whole world to know about the troubles of his drunken son. Even more so on account of who he is and his famous family background."

"I can see his concerns as nothing is private once it gets on the internet. Aussie was only just telling us about what Rory had seen on the internet," said Charlton.

"As you were saying "said Mountie interrupting Charlton in mid flow.

Mountie was shaking his head in disbelief as to what Charlton was about to tell Poppy.

She was trying to muffle a laugh as she already knew the end of his story.

As the zoo's King and Queen there was not much that happened that in the zoo that they didn't know about. They had very good sources who kept them up to date with everything that affected the zoo, the local vicinity and the animals.

"In the end we could see how keen he was about setting up WAAR and his website. It was obvious he wanted to finally achieve something that we would be proud of him for. So, we ended up encouraging him as best we could,"

She leant forward with a hushed voice continued.

"Between the three of us though, Oscar and I were really dreading the launch night. Our contacts had hinted that no-one would turn up for it. We feared he might get so upset after all the work he had put in that he might return to hitting the bottle. We spoke to Aussie who also thought it wouldn't be a success as well and he agreed to Oscar's request to clear out all the alcoholic drinks on the night."

Charlton and Mountie looked at each other and noted that Aussie had failed to mention this.

"Did he have any enemies? Anybody who wanted to kill him." said Mountie changing tact.

"No not our Barnsley. Despite being very in your face at times everyone found him harmless. He did brighten up the place in an odd sort of way. I also loved humming along to that war song that everyone has adopted as well. Whenever I heard it in the zoo it usually let me know where Barnsley was"

Her face then went serious and sipped her coffee. Mountie noticed that the mug was starting to shake and hoped Oscar would appear soon.

"Although he did have some arguments with Crocket. It was because his launch night clashed with his fashion show but in the end it all fizzled out into nothing. I understand Crockett threatened to cover him in champagne if he turned up."

A large smile came across Poppy's face.

"You went to the show, didn't you?" said Charlton looking up from his notepad.

"Yes, I did I arrived just before 8.00, I did say to Barnsley I would keep a spare seat for him, but he left the tent confident that his launch night would be a success. I can still see his large smile as he waved goodbye and set off on towards the café" said Poppy her eyes were beginning to get wet around the edges.

"It was the last time I saw him alive. Then Crocket came and took me to one side about 9.10 and told me the shocking news. I asked him to give it 5 minutes before he made the announcement to stop the show. I went to join Oscar at the café, and he then showed me Barnsley's body. I still find it difficult to get the picture out of mind of his body just lying there with that water bottle stuck in his mouth".

The room fell silent.

Poppy had started to cry and started to wipe her eyes with a handkerchief.

Suddenly a booming voice broke the silence.

"Wow that was a close thing. I just bumped into a boat with two blokes on it. Luckily, they were so high they couldn't work out whether they had just collided with a fully grown lion swimming in the river. I had to dive under the water and swim off quickly,"

He walked into the living room wearing some very tight blue Speedo swimming trunks. He was drying his long golden hair on a large bath towel with a picture of a herd of wildebeest jumping over a stream on it.

"Whoa, sorry I didn't realise we had company" he said quickly after spotting Mountie and Charlton sitting on the sofa.

"I'll quickly get changed."

He disappeared into the bedroom and returned wearing a pair of blue jeans and a Chicago Lion Cubs baseball shirt.

He sat down in his chair, poured himself a coffee and leant back.

"I hope you haven't been waiting too long. It's such a glorious evening I just had to go for a swim in the river to cool down."

Mountie and Charlton both shook their heads in unison.

"So, are you two having much luck finding the murderer yet?" said Oscar looking at Mountie and stroking his mane.

"Not yet really as we have only just started." said Mountie.

He was taken aback at Oscar coming straight to the point.

"We have just been looking around the café and checking the murder scene. We have been speaking to Aussie. We have also been looking at the WAAR website, so it's still early days."

Oscar sat back in his chair nodding his head at the news.

"Oscar, can you tell us what happened on Sunday night?" interrupted Charlton.

He then sat back with his notepad open, and pen poised.

He was keen to make a good impression with Oscar.

Oscar sat back in his chair smiling.

He had known Charlton since he arrived at the zoo. He was impressed with the stubborn nature of his continued support of Manchester United AFC despite every other zebra around him supporting Newcastle United AFC . He hoped this stubbornness might prove useful to help Mountie find the killer, even if it meant ruffling a few proverbial feathers.

Oscar leant forward, refilled his mug of coffee, picked up a chocolate biscuit and leant back in his chair.

"There had been a buzz around the tent all day. Barnsley was on a high about the launch of his new WAAR venture and the website. He showed me all the posters and leaflets. He told me about his website and his plans for the evening. I knew it meant a lot to him so I thought for once I would give him some undivided support and interest in his project."

"Then what happened?" said Mountie taking over the helm of questioning from Charlton.

"Around 6.00 when the zoo shut, he started to get himself ready. I had to go out for a walk as the aromas from the bathroom were playing havoc with my sinus's. You know we lions have great senses of smell, but I wasn't waiting around to have them napalmed by his deodorant. It's called Lynx Africa and if Africa smells anything remotely like that, I am glad I live in Britain instead" said Oscar holding his nose and pulling a disgruntled face.

"He was finally ready at 7.15 and was dressed in a WAAR t- shirt made especially and some designer jeans with rips in them. He left just before 7.30 to go to the café to meet up with

Aussie and get the café ready for his launch party."

"Did you see him after that at all?" said Mountie looking up from his notebook.

"Around 8.00 I decided to go and see how he was getting on, as Poppy had left earlier to go to the fashion show. I arrived at the café just before 8.05," said Oscar.

Oscar turned to Poppy who smiled and nodded that she was okay for him to continue.

"That was very precise how come you know exactly what the time was?" said Mountie looking up from his notebook.

"When I arrived, Barnsley was sitting by himself under the café clock. On a table next to him there were spread out some newspapers and magazines with articles about alcoholism. He told me that there had been one visitor, Theo the dopey elephant, had turned up thinking it was a new war games venture and had left very quickly when he realised it wasn't. I was told he was extremely upset when Barnsley found out that he was some sort of closet "Dungeons and Dragons geek" supposedly." said Oscar with a broad smile on his face.

"He then showed me his website which I must admit looked very professional. I was very impressed by the amount of work he had put into building it. I left around 8.15 as he thought I might be scaring off other visitors. Although I suspected he didn't want me to be around to see

what a flop it was turning into,"
He was still smiling and looked at Poppy to make sure she was still fine.

"What did you do then?" asked Mountie looking up from his notebook.

"As Poppy was at the fashion show and it was a warm night I went down to the river for a swim and cool down, I came back here just before 9.00. I was just drying off when I heard a knock on the door. George was there saying he had some bad news about Barnsley. I quickly got dressed and went over to the café to see what was going on. When I got there, I found him lying dead with a water bottle lodged in his throat."

Oscar leant back and closed his eyes.

A few minutes later Oscar re-opened his eyes.

"Once I got my composure back, I arranged for George to get a message to Poppy telling her to come to the cafe instantly. I also got a message through to Crocket telling him to stop the fashion show and to arrange for all the animals there to come to the café immediately. Poppy then arrived a few minutes later and I showed her Barnsley's body. Then suddenly as requested everyone congregated outside the café."

"I know I was one of them" said Mountie looking up from his notebook and continued "We could all see how extremely upset you were".

"We were both very upset," said Oscar.

He paused and smiled at Poppy who was beginning again to look upset.

"I then told everyone of Barnsley's death and how I suspected he had been murdered. I then announced last night's meeting in the seal house. Poppy and I then spent the night outside the café making sure no one tried to interfere with the dead body or the murder scene. As soon as the morning zookeeper alarm went off, we both left and crept back to our tent".

Everyone sat back reflecting on the events of that night.

"Did anyone see you down by the river that evening" said Charlton breaking the silence.

"I saw Edgar, not sure if he saw me. I couldn't see whether he was with Katrina or not. I wondered whether she and Crocket had finally made up and whether she had now agreed to be at the show modelling for him,".

Edgar was a jackal and the lead singer of a rock band called Day of the Jackals.

His band was regularly in the press for all the wrong reasons, and had a very large animal following.

Edgar was dating Katrina Fross whom he met at Hearts River Zoo.

She was a python and an attractive size zero fashion model who regularly appeared in all the fashion magazines.

She had just set up her own fashion label called "F".

When her relationship with Edgar was

discovered, it had not gone down well with the animal press and fans.

Everyone at the zoo just carried on normally as they were used to accepting and enjoying all the strange things that were reported about the band's antics.

"Did you see anything on your way back from your swim" said Mountie hopefully.

He thought for a minute and then shook his head.

"No, I didn't see anyone other than George and I didn't see anyone on my way to the café either."

"Poor Barnsley" said Poppy sobbing.

The room went silent for a couple of minutes.

Oscar got up and went and comforted Poppy.

Mountie looked at his watch and broke the silence.

"We won't keep you much longer but just a couple more questions. Did you know of anyone who might have had a grudge against him?"

"Barnsley could get up animals noses with his over-the-top nature or whilst he was drunk but deep down, he was harmless, especially for a lion,".

Oscar went and sat back down in his chair.

"Although there was that run in with Crocket recently. He is a funny chap. You must know he was very upset that Barnsley had arranged his launch night at the same time as his fashion show. That soon died down fortunately when he realised that few if anybody would attend the WAAR launch."

Oscar turned to face Poppy.

"There was a rumour that Crocket was going spray Barnsley with champagne if he turned up at the show. Not sure how he would have reacted. I suspect he would have tried to insert the champagne bottle somewhere that would have given Crocket a problem sitting down for a week. Must admit though not sure if flamingos do sit down anyway."

Oscar looked at Poppy and they both started to laugh.

"Are you aware of anyone other than Crocket that might have had a grudge against him?" said Charlton.

He was butting in again to make sure that they had not forgotten that he was also part of the investigation team.

Oscar and Poppy smiled at each other.

"No one else. I must admit it had been hard for me to accept him being an alcoholic. I have been putting up with lots of snide comments and complaints. It got worse when he started going around the zoo drunk. Then Aussie started throwing him out of the café so as to not upset the other guests. Outwardly I tried to not let it not show how it was affecting me but deep down it did upset me. May I say though not enough for me to want to kill him"?

Mountie and Charlton looked at each other as

they had not really considered Oscar as being Barnsley's killer.

"How did you take the news of his proposed WAAR venture and website?" said Mountie.

He leant forward and refilled his cup of coffee and took a biscuit leaving just one biscuit on the plate.

Charlton leant forward to pick up a biscuit and found himself in the embarrassing position of deciding whether to take the last biscuit or to be polite and leave it.

Poppy smiled at him.

"Go on take it I will get some more biscuits and some more coffee."

She picked up the tray and went off to the kitchen.

Oscar leant back in his chair.

"Initially I was very skeptical. I wondered if it might be another one of his mad phases that he went through. I did wonder though if he was now about to settle down, grow up and do something sensible and worthwhile around here for a change."

"Barnsley did go through some funny phases though remember when he went through his vegan phase?" Poppy shouted from the kitchen.

"I couldn't believe it a lion, going vegan what could have been more ridiculous?" said Oscar laughing.

Poppy walked in holding a tray of fresh coffee and biscuits smiling.

"Do you remember that "Meat is Murder" poster he put up in his room at the same time."

"Then there was that new romantic phase where he dressed really bizarrely and had tons of make up on his face. We were subjected to Boy Gerbil and the real Flock of Seagulls droning away to all hours. If only could have listened to some decent animal rock music like Led Zebra or Deaf Leopard"

Mountie looked to the sky in a please give me strength manner.

He gave Charlton a stern look to warn him off entering his musical tastes into the conversation.

"I must admit though I did like his posters of David Bow-wow," said Poppy.

Poppy sat back down and was smiling.

"Oh, but do you remember that Goth phase he went through as well. He had those massive black boots and one of those long black leather coats," said Oscar.

"Yes, I do remember. Typical for him to start wearing all that Goth gear just before that heatwave hit us. Although give him his due he did persevere wearing that coat through the heatwave until someone nicked it...... or so, he claimed."

"At least his musical tastes improved I quite liked the Fields of the Elephants and Nine Inch Snails; you know those animal Goth bands that he started listening to."

There was then a sudden pause as Poppy and Oscar both realised that they had been talking ill of their recently murdered son and looked down ashamed.

Mountie looked at his watch and nudged Charlton.

They both got up from the sofa.

Mountie looked at Oscar and Poppy who were both now looking very upset.

"Well, we best be off. We would like to come back at some point and see his room though. We'll let ourselves out but if there is anything else you can think of which might help us, please let us know."

Mountie started walking towards the door with Charlton following.

They stopped in their tracks and turned around as Oscar started talking to them again.

"I can't think of anything else now. Come back any time to have a look at his room as it hasn't been touched since he left on Sunday evening."

Oscar then brushed a tear from his eye.

"I do hope you two catch his killer because despite all his quirks he was still our beloved son. I do need justice to be seen AND done."

Mountie and Charlton let themselves out of the tent, past the Sphinxes and out of the enclosure.

Mountie looked at his watch which said 10.45.

"Best I get to bed. "said Mountie stifling a yawn.

"We will reconvene in the morning and discuss our next steps. Good night, Charlton."

Charlton heard a loud cheer from the direction of his home and the sound of clinking drinks bottles. He remembered there was a late-night live Animal League football game on the television. He knew his mates would be up watching it and guessed he would not be getting to sleep for a long while.

Mountie sauntered slowly home and was already planning in his head what the next steps would be and who to interview next.

When he got back, he carefully hid the whisky bottle they had found and paused to wonder if it was significant to the case or not.

He fell quickly to sleep in his chair.

CHAPTER 6 – WEDNESDAY
3 AUGUST (AM)

Charlton woke up as usual at 6.00 and had got to bed very late due to the late finish of the animal football match his mates had been watching when he got back. The game had eventually gone to penalties to be resolved.

He was as usual the first to rise in his home.
He was a morning person unlike the rest of the zebras who were invariably asleep till mid-morning and usually missed the zoo opening at 9.00. They only woke up earlier if visiting kids threw things at them over the fence whilst commenting to their parents "How can they still be asleep at this time of the day".
They were not bothered that in a recent visitor's survey they had ranked bottom. Charlton had tried to point out to them the results could mean the zoo splitting them up and being sent off to other zoos. As usual they had all ignored him and carried on getting up late as usual.

He put on a red sleeveless Manchester United AFC football top and a pair of blue jeans.
He made some toast and covered it in his favourite raspberry jam. He then left and went over to Mountie's hut.
It was a sunny morning and it looked like it was

going to be another scorcher.

As he got nearer, he could hear classical music.

Outside he spotted Mountie sitting in a striped folding beach deckchair wearing a white bath robe with a red Canadian Maple leaf on left hand side top pocket.

Next to him was a table with a large cafeteria of coffee and a half-eaten croissant.

He was reading The Animal Times newspaper, and he noticed that the crossword on the back had already been completed.

Charlton cringed as the only newspaper that crossed the his front door was the Animal Sun and he invariably struggled to even complete its quick crossword.

"Morning Charlton. Grab a deckchair, a coffee mug and come and sit down".

Charlton saw a black and white striped deckchair propped up against the shed. He propped it open and sat down with his head and arms instantly blending in with the deckchair's colour scheme.

Mountie glanced over and stifled a laugh.

He saw that there was a spare Hearts River Zoo mug on the table and filled it with coffee.

"Glorious morning" said Charlton taking a sip from the coffee mug.

He was beginning to acquire a taste for the Peruvian coffee that Mountie made.

Unfortunately, he couldn't image successfully introducing it into the zebra enclosure.

He could just picture Mark suspiciously eyeing up the packet and saying in a broad Geordie accent "What do you wanna be drinking this poncy stuff for". Whilst then proceeding to put a heaped spoonful of bargain buy coffee into a stained Newcastle United AFC football mug followed by four spoons of sugar, full fat milk and some hot water.

Mountie put down his newspaper and took a sip of coffee.
"So, what are you planning for us to do this evening?"
"I think this evening we need to interview Theo as he went to Barnsley's launch party. Then speak to Jimi who found Barnsley's body in the café. Hopefully they can give us something more to go on".
"That's a good idea, perhaps we might finally get a lead."
Charlton got out his notebook and started looking over what he had written.
"Do you think we ought to tackle Aussie about not saying he was working with Oscar behind Barnsley's back".
"You can if you want, but Aussie was just helping Oscar out. You do know they have been friends for years. They grew up together in Sydney Zoo although you would never guess from Oscar's accent that he is a fellow Australian. Rumour has it they were both top surfers in their younger

days?". said Mountie smiling.

This was news to Charlton.

"I bet that was a fantastic sight Aussie and Oscar riding a wave together. Unfortunately, they have both ended up here miles away from any sea or surf. It's a shame they can't surf together down the river, now that would be a sight".

Mountie smiled at the thought.

"Any more thoughts around the whisky bottle yet"

"I had a look at it with a magnifying glass and there are no marks on it to help us at all. Alas, animals can buy these bottles of whisky anywhere which doesn't help us either."

He then finished off his mug of coffee and placed it back on the table.

Mountie looked at his watch and got up from his deckchair.

"I need to have a shower and get dressed. I will see you back here at 6.30 this evening".

With that he cleared the contents of the table onto a tray and walked back into his hut.

Charlton gathered his things together and climbed out of his deckchair.

He trudged back home where as expected his compatriots were all still fast asleep.

After Mountie's comment about Oscar growing up with Aussie, he began to realise how little he knew about his fellow zoo occupants.

He realised that this investigation meant he was going to be finding out loads more information about all of them and some stuff they might have wanted to keep secret.

Obviously after the investigation he knew he would still have to keep their secrets.

He wasn't sure though how if it might affect any of his friendships or influence the way he dealt with any of them going forward.

CHAPTER 7 – WEDNESDAY
6 AUGUST (PM)

It had been a really hot day at the zoo and was packed with visitors.

The zebras nursing hangovers had stirred about 11.00. They had as usual been pelted by some upset school kids whilst calling them all lazy.

There had been an incident at the chimp enclosure.

A young couple had been getting very romantic on a rug whilst picnicking outside the chimp enclosure. They were so engrossed didn't spot a male chimp successfully urinating into their half empty bottle of prosecco.

This achievement was executed perfectly to the joyful encouragement of the other male chimps.

The couple had complained after being tipped off by a watching bystander.

The bystander had though successfully filmed the event and uploaded it and was now sitting back admiring the hits it was now getting on-line.

The zoo shut at its usual time with staff keen to get away as quickly as they could to enjoy the weather.

Charlton put on a short sleeved red Manchester United AFC football shirt with POOL FROGBA emblazoned on the back and a long baggy pair of black shorts.

He strolled over to Mountie's and found him once again sitting outside in a deckchair.

On the table next to him was a large pottery jug filled with a reddish-looking liquid with fruit and ice floating on the top.

Mountie motioned him to get the deckchair from next to the hut.

Charlton picked up the black and white striped deckchair, opened it up and sat down next to the table.

"Care for some sangria?" said Mountie filling up his glass with the liquid.

He noticed that Charlton was staring strangely at the pottery jug and obviously didn't have a clue what sangria was.

He refilled his glass and filled up the other glass and passed it to Charlton who was normally a beer drinker.

He took a curious sip of it and found to his surprise that the sangria tasted very good.

"Hey this is alright."

Mountie sat in his deckchair nodding his head in agreement.

They silently finished their drinks whilst Mountie browsed over his notes.

He packed away the tray, glasses, and the jug of sangria inside his hut and returned.

"Let's start at the elephant house and speak to Theo about his visit to the launch party."

Charlton got up from his deckchair and packed it

away.

They walked towards the elephant house where a family of Indian elephants lived.

It had been designed by the 2nd year class of Hearts River Lower School.

An enterprising mum who worked in the Hearts River town tourist information centre had suggested to her daughter that it would be good idea if the elephant house, being a large building, could be designed to mirror the picturesque part of the town's high street.

She hoped it might encourage more visitors into the town after they had visited the zoo.

As there were no other suitable ideas received by the class's teacher the suggestion was successfully put forward to the designers.

The front and rear side of the house was covered with large photographic pictures of the more picturesque parts of the high street. The pictures conveniently missed out the boarded up empty shops and £1 stores that were the last survivors in the other half of the high street.

The town had a large village green, some old white stone-built buildings with black thatched roofs and a small chapel with a thatched roof that was built in 1536.

There was a park with two large black entrance gates. One gate had a large "H" on it and the other had a large "R". The gates design incorporated a flowing replica outline of the stretch of Hearts

River that ran through the town.
Inside the park there was a large "H" shaped boating lake.
The elephant enclosure needed a swimming pool and so the final design included a replica village green, "H" and "R" gates and a "H" shaped swimming pool.

Opening the gate to the elephant house they then saw Rowena walking towards them.
She was the eldest of the two elephant children.
Few of the animals had seen her since she returned from, by all accounts, a torrid time working at a call centre.
"Oh no I forgot she was back" whispered Charlton.
Rowena met up with them at the entrance.
On her head was a large telephone answering headset including a microphone. Its loose cable swung in front of her white T-Shirt that had in big red letters "Monkey's Electricals Wild Goods@Wild Prices4Wild Animals".
Charlton agreed with the last comment as he had been an extremely wild animal after the service he had received. They had delivered him a microwave that didn't work. Also, the delivery box looked like it had been used as a football. He had unleashed his full anger on an unsuspecting Call Centre assistant and now had a pang of sympathy upon seeing Rowena the way she was.
"Hello, you have come through to Elephant

Deliveries and my name is Rowena."

They stared in shook at her.

"How may I help you both today."

Rowena pretended to read from an imaginary script she was holding.

"Hello Rowena. We are here to see Theo about Barnsley the lion" said Mountie in a soothing way.

"OK, Please can I take your down your name and address."

Rowena was poised and ready to type something onto an imaginary keyboard.

"Rowena, it's me Mountie I live here at the zoo with you" said Mountie in a friendly manner.

"So that's Mountie and you live here at the zoo, I am Rowena your support tonight. You mentioned something about a lion called Barnsley. Please can you tell me what is wrong with it."

Rowena carried on reading from her imaginary script.

"Well, he's dead" said Charlton with a smirk on his face.

Rowena again looked down at an imaginary script.

"Was he working when we delivered it to you?"

Mountie decided to resume doing the talking and took over from Charlton.

He sensed Charlton was going to be extremely rude with his next comment.

Mountie, like the rest of the zoo, had been

forced to hear Charlton on the public phone near the café chastising someone from an Indian call centre for over an hour concerning the microwave that had been delivered and didn't work. Charlton's levels of abuse had escalated by the minute and by the end he was being extremely abusive.

Charlton on the other hand was feeling guilty as well. He was trying to work out whether it had been Rowena who he had been abusive to on his call. He began to wonder whether his call had been the final straw in her downfall.

"Barnsley, you know Oscar the lion's son" said Mountie calmly.

"Oh, Oscar's son has a Barnsley as well, was his delivered okay or was his dead as well on arrival" said Rowena again referring to an imaginary script.

"No, it's Oscar's son Barnsley that is dead," said Charlton.

Rowena again looked at her imaginary script.

"That does sound like a coincidence, yours and Oscar's sons Barnsley the lion's being dead. I can assure you that they would have been working perfectly when they left here. We do have strict product testing before delivery."

"Sure, you do" murmured Charlton under his breath.

He remembered the state his microwave had arrived in. The box looked exactly like it had been used as a football by the dispatch staff.

Mountie turned and held a finger over his mouth to get Charlton to be quiet.

"I think you will find that it is usually the delivery firms that are at fault. Have you spoken to them as we are always getting reports of them breaking things when they deliver them?".

Just then Theo appeared and seeing Mountie and Charlton cornered by Rowena came walking slowly down to see them.

Rowena turned and saw him.

"Here is one of our engineers now. I will pass you over to him as I am sure he will be able to sort you out with a replacement Barnsley the lion."

She turned and walked back into the elephant enclosure.

"Sorry about that" said Theo who was dressed in a pair of blue shorts and a white England rugby top.

"She is slowly getting better though after being diagnosed as suffering from Call Centre Syndrome. It's where someone stops listening when people speak to them, they break into sweat if they hear anyone swear at them and their lives are run from an imaginary script. Thankfully it is curable. Another side effect is that she does occasionally wake up in the middle of night shouting with a Geordie accent about having a fooking microwave inserted somewhere."

Charlton went as bright red as his Manchester United AFC.

Mountie stifled a laugh as well.

Theo looked at them both confused as he had been fortunate enough to have missed Charlton's epic phone call.

"I assume you have come to ask me about last Sunday evening. You know I turned up at Barnsley's launch evening, don't you?"

They both nodded.

"Well, you better come and join us relaxing around the pool."

He turned around and they started walking towards the pool at the back.

Walking through the gates they approached four sunbeds. Two were vacant and the other two were occupied by Theo's mother Heather and father Jonathan.

Seeing Mountie and Charlton they put on some beach robes and returned to their sun beds.

"Sit down" said Jonathan motioning for them to sit on the two vacant sunbeds.

"I'll sit on the ground. They have come to see me about Sunday night." said Theo.

"Shocking, absolutely shocking and to think it happened right here and not in some American zoo" said Heather adjusting her robe.

"Please can you tell me what happened that evening?" said Mountie getting his notebook and pen out.

"Well mum and dad went off to start working on the fashion show as soon as the zoo shut. Mum was assisting Crocket and dad was helping

Lemming get the stage ready. I was left looking after Rowena. I'd made her go to bed early as she would have wanted to go to the show if we had let her know about it. We knew though if she had gone, she would have wreaked havoc."

Heather and Jonathan nodded in agreement.

Theo pulled a piece of paper from a pocket in his shorts and handed it over to Mountie.

Mountie looked at it and showed Charlton that it was one of Barnsley's launch night flyers .

"I found it on our doorstep. Unfortunately, being dyslexic, I misread it and thought it was an invitation to a new war gaming club that was meeting at Aussie's café. So rather than staying here by myself I decided to go along to find out more about it."

Theo reached under Mountie's sun bed and picked up a can of fizzy orange drink that he had left there.

"Go on," said Mountie.

"I left here around 7.55 and arrived just before 8.00. I was the first person there. I walked in and Barnsley welcomed me and said he didn't realise I had a drinking problem. I scratched my head, and I said that I didn't realise that he was into war gaming. I asked him whether he was into Dungeons and Dragons and the Warhammer gaming side as well. I must admit I was totally confused as to what was going on until he explained that WAAR was about helping to reform alcoholic animals."

"I think I would have been too" said Mountie laughing to try and lighten the atmosphere.

"So, what happened then?"

Charlton nodded in agreement too and was just about to say something when Mountie gave him one of his don't say a word please looks.

"Barnsley then called me a dopey idiot. He asked me whether I had read his posters. I shook my head as I am not a great reader. He then carried on at me and I felt a right idiot."

His parents were giving him encouraging smiles.

"So, what happened then."

"Barnsley always was a lot smarter and quicker than me. He started singing in a mocking way "Brains what are they good for" I was mortified I apologised profusely and made a quick beeline for the exit nearly knocking the doors off their hinges. He did call after me to make sure I told the rest of my Dungeons and Dragons geeks what had happened and to make sure that they did not mistakenly turn up as well. I was so embarrassed."

Theo was blushing profusely and crushing the can of orange in his hand.

"Did you see anything else."

"No, I just rushed back here as quickly as I could before anybody saw me and wondered why I had been at the cafe."

"Theo why don't you go and get some more cans of orange from the fridge for all of us. Please can you also check what Rowena is up to," said

Heather.

She took her sunglasses off and repositioned herself on the sunbed to face Mountie.

Theo got up and went to get some drinks and disappeared inside the house.

"He was looking extremely shaken when we got back after Oscar's announcement about the murder," said Heather.

"He was even more shocked when we told him about the murder. The poor lad poured his heart out to us about how he had mistakenly been to the café earlier that evening. He was worried about being a possible suspect as a result," said Jonathan.

"And as soon as you two agreed to run an investigation, well we knew you would be round here quickly to see him. We are both sure he didn't kill Barnsley." said Heather.

Mountie and Charlton made some notes in their notebooks.

Theo then returned with 5 cans of orange and handed them out to everyone.

"Just to let you know Rowena is sitting on the sofa arranging delivery for some replacement Barnsley the lions to be delivered to Mountie and Oscar. They supposedly got sent dead ones."

Heather and Jonathan looked at each other confused and then looked at Theo who was smiling.

"Long story. Don't ask"

"Please can I ask where you were on the

evening?" said Mountie turning to Heather.

"I had been working hard on the fashion show with Crocket. We elephants never forget anything, so I was Crocket's proverbial right-hand man."

She pointed to her head.

"In here I remembered which model was wearing which outfit, with which shoes, with which pieces of jewellery, for every costume that was part of the fashion show".

She paused.

"And also, I knew who should be on when and where. Crocket would have been completely lost without me. On the night all he craves for is to be the star and to get all the accolades for a successful show"

"Yeah, that Crocket underestimates your value, he gets all the glory, and he never gives you any thanks," said Jonathan.

He leant forward and put his empty can on the floor next to him.

"So, Jonathan where were you on Sunday evening," said Mountie.

He took a sip from his can of orange. To his surprise the heat of the sun had made it taste warm and disgusting, but he swallowed it out of politeness.

"Lemming needed a hand setting up, lugging the scaffolding, walkways, and lighting. I was just on my way home after finishing when that cheeky sod Crocket had the audacity to ask whether he could sit on my back during the show. He wanted to rule over everyone, bark down orders and oversee what was going on. I was too polite to say no to him."

Jonathan leant forward.

"Not even a thank you, never again will I help that ungrateful little swine."

Mountie turned to face Heather.

"Was the rumour true that Crocket really did have something planned for Barnsley if he had turned up at the fashion show?"

Heather sat back and let out a big laugh.

"Poor old Barnsley. Crocket was initially really upset when he found out that he arranged his launch event to clash with his fashion show. He even had a row with him over it. He did threaten to do something to him at the show if had turned up. He then saw ticket sales increase, so he milked it for a little while. As the show got nearer the talk of the WAAR event died down and was then forgotten about. Crocket didn't want anything to spoil or distract from his crowning glory. I think if Barnsley had turned up then he wouldn't have done anything to spoil his evening."

"Knowing Crocket, he would have given him a job to do like selling ice creams" huffed Jonathan.

"How did Crocket take the news about Barnsley's death" asked Charlton.

He took a sip from his can but unlike Mountie he spat out the disgusting warm liquid that was in the can. Luckily, he just missed Heather's white bath robe.

"Oops sorry about that"

She adjusted her robe and moved away from Charlton's orange coloured mess.

"I saw him talking to George and I thought it looked a bit strange. At first, he wanted nothing to do with George. I initially thought it was something to with the bar."

"Please carry on."

"Then suddenly his mood changed. He said something to George who left quickly. Then he went off and spoke to Poppy who left instantly. This was looking very strange to me."

Heather started fiddling with a ring on her finger.

"I knew something was up when he stopped looking at the show and started looking at his watch instead. Then about 5 minutes later he grabbed a microphone and brushed past me and went on stage. He made the announcement about Barnsley, that the show was over, and that Oscar wanted everyone to meet at the café."

Jonathan nodded his agreement from his seat.

Heather was now fiddling with her watch.

"We all silently left the show and went to the café. You know the rest as I remember seeing you there" she said directing her comment towards Mountie.

"Indeed, I was" said Mountie nodding at the same time.

"Anything else that you thought strange or odd that evening," said Charlton.

Jonathan saw an opportunity to further dig the knife into Crockett, who he really didn't like, butted in

"If you ask me there is something very odd about Crocket. It's strange how everyone does whatever he asks them to even though everyone hates him."

"Come off it he is a great event's organiser and no one else is that good at it."

Jonathan climbed off his sun bed, stood up.

"If you would let me finish. I reckon he saw Barnsley as some kind of opposition. He finally realised that there might be someone else who could take over his role as the zoo's event organiser. Just imagine if the WAAR launch had been a big success for Barnsley. It would have killed him to not be the star around here anymore."

There was silence for a few minutes.

Jonathan realised he was standing up and no one had responded to his comments.

He sat back down feeling rather foolish.

Mountie made eye contact with Charlton and they both climbed up from their sunbeds.

Mountie turned to Heather, Jonathan, and Theo

"Thanks for all your help, if you do think of anything that may help, please let us know."

Mountie started to leave and Charlton followed behind.

All sudden he then ran past Mountie who looked confused.

"Hold on I have just seen the complainant now. I will go and ask him where we need to deliver the replacement Barnsley to."

Mountie now started running and finally caught up with Charlton.

They found a safe spot to sit down for a couple of minutes to catch their breath.

"Wow that was close." said Charlton.

Mountie was deep in thought and Charlton looked at him curiously.

"Did I miss something important in there?"

"I'm not sure. Theo as we know attended the launch party."

"Right and he told us it was all a big mistake."

" But what if it wasn't a mistake?"

"Well, we know Oscar visited Barnsley after his visit, so we know he didn't kill him."

"What if hadn't been a mistake and he was using this wargaming excuse as a cover."

"Ah I think I am beginning to see what you mean."

"What if Theo went at the start of the event to check out what was going on and do a recce of the place. He returns later knowing what is going on, he could have already chosen to use the water bottle as his weapon, and he then decides to kill Barnsley for whatever reason."

"Interesting I hadn't thought of that. Although I am still not sure I would have had Theo down as the killer"

"I probably agree with you, but we must keep an open mind and not eliminate any possibilities. Let's not forget that currently Theo doesn't have an alibi."

You're tight he doesn't unless Rowena was still awake and can vouch for him. I think I may have to let you deal with checking that one out and you can sort out your Barnsley delivery at the same time."

"Very funny." said Mountie.

They both started laughing.

"Okay let's go and visit the gorillas then." said Mountie,

.

CHAPTER 8 – WEDNESDAY 3 AUGUST (PM – LATER)

They started to slowly walk towards the Gorilla enclosure.
"Looks like Jonathan has got a grudge against Crocket, hasn't he?" said Charlton.
"Crocket is like Marmite; you either love him or you hate him. I do give him some credit though because despite most of the animals hating him, he does still somehow manage to get their help and support to run his fashion shows. Somehow, he manages to galvanise them all into action, and they always respond to make the shows a success for him."
They were getting closer to the gorilla enclosure.
"So, what do we want to achieve from our next visit?"
"We need to speak to Jimi as he found Barnsley dead in the cafe. Hopefully we can pick up some valuable information from him. I am very curious as to why he decided to visit the cafe that night. He must have known Barnsley's WAAR launch party was going on and his appearance could have upset any alcoholic animals that were attending."
They stopped abruptly at the entrance gate and looked at the sign.
"Private Property No Entry unless carrying

BEER!"
They both started smiling as they made their way in.

The gorilla enclosure design had fallen to Year 2 of Hearts River Upper School.
The winning idea had come from a boy who loved the cartoon movie "Cars".
His design replicated Luigi's tyre garage from the film, complete with a repair ramp, a tower of tyres outside and some petrol pumps.
There were a few raised eyebrows as the son's father was the owner of a large car sales garage in town.
There were further raised eyebrows after it was agreed that the garage would be named after his father's garage.
A deal had been agreed with the boy's father to provide a car to go on top of a podium. Although he did say it wouldn't be a veteran car like in the film.
Amazingly the car he had chosen for the podium was a bright red convertible Ferrari 328 GTS that had been written off after crashing into a big oak tree just outside of town.
It had also not gone unnoticed that the car had some rather large strategically placed stickers advertising the father's garage plastered on it as well.

Lemming had been over the moon when he saw the podium had a Ferrari mounted on top of it.

He had rebuilt the engine and managed to get it running despite it being stuck on top of the podium.

He had also kitted it out with a large loud stereo system with big speakers so he could just chill out in it.

There were several engine bits he had needed and he had used TESCOW to get them delivered to him.

TESCOW was the brainchild of two cows called Harry and Glen.

Harry lived in a field in North Norfolk and one day found that he needed to get a birthday present to his friend Glen in Devon.

Harry worked out a route that involved passing the present from cow field to cow field all the way down to Devon.

This worked out so well soon that all the cows then agreed to start passing goods backwards and forwards for other animals.

They then decided it needed a more structured approach.

They then set up TESCOW giving all the animals the ability to order goods initially by phone and then via the internet from them.

The items were then delivered throughout Britain.

Animals and humans delivered goods to various warehouses they had either purchased or rented all over the country.

Then by night they employed teams of animals, mainly chimpanzees and other apes, to deliver all the ordered goods to their animal customers via local animal delivery services.

The delivery lorries and vans intentionally had the same distinct blue and white design as the human firm with the similar name. This was done to help make their delivery service as inconspicuous as possible to humans.

Suddenly the Ferrari engine started up and let out a loud roar.

They both looked up at the car.

Lemming looked down from the driver's seat and saw them and started smiling. He turned off the engine and climbed down the podium to greet them.

He was dressed in blue jeans and a Cobrahead tour t-shirt.

After escaping from Birmingham Zoo, he became a roadie for the animal rock group Cobrahead and lived in their lorry.

He loved working on their lighting, special effects, and anything to do with electrics.

Unfortunately, he made the mistake of visiting his cousin Jules at Edinburgh Zoo whilst Cobrahead were playing there.

Whilst there a zookeeper had begun to become very suspicious of him and had decided to challenge him. He thought he had done a rather convincing act of pretending to be a member of the Honda Gold Wing Owners club. Unfortunately, the zookeeper by sheer coincidence was the Chairman of the Honda Gold Wing Owners Club and didn't recognise Lemming from any of their events. As a result, he had been captured and sent to live at Hearts River Zoo.

"What a shame a road ready Ferrari. I would love to get it off the podium and take it out on the roads and really give it good drive." said Lemming staring solemnly up at the Ferrari on the podium.
"Certainly, is a great looking car and that amazing Ferrari engine sound" said Charlton looking at the Ferrari with a big smile on his face.
"How's the investigation going? I assume you have come here to chat with our young Jimi."
Mountie nodded.
"Still early days and yes we have come to have a chat with Jimi."
"Well, you better follow me then."
Lemming led Charlton and Mountie into the garage.
It was split into a kitchen, two bedrooms and a living room with a couple of big chairs and some sofas. There was a modern ultra–HD Smart television and a new music centre.
Jimi was sitting at a table playing a computer game on a laptop.
He was dressed in a Day of the Jackals T shirt

displaying the album cover of their latest record "Death to Wildebeest". He also had on a pair of blue denim jeans.

"What game are you playing" said Charlton looking over Jimi's shoulder.

Charlton tried to appear interested and then spotted that the screen was filled with the image of a dead human body with blood pumping out of it.

"Warden Destroyer III" said Jimi not looking away from the screen.

"It's where you choose to play at being a lion, a tiger, or a leopard. You get to track and kill game reserve keepers on a selection of game reserves across the globe."

After hearing Charlton's voice Beth came out of the kitchen

She was short and very attractive and was wearing an apron with a picture of a cartoon naked female human's body on the front with fig leaves in strategic places.

She had been resident here when Lemming had arrived after his capture, and it was love at first sight for them both.

"Jimi, turn that thing off as I suspect Mountie and Charlton have come to talk to you" she said drying her hands with a tea towel.

Mountie and Charlton both nodded

"That is correct yes, we have come to ask Jimi a few questions about what happened that evening at the cafe," said Mountie.

Lemming had walked into the kitchen and then the sound of water and then the sound of dishes clanking together.'

Charlton tried to strain his head to see into the kitchen. He was intrigued to know if Lemming was dressed in a similar apron but with a picture of a naked man instead.

Beth looked suspiciously at Charlton and wondered what he was trying to see.

Mountie gave him a tug.

"You two sit there. Jimi, please answer their questions whilst we finish the dishes and then we will bring in some beers and join you."

She went into the kitchen to join Lemming.

They sat down on the sofa whilst Jimi shut the laptop lid.

"Hi Jimi, so what happened that evening" said Mountie opening his notebook.

"Well, I was home by myself. Mum and dad were helping at the fashion show."

He was nervously fiddling with the laptops mouse.

"I was watching the Day of the Jackals gig at Glastonbury Zoo from earlier this year and that finished around 8.45.

During it I received a text message about a new Antarctic Monkey's track called "Meadowhell" that was now available to download from their website for free for a limited time period"

Mountie had stopped writing and looked confused. He didn't like to admit that he was a real technophobe.

Unfortunately, Charlton wasn't that much more technically astute either although he managed to hide it better.

Jimi smiled and pulled out his green Crocodile phone.

It had been designed so that when folded it looked like a crocodile's mouth complete with false crocodile teeth running up and down the sides of it.

"The phone has 4G wi-fi, text, plays music, full internet access, digital and video camera. Also, amazingly you can even make phone calls on it as well!"

Jimi was met by blank expressions from Mountie and Charlton.

"I suspect Mountie you still have a camera the size of a brick that still needs film in it."

"Less of the lip you. And I do have a brick sized camera and I still take some very good pictures with it."

Mountie paused and wrote some more information into his notebook.

"So, you then went to the café to download this new song that you had got the message about?"

Jimi sat there nodding in agreement.

"Whilst your parents are in the kitchen there is something I must ask you. Was the real reason you went there because you needed to attend the WAAR launch party. Perhaps you have a secret drinking problem. You see we need to know because you must have known it was on ?" said Mountie.

Jimi burst out laughing.

"NO WAY! You know I like my beer too much to want to give it up. In fact ,there is as much chance of me giving up drinking beer as Charlton giving up supporting Manchester United AFC!!"

They all started to laugh loudly.

"But seriously Dad keeps me in check after witnessing the dangers of excess drinking from his days of being a roadie."

Mountie wrote in his notebook.

"As I said I had to ask you the question even though I probably knew the answer. Now tell me what happened on the night."

"Well, I set off and, on the way, I did remember that Barnsley's event was going on at the café. I decided to carry on but to check to see what was going on before making my next move. It was all very quiet when I arrived. I assumed it was all over, so I went in and closed the door behind me. I decided I was going to play on the computers as well as download the song."

Jimi continued to fiddle with the computer mouse without looking at Mountie or Charlton.

"As I was walking over to the computers it was then that I saw Barnsley lying still on the floor. I saw there was a water bottle sticking out of his mouth and he was looking dead. I know I play too many violent computer games, but my first instinct was that it all looked odd and that he had been killed by someone. I was so scared as you can imagine. It then struck me that his killer might still be around and might try and kill me as well. So, I ran out of the café shouting and headed for the fashion show. I then bumped into George. He said he was going to the café to get some more gin for the fashion show bar as they were running out".

Jimi's eyes were beginning to swell up.

"I know this is very difficult for you but please tell us what happened then" said Mountie looking up from his notebook.

"I told George that I had found Barnsley dead in the café. He told me to go home. He said he would return to the show and send my Dad home as quickly as he could".

"George came and told me what had happened and I came back here as quickly as I could," said Lemming.

He walked out of the kitchen with an arm full of beers and placed them on the table.

He then placed a comforting arm round Jimi's neck.

"Poor little chap is still struggling to get over it. It was a very nasty shock for him."

Beth reappeared wearing black denim jeans and a black Honda Gold Wing Owner's Club T shirt. She wore it as a reminder as it was thanks to them that the love of her life had been captured and sent here.

"You lot not drinking?" said Beth.

She walked to the table and separated the cans of beer and threw a can to Lemming, Charlton and Mountie and then opened one for herself.

Mountie waited a couple of seconds for a glass and then realised one was not going to be forthcoming. He opened the can and took a sip of ice-cold beer.

Charlton did the same whilst Lemming and Beth parked themselves in their chairs.

"Beth where you were that night ?" said Mountie after waiting till everyone was settled.

"As Jimi said I went to the show. I got myself ready by 7.45 and arrived at 8.00 when it started. I stayed there till the announcement was made and went to the café like everyone else did including you" said Beth directing her reply towards Mountie.

Charlton was beginning to get a bit of a complex about this. He had also been at the café as well, but no one had yet mentioned remembering seeing him there despite him having a bright green Mohican that night.

Beth took a sip of her beer.

"I bumped into George who told me what had happened. He said Lemming had gone home to comfort Jimi. So, I stayed at the café to see what was going on and then came home to comfort my beloved Jimi".

Jimi went bright red with embarrassment and looked down at an invisible spot on the top of his laptop

"And what about you Lemming?" said Mountie.

"Well because of my roadie skills Crocket had roped me into setting up the stage and arranging all the lighting. I managed to get Jonathan to help me out. Although he was a bit upset as just as he was about to leave Crocket collared him to help him with something else not sure what, but he didn't look too pleased."

Lemming sat back in his chair and took a drink from his beer can.

"I was settled behind the sound and light monitoring desk at 7.45. At 8.45 there was an interval, but I had to stay in place as I was providing the lights and music for the seal demonstration that took place during it. The show restarted at 9.00 and I carried on until about 9.15 when Crocket made his announcement on stage. Just as I was leaving George told me what had happened, and I dashed back here to comfort Jimi."

"Where were you positioned?" said Charlton.

Lemming thought for a minute.

"I was positioned high at the back of the seats, why does it have any relevance?"

"Well, I was just wondering from there if you saw anybody leave the show whilst it was on or see anything that you thought looked a bit odd." said Charlton.

He was enjoying his chance to contribute to the interview process.

"You mean apart from the outfits in the show.

Some of them were extremely odd. I couldn't for the life of me work out who would have been seen dead wearing half of them."

Lemming was smiling and then his face changed as he realised what he had just said.

"Sorry it was just a figure of speech. Actually, I was concentrating hard on managing the show. Crocket is a perfectionist as we all know. I didn't want to put a foot wrong even though A- he wasn't paying me, and B- I can't stand the sight of him."

"Anything else happen that you think might help?" said Mountie finishing off his beer and placing it on the floor by his feet.

Beth pointed to another can and Mountie shook his head.

Lemming sat forward in his chair.

"Not sure if it is relevant, but there were a few sparks between Crocket and Edgar. You see he wanted Katrina to be one of his models. Edgar, you see, has never liked Crocket. So much so he persuaded her not to do the show and instead spend the evening with him. Crocket was mad about it. He is persistent though and did carry on trying to get her to do the show, but she always refused. I suspect she did spend the evening with Edgar instead as I didn't see her at the show."

"Not sure if this relevant but we will look into it when we speak to Crocket," said Mountie. scribbling a not in his notebook

Lemming's face became animated, and he leant

forward.

"I also love reading thrillers and detective novels and has got me thinking about this murder case. Now hear me out, suppose there was someone who wanted to kill Edgar for whatever reason. He's not the world's most popular singer, is he? So, what if they hired a hit animal, who's not very bright, to come here to kill him? They misread the WAAR posters and think Edgar will be there as alcohol is mentioned. They go to the café and for some reason mistake Barnsley for Edgar. They kill the wrong animal and leave quickly after hearing Jimi approaching. What do you think?"

He sat looking very smug and then finished his can of beer and motioned for Jimi to throw him another one.

Charlton and Mountie both nodded in agreement and wrote notes in their notebooks.

"Hmm that is interesting as we hadn't considered Barnsley not being the target. Although I do believe he was the intended victim, but we won't rule out your idea that there could have been a mistaken identity with the killing. There is some logic with your suggestion concerning Edgar being the real target and how someone could have assumed him being at the WAAR launch. Although we all know Edgar would not have been attending from a giving up the booze perspective though."

Charlton got all excited and sat forward.

"Although what if Edgar was secretly at the WAAR launch to try and give up the booze. What if Barnsley had mentioned that he might leak it to the press? If so, it might have then been in his interest to kill Barnsley. He does have a new album coming out and for sales reasons it has always been best for Edgar to remain the animal world's number one wild drinking bad boy."

"It's something to ponder on Charlton," said Mountie as he rose from his chair.

"If you do think of anything that might help you know where we are."

Charlton got up and started to follow Mountie out.

As they were leaving, they heard the jingle of Jimi's computer starting up.

When they got outside Mountie looked at his watch

"Sorry I need to dash back for the start of a Moozart concert on the radio that I wanted to listen to. I will see you in the morning as usual Charlton".

Charlton nodded and felt in need of another beer and saw that the café was still open.

He joined the other zebras at a table and was able to switch off for a while from the pressures of the investigation.

His friends had agreed not to discuss the investigation with him and had all offered him their support when needed.

CHAPTER 9 – THURSDAY 4 AUGUST (AM)

Charlton awoke after having a bad night's sleep due to the previous night's interviews going around and around in his head.

He put on a red Manchester United AFC football top with FATCOW emblazoned on the back and put on a pair of blue jeans.

Fatcow was their new striker and although he had scored loads of goals at other clubs he was struggling to make an impact at the club.

He made himself a mug of coffee and washed down two paracetamol tablets.

He was feeling a bit groggy when he started to leave.

As soon as he got outside, he had to shield his eyes as the sun was shining very brightly and went to get his green and yellow reflective wraparound sunglasses.

He found Mountie sitting outside in a deckchair fully washed and shaved. He was dressed in his black trousers and red tunic which had the top button undone.

There was a small table with a pot of coffee, two green Hearts River Zoo mugs and a plate with four croissants on it.

Mountie wrote something on the back of his Animal Times newspaper and then folded it to reveal that he had just finished the crossword.

Charlton picked up the black and white striped deckchair and parked it next to the table and poured himself a mug of coffee.

Mountie motioned for him to take a croissant as well which he did.

"You look a bit rough this morning."

Charlton nodded and took a sip of his coffee.

"I couldn't sleep at all last night. All that information about this case just kept swimming around in my head."

Mountie picked up a croissant and started to eat it brushing the crumbs off his tunic.

"Me too. I had everything going around in my head as well."

Mountie opened his notebook.

"I have a feeling we missed something last night, but I can't figure out for the life of me what it was."

Charlton scanned through his notes but ended up scratching his head.

"Sorry you have lost me as I didn't pick up anything from last night."

Mountie picked up the pot of coffee and refilled his mug.

"Well, we know a bit more about the murder and slowly identifying where everyone was. Unfortunately, most of the animals will have the fashion show as their alibi."

Charlton twiddled his coffee mug and started to look concerned.

"Something has been concerning me though."
"What's that?"
"It was Beth's comment about stopping the killer before they struck again. Also, Jimi saying about running for safety in case the killer wanted to strike again. Plus, Lemming's thoughts about a hired killer. All this has got me really worried about our safety."

Mountie smiled and sat back in his deck chair.

"I have been giving that some serious thought as well. My gut feeling is that this was a one-off murder. Although that's not to say they won't strike again especially if they think we are getting close to finding them"

This comment made Charlton look even more concerned.

"Also, I can't decide yet whether it was a spur of the moment killing or a premeditated killing. I was wondering if our killer had drunk the whisky to give them the courage to kill Barnsley. If so, then the whisky bottle is our first real piece of evidence and a big clue to helping us find our killer."

Charlton poured the last of the coffee into his mug and sat in the deck chair trying to calm down a bit.

"I will be a lot happier when we finally catch whoever did it."

Mountie nodded in agreement.

"We need to be very careful and not forget that we are trying to find a killer. The last thing we

must do is provoke them into killing either of us two or worse still killing anyone else in the zoo."
Mountie looked at his watch.
"Any way it's nearly time for the zookeepers to arrive. Keep your chin up as I'm sure we'll find the killer in the end."
Charlton climbed out of deck chair slowly and turned to Mountie.
"So, what are the plans for this evening then?"
Mountie climbed out of his chair as well.
"I suggest we reconvene here around 6.30. We then go and see Crocket and start interviewing the rest of the animals. We need to concentrate on who wasn't at the show."
"Fine by me and I will see you later."
He turned and started to walk back.
"Also" said Mountie.
Charlton stopped in his tracks and turned around.
"I have been thinking. We need to get into the vet's surgery to see if there was an autopsy or report on Barnsley's death. It might contain some vital information that will help us. So, we both need to start thinking about how we might achieve this."
"Can't we just break in and get it overnight?"
"Not as easy as that as it is heavily secured because it is full of drugs. Security was upgraded after the attempted burglary last year. We don't want to be breaking in and setting off any alarms do we. I think our best plan is a diversion of some

sort. We need a reason to get Doctor Mike to leave the surgery unattended long enough for us to sneak in undetected and see what we can find. "

"I'll give it some thought."

Charlton was beginning to cheer up at the thought of this.

Just then the sound of the zoo opening alarm rang out around the zoo.

Charlton turned around and hurried back home.

CHAPTER 10 – THURSDAY
4TH AUGUST (PM)

Another hot day with the zoo packed with lots of coach parties and children's parties.
The last visitors hadn't left till 5.45 as they were making the most of the glorious weather.
The staff had finished off their chores quickly to get off as soon as they could.
Andy Cousins finally locked up at 6.15 and handed everything over to the zoo security.

Charlton had showered and sculptured his trademark Mohican into a gleaming black construction.
He again found Mountie sitting outside in a deckchair.
He was dressed in his black trousers and red tunic with all the buttons undone.
He had on some gold rimmed aviator style sunglasses and was staring at his notebook.
On the table was a pottery jug of sangria, two glasses and a brown earthenware plate filled with green and black olives.
Charlton collected the black and white striped deckchair and parked it next to the table and poured himself a glass of sangria.
He didn't want to start getting a taste for it because he knew if he started drinking it back at

home, he would never hear the last of it.

"Found the clue yet" said Charlton hopefully sitting down in the deckchair.

Mountie shook his head and carried on looking at his notepad.

"Good job we are not seeing Edgar today. I hear he is still pretty mad with Bruce the scorpion."

Mountie just nodded and carried on reading from his notebook.

Charlton decided to get his notebook out as well and sat back with his glass of sangria. He started reading through his notes to see if he could see anything they might have missed.

The morning had got off to a very eventful start.

A zookeeper had gone to Bruce the Deathstalker scorpion's enclosure to put some more food in it and found that it was empty. The alarm had gone off and everyone then started hunting around the zoo for him.

He had finally been found in Katrina's enclosure where he had spent the night.

Bruce had been drinking at the café and had got very drunk, which by a scorpion's standard was 2 pints of beer. On his way back he had accidentally ended up in Katrina's enclosure where he had fallen asleep.

She had initially been shocked by his intrusion.

She found it amusing to have a beer smelling scorpion in her enclosure rather than a beer smelling Jackal in there.

Edgar was livid when he found out.

A message of apology from Bruce had been passed to him via Postie Stevie.

Katrina had passed messages to Edgar as well telling him not to make such a big deal of it and agreed to go out that evening with him to help calm him down.

Early on the animals had realised the need, whilst the zoo was open, for messages to be passed between them. Especially as mobile phones were impossible to use during the day.

Oscar had befriended a seagull called Stevie.

Unfortunately, his parents were into action movie and big fans of Steven Seagal. They also had a sense of humour and had called him Steven. He soon tired of the jokes and changed his name to Stevie. Although even this still caused some merriment.

He had quickly become known as Postie Stevie.

He had a code of honour to never read any of the messages or divulge the sender.

He had access to all animal enclosures.

In exchange for doing this role he was kept fed and watered, usually at the café.

As such by seagull standards he had a very good lifestyle.

Finally, Mountie put down his notebook, finished his sangria, got up from the deck chair and then did up all the buttons on his tunic.

"Come on Charlton let's go and see what Crocket

has to say for himself".
Charlton finished his sangria and put the empty glass on the table.
He then joined Mountie who had started walking in the direction of the flamingo enclosure.

The design for the flamingo lake fell to the Hearts River music college and not surprisingly they had come up with a music-based design.
The lake was shaped like a large flying V electric guitar.
All around it were green-coloured poles and on top of each was either a green or gold coloured cast iron instrument. These included a violin, a saxophone, a trombone, and even a French horn. The stringed instruments had electronic bows moving across the strings in time to some classical "elevator" music that blared out during opening times. It was instantly switched off soon as the zoo shut.
All the animals hated the music and regularly managed to sabotage it much to relief of any animal in earshot whenever they were successful.

They carried on walking into the enclosure.
They found Karen, Lindsay and Joanne standing in the lake chatting.
They were all dressed respectively in blue, green, and pink two-piece velvet tracksuits.
Mountie was constantly confused by animals such as zebras and flamingos who liked to dress

themselves in outfits that matched the colour of their bodies or feathers.

He looked at Joanne and decided now was not a suitable time to pass comment.

Mountie coughed loudly to get their attention.

They stopped talking and looked over.

"We were hoping to have a chat with Crocket" said Mountie looking around in vain trying to spot him.

"Sorry our zookeeper thought he looked a bit off colour this morning and took him to the vet's surgery to be checked over. He did text me to say he should be back tomorrow though," said Joanne whilst preening her feathers.

Mountie and Charlton's hearts sank as they didn't really want to wait till the next day.

Spotting their disappointment Joanne nudged Karen and Lindsay

"Why don't you interview us about the murder, you never know we might have some useful information for you".

He knew they had been cornered and that it would be rude to say no.

He suspected that the conversation was going to prove utterly pointless.

They both knew the flamingos considered themselves hot shot American detectives as they had starred in the opening sequence of the Miami Vice television detective shows.

They constantly watched old clips of it on

their television and paused to point out which flamingos they recognised.

They also pointed out how some of them had now changed. Cousin Joe now has a beer belly or Uncle Nigel's feathers were now going grey. This was not surprising as it had been at least 20 years since the filming had taken place.

It was rumoured that Crocket had also starred in the opening sequence but as yet no one had proven it.

Ignoring Charlton, looking like a rabbit caught in the headlights Karen launched in.

"So how are you getting on with the hunt for the killer?"

"We are beginning to make some progress" said Mountie who was in two minds whether to open his notebook or not and chose the latter option.

Joanne warming to the discussion chipped in

"Now what would Tubbs and Crocket have done?"

Oh no here we go thought Mountie and Charlton in harmony, their faces not hiding this thought either.

Karen ignored their negative body language and carried on with the conversation.

"They would have guessed that Barnsley was dealing drugs in Hearts River town and then there was a bust up with some rival drug dealers. There followed a shootout behind the Ye Watered Down Ale public house and

Barnsley then escapes back here in his sky-blue convertible Lamborghini Gallardo."

Joanne was getting excited.

"No, a nice pink 1950's Cadillac convertible with big fins at the back"

Lindsay also started warming up to the conversation.

"No, it's got to be a red Ferrari Testarossa, they would have no chance catching him in one of them."

"Give me strength" muttered Mountie and tried desperately to catch Charlton's eye in vain.

"Then they chase and follow him back to the zoo's car park where they then have him cornered. They then strangle him and drag his body to the café. They then stuff a bottle of water down his throat to disguise the fact he was strangled and then they leave." Joanne continued with enthusiasm.

"Did you check the car park for Ferrari tyre tracks and signs of his body being dragged towards the zoo?" Lindsay excitedly butted in.

"Surely it was Cadillac tyre marks." Joanne chipped in

"No you are all wrong it would have been Lamborghini tyre marks" said Karen smiling whilst noticing Mountie and Charlton's discomfort.

There was a pause during which Mountie decided how to use to get the conversation back on track.

"Well thank you all for your ideas. Let's not forget this is sleepy Hearts River town and not downtown Miami. Although I did say we will leave no stone unturned in our investigation"

Charlton was drifting slowly back to the land of reality and like Mountie he had decided not to get out his notepad either.

"Now where were you all between 8.00 and 9.15 that night?" said Mountie.

Karen looked at the others first then decided to take on the lead role.

"We were all helping Crocket put on the fashion show."

"As you know no one escapes Crocket. What a task master he is and never a thank you. Still being the only male amongst us females we do get our revenge all the time though." said Lindsay testily.

All three of them laughed in unison.

"Lindsay and I were asked to be models along with the giraffes Claire and Michelle. As Joanne didn't fancy modelling this time" Karen resumed.

"Time of mouth" mouthed Lindsay who started laughing.

She was given a hearty whack from Joanne who had gone an even brighter shade of pink.

Karen glared at them both.

"Joanne was asked to show the animals to their seats and give out programmes. We were all busy until the show stopped, and Crocket made his announcement".

Mountie turned to Joanne.

"As you were manning the door did anyone leave and return at all during the show?"

Joanne stood on one leg pondering the question finally.

"No one left early except for Poppy who was looking very upset. She left about 5 minutes or so before Crocket's announcement."

There followed a minute of reflective silence.

"What were you all doing during the interval?" said Mountie.

"Well Lindsay and I stayed in the changing room to get ready for the second half of the show. I think we both went to the loo, but we didn't venture much further than that. Obviously, we all met up at the café after the announcement and we saw you there Mountie".

Charlton was upset again at not been noticed as being at the café.

Lindsay nodded in agreement.

Mountie turned towards Joanne.

"I stayed in my seat as I knew if I wandered around, I might get nabbed by Crocket to help him out with something else. I watched the excellent seal show and stayed in my seat till the announcement. As Karen said I then joined them at the cafe"

Charlton decided to take over the questioning.

"Before we go do you know anybody who had a grudge against Barnsley."

Karen laughed "Obviously you know about Crocket's run in with him over the clash of events".

Mountie and Charlton both nodded in agreement.

"Well that soon subsided when he thought no one would be going to Barnsley's do anyway. He also started spreading a rumour as to what he would do if Barnsley turned up at the show. Suddenly he saw ticket sales rocket. Although knowing Crocket if Barnsley had turned up rather than making a spectacle of him, he would have roped him to doing something like selling ice creams "

Lindsay with a big smile on her face nudged Karen

"Although do you remember the mood he was in when he first found out about Barnsley's event clashing. HE manages all the events in the zoo thank you very much and no one, especially Barnsley, was going to take that away from him."

"Yes, we ribbed him rotten for a couple of days. We kept saying that we had heard that lots of animals were going to Barnsley's do just to see how he reacted. See we can get our revenge when we put our minds to it. He does get so puffed about his self-importance and he is an easy target for us." said Joanne smiling.

Mountie, seeing an opportunity to escape, nudged Charlton.

"Ok well thanks a lot if you think of anything

more please let us know"

Joanne, Lindsay and Karen nodded their agreement.

Mountie started walking out and then stopped and turned around.

"When he gets back tomorrow can you tell him that we visited and would like to have a chat with him."

Joanne, Karen, and Lindsay again nodded their agreement.

As they left Charlton breathed a sigh of relief

Mountie stopped and turned to him.

"That was very interesting. Very interesting in deed"

"What was? the Ferrari, Lamborghini, or the Cadillac car choices . Although you can't beat a good old Aston Martin any day"

Mountie shook his head.

"No not that. We have only been thinking that he was killed in the café. But what as they suggested he was killed somewhere else and then moved to the cafe."

Mountie got out his notebook and started writing something in it.

"Surely if that happened the killer need to be pretty strong to be able to have dragged Barnsley to the café from wherever they had killed him." said Charlton deep in thought

"Or persons. Although I still think we are looking for just one animal and I am convinced he was killed in the café. I can't see him leaving the café during his event to meet someone else. He would have stayed at the café to meet and greet."

"Or if there was someone wanting to see him, he would have arranged for them to come to café either before at the end instead."

"Exactly. Also, I'm pretty sure the killer or killers would want to avoid being spotted moving a dead lion around the zoo."

"There was another very interesting comment though which I hadn't considered."

Charlton stopped writing in notebook, looked curiously at his notes and then scratched his head.

"Err what was that?"

"What Joanne said about stuffing a bottle down Barnsley's throat to disguise the fact he had been strangled. I hadn't really thought about him being killed other than by being choked with the water bottle. We do urgently need to check out the vet's surgery for an autopsy if there is one at all".

"I might have a plan. It's a bit far-fetched and still needs work on it reviewing before I tell you about it" said Charlton smiling proudly.

Mountie nodded his head and smiled.

That's good news perhaps we can discuss it tomorrow."

"Fine I will give it some more thought later. We have still have plenty of time to see someone else who do you fancy seeing".

"I reckon we still need to see Edgar and the

jackals, but under the circumstance this is best left till tomorrow. Not much point seeing Katrina either."

Charlton nodded in agreement.

"Well, we still have to see the rest of the reptiles, the zebras, the wild cats, the giraffes, the rhinos, the camels, the seals and those mischievous monkeys where do you fancy starting."

"Well, I know I might regret saying this, BUT it is still early and as there is no football on tonight, we could go see my lot and cross them off our list"

Mountie looked down at his list.

"I did consider seeing the camels. Although we really need to see them as soon as the zoo shuts as we mustn't give them time to start drinking, perhaps we can make them our first port of call tomorrow evening."

Charlton nodded in agreement.

"That's a great idea. Come on, let's go and see my lot. I just hope we don't get too much stick from the lads."

Mountie, still smiling, closed his notebook.

"Well, if we do get any stick, I will mention about Oscar joining us next time."

They both laughed and started to make their way towards the zebra enclosure.

CHAPTER 11 – THURSDAY 4TH AUGUST (PM-LATER)

"How's the investigation going?" a voice suddenly called out after them.

They turned around to see a tiger called Troy walking towards the big cat's enclosure carrying a crate of lager that he had collected from the café.

He was dressed in a pair of long red shorts and a red Ferrari Formula 1 t-shirt.

They both walked over to him.

"Thanks for asking. Still early days." said Mountie.

"The sooner you catch the killer the sooner we can get back to sleeping safely at night."

He adjusted the crate of lager he was holding.

"I suspect you will want to speak to us soon, not that I think we will have much to add".

Mountie looked at his watch.

"Are you all free now?"

"Sure, the place is a bit of tip, but we should all be free now. Follow me"

Troy carried on walking and waited by the gate and Charlton opened it for him and then they walked in.

In front of them stood a large sheet metal Red Indian tepee painted light brown.

The design was done by the 5th year of Hearts River Upper School.

It was agreed that after completion they could all come and decorate the outside of it. They painted a large mural of a Wild West scene all the way round the tepee and it contained buffalos, cowboys fighting red Indians and some mustangs.

Sally Ritchie, a pupil in the class, had designed it and had won an annual family pass to the zoo.

The inside of the tepee had been split into three enclosures and each one housed Troy, a jaguar called Paul and a leopard called Victor.

Troy led them inside and they walked into the living room where there was a large 50-inch television in the corner that was on.

A voice boomed out from it.

"We have a new Maserati to test tonight and who better to put it through its paces than our mysterious superstar. He claims he actually knows 60 shades of grey elephant and has the marks to prove it. All we know is his name is The Squid."

On the screen appeared a giant squid in a white racing outfit, white crash helmet and a white visor who then climbed into a new blue two door sleek Maserati sports car.

All the top animal car racing drivers were giant squids as they were very large and had intelligent eyes.

Also, their ten tentacles provided them with the ultimate multitasking driving experience. They could have two on the steering wheel, one on each of the clutch, brake, and accelerator foot pedals, one for the manual gearbox and one for the other car controls like indicators. This left them with three free tentacles to either change a CD, use a mobile phone, eat a sandwich or smoke a cigarette all at the same time.

Troy coughed loudly "Gentlemen where are your manners we have guests?"
There were two big black sofas with Victor and Paul sprawled out on both.
Upon hearing Troy's voice, they both turned around to see who the guests were.
Both were dressed in jeans with Victor wearing a T shirt with a Ducati motorcycle on the front.
Paul had a black T-shirt featuring a figure dressed in racing whites, white visor helmet and white writing above it "Who is The Squid?".
They were both surprised to see that their guests were Mountie and Charlton.
Paul hit the television remote control pause button and the Maserati was frozen mid corner and partially obscured by some white tyre smoke.
"How is the murder enquiry going" said Victor beckoning Mountie and Charlton to sit down on the empty third sofa.
"I was just saying to Troy it still early days but I

think we are making some progress."

Troy placed the crate of lager on the table and threw a can to Victor and Paul.

Mountie and Charlton also nodded their acceptance and were thrown a can as well.

"It's good to hear you are making some progress though. I know Oscar and Poppy are very upset. It will be good for the rest of us when this killer has been caught" said Paul opening his can

Victor and Troy nodded in agreement.

Charlton started looking at their t-shirts.

"What were you all doing that night, I assume you were not at the show?"

Troy, Victor, and Paul all laughed.

"PLEASE Can you really see us at a fashion show," said Paul.

Mountie and Charlton both looked at each other and shook their heads in agreement.

"Anyway, it was a Sunday night and it started at 8.00. What does any normal red-blooded male animal do at that time?" said Troy enthusiastically.

Mountie looked blank on account of him not having a television.

Charlton was just about to answer.

Troy, Paul, and Victor then shouted out.

"It's 8.00 and it's time for Top Deer".

All three of them then hummed the theme tune out loud.

Mountie was taken aback and a bit shocked as he didn't have a clue what they were on about.

"I think that Jeremy Hartson is brilliant" said Troy opening his can of lager and sitting down in a chair next to the table.

"I really thought Rich (a Siberian hamster), and James (a Canadian Wolf) were going to beat Jeremy in the race this time" said Paul excitedly then taking a drink of his lager.

"Still not sure how Hartson managed to get that Aston Martin Vanquish S down the Amazon to win though" said Victor laughing out loud.

Mountie still looked totally blank.

"I will update you later" Charlton whispered a bit too loudly to him.

Troy, Victor, and Paul looked at each other as though an alien had just landed in their tepee. They couldn't believe there actually someone who had never seen Top Deer.

"Mountie hasn't got a television" Charlton piped up in a vain attempt to spare Mountie's blushes.

This remark resulted in three even more blanker faces.

They were all struggling desperately to understand the concept of not only living without a television but also living without their weekly fix of Top Deer.

"Back to Sunday evening." said Charlton trying to break their trance.

Life began to visibly reappear on their faces.

Troy was the first to realise that the conversation was back on home territory.

"And last Sunday's episode was extra special.

Paul's jaguar cousin Alex was on it. They were trying to see on a pro rata basis whether Alex could jump over more caravans than a Jaguar XKR sport car"

"I still think they fixed it with that last caravan. We knew Alex would normally have cleared it. Also, not sure why he wasn't wearing a crash helmet. Still at least I know he is Okay" said Paul sipping from his can of lager.

"And what time did the show finish?" said Charlton.

He was taking over from Mountie in doing the questioning in a bid to save him further blushes over his ignorance of the show.

"Well, the show finished at 9.00. I then called Alex to make sure he was OK and he said he was fine now." said Paul leaning back in the sofa and drinking his lager.

"I then got everything ready for us to watch the show again" said Victor drinking from his can of lager.

Mountie and Charlton turned their attention to Troy, who took a drink from his lager can.

"We'd all had a curry the night before, so my stomach was a bit iffy. As soon as the show finished, I zoomed off to the bog and I was in there for about 10-15 minutes. The new Top Deer magazine had arrived the day before, so I was reading that in there as well".

There were some loud sniggers from Victor.

"There I was thinking that males couldn't

multitask only to find Troy displaying a perfect example of it" said Paul with a big smile.

"Although if I recall it was definitely "I would give it 20 minutes" job" said Victor,

Everyone laughed although Mountie frowned.

"When I had finished, I came back in took some drinks and food orders and I started walking over to the café to place our orders with Aussie as usual" said Troy crushing his can in his hand.

"On my way I met up with the rest of the animals that were also on their way to the café. Karen the flamingo told me what was going on. So, I went and heard Oscar's announcement. I think I stood near you Mountie. Afterwards I came back here and told the lads"

Victor and Paul nodded in agreement in unison.

Charlton was even more upset as he had been standing in front of Troy and again, his presence at the café had not been mentioned. He started to think about future outrageous colour schemes for his Mohican to make sure everyone remembered him next time.

Mountie finished his can of lager and stood up and put it on the table.

Charlton got up as well and placed his can next to Mountie's.

"Sorry we couldn't have been more help "said Troy getting up from his chair.

Victor and Paul again nodded in agreement.

Mountie stopped and turned to Troy.

"Sorry you said you took a drinks and food order

with intention of going to the café. Did you not remember about it being shut because of Barnsley's WAAR event?"

"You can see we enjoy our beer, but not too excess, so it would not have been on our calendars. I must admit though I had completely forgotten about till I bumped into the Karen. We have a Sunday night routine here where we watch Top Deer live. Then we get some drinks and food from the café and then watch it all over again"

Victor and Paul again nodded in agreement.

"Did you see anyone else about on your way to the café? Somebody not going to the café or somebody acting suspiciously?"

"Ah I see what you mean. Did I perhaps see the killer by accident. No, I don't recall seeing anyone until I bumped into Karen who was at the back of the animal group. She was jealous that I had missed the fashion show. Sorry I can't help you further."

"Well, if you do think of anything that was strange or odd please let us know "said Charlton.

"You mean other than not owning a television or watching Top Deer?" said a smirking Paul.

Troy and Victor burst out laughing.

Mountie went bright red and carried on walking out of the tepee

Charlton stopped in his tracks.

"Hold on a minute I need to go back and borrow something".

Mountie gave him a puzzled look.

Charlton disappeared into the tepee and returned holding a Top Deer magazine.

Mountie looked strangely at the magazine.

"Run out of reading material? I have some good detective books I can always lend you."

Charlton shook his head.

"I think I might need this as part of my vet diversion plan".

"Okay" said Mountie looking confused

The sound of squealing tyres then filled the air.

"Well at least on a positive note that's a few less animals we need to interview".

Mountie nodded in agreement.

"Also, unfortunately Troy didn't see anyone on his way to the café."

Mountie nodded in agreement.

They carried on walking and Mountie suddenly stopped.

"Hang on a minute. They said Troy was out of sight for 10-15 minutes as he was stuck in the loo."

"So, they did but why is that important?"

"Well with his speed and physical size he had a window of opportunity to go and kill Barnsley. He could have returned in time without being noticed by the other two" said Mountie looking concerned.

"It would have been a bit risky. How would he have known that Barnsley was still there and alone or was it just a lucky guess".

"If it was Troy, then it explains why even with a dodgy stomach, he was still keen to do the food and drinks order. Perhaps he needed to return to the café and see if he had left anything incriminating there or to see if anyone had spotted him.".

There was a pause as they both started to think this idea through.

Charlton's face then went shocked.

"Do you think Troy has just stage-managed bumping into us and our invite in order to pick our brains as to what we know."

"I hadn't considered that, but it is a possibility. If it was Troy, then I don't think the whisky bottle had anything to do with him. Although if we assume the bottle is relevant to our investigation then perhaps its owner saw everything".

There was a further pause as Mountie and Charlton both thought this through.

"Well, that meeting has definitely given us lots more food for thought." Said Mountie.

"And a possible suspect."

"Come on let's go to your enclosure and get them out the way whilst we can hopefully get some semblance of intelligence out of them".

They started to make their way with Charlton enlightening Mountie on the delights of the Top Deer television programme.

Mountie was now even more convinced that his lack of a television was still a good idea.

CHAPTER 12– THURSDAY 4 AUGUST (PM – EVEN LATER)

Although Mountie knew Charlton quite well, he had never actually been in the zebra enclosure before.

Charlton opened the gate, and they walked in.

Inside was a life-size blue replica of Thomas the Tank Engine and attached to were replicas of Annie and Claribel's passenger carriages.

The design came from the Year 1 students at Hearts River Lower School who were all big Thomas the Tank Engine fans.

Thomas had been converted into their kitchen area. Annie's carriage was used as their living room and Claribel's carriage contained their bedrooms and bathroom.

Charlton led Mountie in through the front door and straight into the kitchen area where they found Laura, Alice, and Gail.

They were all dressed in very short skirts, Gail's was bright red, Laura's a bright purple and Alice's was a bright green. They all had similar low cut small sleeveless white t-shirts that were short enough to leave their navels exposed and to show off their various piercings that they attached and removed each night. They were all wearing high heeled white shoes and were just finishing off applying their make-up.

Charlton's mum Deidre then entered and was similarly attired but wore a short black skirt.

All of them had full wine glasses and were just about ready to go out drinking at the café.

"Well look what the cats dragged in" said Alice laughing loudly.

"Well look what the cat is about to drag out". said Charlton rising to the bait.

Mountie moved behind Charlton in order to avoid being in the crossfire.

"Tweedle Dee and Tweedle Dum" said Laura drinking from her wine glass.

Mountie was going red behind.

"Leave them both alone" said Deidre fluttering her eyes in Mountie's direction.

Mountie chose to ignore this and took the opportunity to look around the kitchen.

He was hit by the eclectic collection of different coloured appliances. There was a large electric blue American style walk in fridge freezer with a cold drinks dispenser that had been adapted by the lads to dispense cold lager.

Next to it was a large shocking pink fridge freezer.

He then noticed that the cooker, washing machine, dishwasher, kettle and even the toaster were all the same shocking pink colour.

Mountie looked in disbelief that someone would have chosen to buy such a collection of awful coloured objects.

"Don't look like that" said Deidre who was watching Mountie's every move.

She had noticed his disapproving look.

"We didn't pay for any of it you know. Our Alice here is a dab hand at entering and winning competitions"

Alice proudly nodded.

"The electric blue fridge I won by sticking my name and address on a postcard entry competition. The pink electrical goods I won from Monkey's Electricals for coming up with the winning slogan in their competition. "Wild Goods@WildPrices4Wild Animals". They are using it now as their marketing slogan"

Not for the first time that evening Mountie hadn't got a clue what someone was talking about.

Charlton spotting Mountie floundering again.

"Mountie most of things in here have been won by our Alice. She seems to have this lucky golden touch when it comes to entering and winning competitions run by different firms."

Laura, Gail, and Deidre all nodded in agreement.

"You should have seen the place when we first arrived from Newcastle Zoo. It was so drab and awful," said Alice.

Mountie had seen it before they moved in as he had lived in it a couple of days whilst his hut was being finished. He was reminiscing how much better it had been without all the gaudy junk that it had now had been filled with.

Charlton went over to the pink fridge and opened it to reveal that it was filled with bottles of Newcastle Brown Ale. Charlton got two bottles out, took off the bottle tops and passed one to Mountie who took a drink.

Mountie was beginning to think that he was going to have to put this down as a wasted night and so decided to take a back seat and let Charlton be the lead.

"Well you know why we are here" said Charlton taking a drink from his beer bottle.

"Well we assume you're not our gigolos for the evening" said Gail laughing and adjusting her top.

"Come on you lot be serious" said Deidre giving Gail a stern look.

" Charlton as you know we all left to go the fashion show just before the football match started at 8.00."

"We did. But it was really boring" said Gail butting in and then did a faked large yawn.

"I know it was billed as being the forthcoming winter collection, but it was all coats and jumpers not a short skirt or skimpy top in sight" commented Alice.

Alice folded her copy of Ellie magazine that she had been reading whilst waiting for the others to get ready.

Ellie magazine was an animal fashion magazine and was the brainchild of an African elephant called Ellie.

She had been born in Paris Zoo and become an unlikely supermodel despite her size.

During her modelling career, she had noticed a gap in the market for animal specific fashion magazines. So, she decided to launch her own called Ellie. It had been an overnight success and was now the benchmark for competing animal fashion magazines.

"All the costumes were black and white, please, do us zebra's need any more black and white things" said Laura finishing off her glass of wine. This comment warmed the cockles of Mountie's heart as he had finally found somebody with similar fashion views to himself.

"We stayed at the show till 9.15 when Crocket made his announcement and then we went to the café like everyone else including you Mountie" said Deidre smiling at Mountie who was starting to go bright red.

Charlton looked first at his mum and then at Mountie and a large smile spread across his face.

Although it quickly disappeared when he realised that even his mum hadn't mentioned him as being outside the café. A fact that Mountie had picked up on and had stifled a laugh.

"Charlton is there anything else you want to ask us. As we girls are losing valuable drinking time standing here chattering away with you two" said Laura impatiently looking at the kitchen clock and continued"

This confused Mountie as all the girls were holding wine glasses and he chose not to comment though.

Charlton shook his head.

"No nothing else but if you do think of anything you will let me know."

"Right come on girls," said Laura.

She brushed past Charlton and headed for the door.

Charlton and Mountie both stepped aside as she was followed out by Gail, Alice and Deidre who winked at Mountie as she passed him.

When they were all gone Charlton turned to say something to Mountie who started to shake his head.

"Don't ask as there is nothing and I mean nothing going on between your mum and me".

Charlton shrugged his shoulders.

"Well, that was the easy part out the way lets go and see the lads."

Mountie looked longingly at the door the girls had just departed from.

Charlton spotted this and smiled.

"Don't worry their bark is worse than their bite. We'll be fine and if we have time we can go and have a last drink at the café afterwards"

A very shocked expression came across Mountie's face

Charlton saw it and laughed.

"OK Perhaps that's not a good idea after all."

They went into the main room where there were three large sofas.

Sprawled out on each of them were Mark, Richard, and Alistair.

They were all dressed in jeans and black and white Newcastle United AFC football tops.

"Well in my dream Newcastle United AFC team I would have Shay Gibbon in goal. He has done some sterling work for us this season and has a safe pair of hands," said Mark. Richard and Alistair were both nodding in agreement.

They did not notice the arrival of Mountie and Charlton.

Against one wall was a 85 inch television.

Mountie stared at it in stunned amazement as he had never seen a television screen that size before. All the animals on the screen were nearly life size.

Playing on the screen was the highlights from the previous weekend's football game between Manchester United AFC and Everton AFC.

Charlton nudged Mountie.

"Watch this Rhinoaldo will skip past their last defender, put in a dipping cross then Storksjaer will smash the ball into the top right-hand corner of the goal."

As the ball hit the back of the net Charlton shouted "GOALLLL UNITED".

Mountie tried to feign interest but he had never been a sports fan.

Mark, Alistair and Richard stopped their

conversation

"Look what we have here the Lone Ranger or should it be the lone Manchester United AFC fan" Mark muttered out loudly .

"And you must be Tonto?"

Alistair and Richard both started laughing.

Mountie was still standing transfixed by the massive screen.

Richard saw it was showing the Manchester United AFC game and slapped his forehead.

"Oh NO, please tell me he's not another Manchester United AFC fan. It's bad enough having one in the zoo who also lives with us. I don't think we could cope with a second one around here."

"No nothing like that. He hasn't got a telly in his hut" said Charlton butting in and answering for Mountie.

Luckily the comment flew right over the heads of Mark, Alistair and Richard as all they heard was the word "No" which was more than sufficient information for them to digest.

Charlton gave Mountie a hefty tug.

Mountie was still awestruck by the television.

"I really didn't realise that they made television sets that big."

"We didn't either till Alice won it. It seemed fated really. She came in during the half time of a live Newcastle United AFC football game to top up our beers just as they announced a competition to win this telly. We told her what the answer was and she went off to text in the answer. Next thing we know she has only gone and won it. Next day TESCOW delivered this massive television set" said Mark

Richard with a big smile on his face joined in

"I remember it was a cracking question about one of our previous managers Glenn Roedeer. The question was what is Glenn doing now is it A- West Ham United AFC manager B- England AFC manager or C- Dead?"

Mark butted in

"Alas for poor old Glenn the answer was C. He was a deer and had to explain a run of bad results to the Directors who were a mix of lions, tigers, and a vulture. The outcome was always going to be inevitable and also very messy!!"

Mark, Richard and Alistair all laughed out loudly. Alistair spotted the bottle of beer in Mountie's hand and shouted out "Alice, three more beers please"

Charlton laughed.

"You'll have to go and get it yourself as they have all gone out for the evening."

Alistair climbed out of his chair and returned holding three bottles of Newcastle Brown Ale. He handed them out to Richard and Mark.

Mountie made an unsubtle glance as his watch and Charlton got the hint.

Seeing as they were all quiet and drinking in their chairs Charlton thought it was a good time to tackle them with his questions.

"As you know we are investigating what happened on Sunday evening and wanted to know what you all were doing then."

"We were here as it was 4th Round FA Cup night. Channel Roar was showing live coverage of Newcastle United AFC versus Arsenal AFC game," said Mark.

"We were cheering for the first 30 minutes then Arsenal AFC scored. After that we were never in the game" said Alistair leaning forward in his chair and drinking from his beer bottle.

"We didn't have the same desire for the game" said Richard, taking a sip from his beer bottle.

"Now if you look at the Arsenal AFC team you will see all their animals were born in the wild. Whereas our manager Sam Alligator was fielding more animals born in a zoo. I'm telling you there is a real noticeable difference." Said Richard.

"The zoo born players just don't seem to have the same hunger for the game" said Alistair stopping to take another swig from his beer bottle.

"You can say that again. That referee was spot on though for sending off their midfielder Dennis Bearkamp after eating our right back just after the break," said Mark.

Richard and Alistair nodded in agreement with big smiles on their faces

Alistair laughed.

"I bet they will make sure he gets his fair share of half-time oranges next time he plays"

To which Mark and Richard joined in with him

laughing.

Charlton looked at Mountie who wasn't laughing.

Although he had been trying to keep up with the conversation, he had lost the plot completely and couldn't wait to escape and go home.

"Our problem was not getting the crosses into the box. What we really need is a Trent Alligator Arnold" said Alistair sitting back in his chair

"Yeah, I reckon he would be good for us. He would have scored from that free kick we got for having our player eaten" said Mark twiddling with the beer bottle causing some to spill onto his already beer-stained Newcastle United AFC football top.

Mountie got up and rather rudely said "Well thanks for the drink and if you do think of anything else that might be useful then you will let Charlton know won't you."

Mark, Richard, and Alistair were a bit taken aback at Mountie's show of rudeness and they looked at Charlton.

Charlton indicated to let it go.

He started to get up to escort Mountie out.

"No, it's OK I will make my own way out. I'll see you as usual in the morning".

Mountie then left.

They were quiet until they heard the back door open and then shut.

"Was it something that we said" said Mark looking confused.

Alistair and Richard also looked confused.

"Time of the month" said Charlton and burst out laughing.

The others started laughing as well.

This was the answer they usually used for something that couldn't be explained away normally.

Mountie left and breathed a huge sigh of relief.

He quietly made his way home keeping a watchful eye out in case Deidre was on the prowl after waiting for him to leave.

Luckily, he didn't see anyone on his way back home.

He crashed down in his favourite chair with a large glass of Canadian scotch.

He looked at his notebook and wrote up a record of the evening's activities and his thoughts.

He then promptly fell fast asleep in his chair.

CHAPTER 13– FRIDAY 5 AUGUST (AM)

The vet's surgery is a small green and black camouflaged building located behind a fence near the entrance to enable easy access.
It is fenced off to stop visitors seeing it and viewing what was going on inside.
It has a surgical area, a recuperation area, and an office.
It is run solely by the zoo's vet Doctor Mike, as he is known to all the animals and zookeepers.

Charlton woke up at 6.00 and pulled back his curtains and saw that the sun was slowly rising.
It looked like it was going to be another hot day.
He put on some black shorts and a black Manchester United AFC football top with "RHINOALDO" embossed on the back in large silver lettering.

Rhinoaldo was a Portuguese white rhino they had signed.
He was slowly going up in his estimation following a slow start at the club and in the previous game he had scored and laid on a goal for Storksjaer.

He went into the kitchen and saw all the worktops were covered in empty wine glasses, wine bottles, corks, and empty bottles of

Newcastle Brown Ale.

He couldn't be bothered to clear up and left.

Mountie was sitting outside in his deck chair and on the table was a large pot of coffee, two green Hearts River Zoo mugs and four chocolate croissants.

He was engrossed with the Animal Times newspaper.

Charlton went to get his now usual black and white striped deckchair, and he glanced over Mountie's shoulder and saw there was one answer needed to finish the crossword.

Charlton sat down and grabbed an empty mug and filled it with coffee. He took a croissant and dunked it in the coffee, as he had seen Mountie doing previously.

Mountie looked at him over the top of the paper and weighed up whether to ask for help with the last answer.

He was just about to when he guessed what the answer was and wrote it in the gap. He then folded up the paper and put it down on the floor by his side with a contented smile on his face.

He picked up his notebook and started to read through it and then stopped and looked at Charlton.

"So can you tell me about your ideas for getting us into the vet's surgery to look for an autopsy, assuming there is one."

Charlton smiled, wiped some chocolate off his shirt.

"I'd hoped you would ask me that."

He then took a drink from his coffee mug.

"Any plan needs us to get Doctor Mike and the rest of the zookeepers away from the vet's surgery long enough for one of us to go in and have a rummage around."

Mountie nodded his head.

"I see the person doing the rummaging around is you."

Mountie continued to nod his head in agreement.

"We know Doctor Mike arrives at 8.30 each morning in case any animals have been taken ill overnight. This gives him time to look at them and if necessary move them to the surgery before the zoo opens to the public at 9.00."

Mountie nodded in agreement and made a note in his notebook.

"That's correct. Doctor Mike saw me at 8.45 when I hurt one of my antlers three months ago"

"So, the plan is one morning around 8.50 Deidre and me".

Mountie looked surprised at the involvement of Deidre.

Charlton spotted the surprised look.

"My plan will work best if only two animals are involved, and they will be my mum and me. Mum is the only one of the zebra's I can trust to take this seriously and help me with my diversion plan."

Mountie picked up his mug of coffee, took a sip and with a frown on his face.

"Do you think she will do it?"

"I think so, though she might need an incentive, are you up for taking her out for a meal at Aussies café?"

Mountie forcefully ejected a mouthful of coffee.

"I was only joking. Of course, she will do it. She is really proud of me helping you with this investigation"

Mountie pulled a white handkerchief out of his trouser pocket and started drying himself off.

"So, what is the rest of the plan".

"At 8.50 we will be helped over the perimeter fence by Mark, Richard and Alistair."

"Flaw number one, it's 8.50 in the morning. Those reprobates don't normally surface till 11.00 on a good day. How on earth are you going to get them up at that time and not only that, up and doing something useful for a change"

Charlton nodded in agreement and laughed.

"I have thought of that. I reckon an inducement of some free beer at the café should help solve that problem."

Mountie made a mental note to approach Oscar to see if he would pay for the beer. He suspected it would be fine but best ask him anyway.

"Right, once we get over the fence Deidre will run around the car park causing havoc until she is caught. I will point out some expensive cars for her to head towards and cause havoc by. That is why I borrowed the Top Deer magazine. I will ask her to keep the zookeepers entertained for as long as she possibly can."

Mountie was silent for a minute imagining Deidre running around the car park being pursued by zookeepers and started smiling.

"My plan is to make it out of the zoo grounds. I will run past the gates and out onto the main road. Doctor Mike will have to chase me and stop me by using a tranquilizer gun. I am hoping both our diversions will then give you enough time to visit the surgery and rummage around looking for clues."

Charlton sat back looking pleased with himself.

Mountie thought about the proposition put before him.

"You know what Charlton I reckon that might just work. How quickly do you think it can be arranged?"

Charlton sat beaming and was really pleased Mountie had liked his plan. He had thought he might reject it straight off or have an alternative plan.

"Possibly a day or two. I need to check Doctor Mike still comes in early. I can't see a problem getting agreement from the others., I need to make sure I haven't missed anything with the plan."

"That timescale sounds excellent. Obviously sooner the better as I am keen to see the autopsy if it exists."

Charlton nodded in agreement and then a thought struck him.

"I am planning to show Deidre the Top Deer car magazine so she has an idea of alternative expensive cars to go for in case she can't get to the ones I point out for her."

Mountie nodded his agreement.

"Also, I will need to book a table at Aussie's cafe for you two as well".

Mountie shot bolt upright in his deckchair and saw that Charlton was laughing.

Mountie then looked at his watch.

"Very funny. Right the plans for later are to meet at the camel enclosure at 6.30. Hopefully Crocket will be back from the vets, and we can see him afterwards."

"Thinking about Crocket he will have information about the current activities of Doctor Mike in the morning".

Charlton climbed out of deckchair put his mug on the table.

"Okay I will see you 6.30 at the camel's enclosure."

He put his deckchair back by the side of the hut and started to walk back to his enclosure.

CHAPTER 14 - FRIDAY 5 AUGUST (PM)

Another scorching hot day and the zoo had enjoyed another packed house.

The animals had been resting in any shade they could find as the temperatures soared.

They had all looked enviously at the kids wandering around eating their ice creams and were eagerly waiting for closing time so they could eat their own.

Mountie and Charlton had quick showers then met outside the camel's enclosure.

Charlton arrived wearing a white short-sleeved England AFC football shirt . On the back was the name of their top goal scorer CRANE . He was also wearing a pair of long baggy red shorts with a Manchester United Football AFC Club logo on the front. He had also turned his mane into a bright red coloured Mohican.

He was already sweating when Mountie arrived.

Mountie looked cool even though he was dressed in his black trousers and a red tunic with the only concession being that the two top buttons were undone.

"Sure, has been a very hot day. I have some good news from Crocket saying he is back and will meet us at the café at 8.00 tonight."

"That's excellent news," said Charlton.

He started to walk up the path to the entrance to

the camel's house and Mountie followed a little behind him.

The camel's house had been designed by the 4th Year of Hearts River Lower School and its design centered around their love of fairytales and sweets.
They had designed a large gingerbread house.
The walls and roof were a light gingerbread colour and it had bright red slated wooden windows and a large bright red front door.
The children had decorated the outside of it with various coloured/shaped sweets that the builders had made for them.
On each wall there was a large wooden pink heart covered in fake jewellery that the children had made in their arts and crafts lesson.
Outside the house stood a life size statue of a gingerbread man, woman, boy and girl all holding hands. They had also been decorated in sweets by the children.
The children who visited the zoo loved the enclosure.

Unfortunately, the camels that lived in it absolutely hated it and they constantly cited it as the reason that they had turned to drink as they claimed they could only face its hideous façade when they were drunk.

As they were walking up to the entrance Mountie stopped as he spotted a strange plant partially sticking out from behind the gingerbread man's right leg.

He stopped to register what it was and then wandered behind the other gingerbread characters and saw about thirty more plants growing there.

"Well, you don't see them in many gardeners' magazines." said Mountie smiling.

Charlton was looking at the plants and scratching his head in puzzlement.

"What's that plant then?"

"That Charlton looks like some top-quality cannabis,"

He then made a sniffing motion in the direction of the gingerbread house.

"And so is that."

Mountie knocked on the door.

After a few minutes George peered around the corner of the door and smiled.

"It's OK Willie it's only Mountie and Charlton".

George fully opened the door and ushered them into the front room that contained two sofas.

On the floor and around the edges of the wall were various bottles and barrels that were all in the process of making an array of various homemade wines and beers.

On one of the walls was a massive poster of a packet of Camel cigarettes.

Beneath which sat on one of the sofas 's was Willie who was wearing some rainbow-coloured walking trousers and a light green T-Shirt with a cannabis leaf on it and "Legalise Cannabis" above it in large black text. The T shirt was gamely trying to fit over his rather large belly.

Mountie and Charlton started looking at the poster.

"That is great Uncle Cedric, god rest his soul. One of the most famous camels in the world. Luckily, he had the foresight to include in his contract that after he died all future family members would be entitled to as many free Camel cigarettes as they wanted. Now that is what I call a legacy," said Willie.

He motioned to the table where there were six large boxes of Camel cigarettes.

"Take some if you want."

They both shook their heads as neither of them smoked.

"Very wise, disgusting habit but as you will appreciate, I have don't any incentive to give them up."

George appeared wearing jeans and a T-shirt with the Camel cigarette logo on it.

He was holding a tray with four glasses of beer on it.

"You have got to try this. We have just finished brewing it and it is really smooth with a real kick at the end".

He sat down on the sofa next to Willie and motioned Mountie and Charlton to sit on the other sofa.

George then passed them each a glass of their

new home brew and each took a sip and all commented in unison "Wow that does taste good"

"Good to enjoy the fruits of our labour," said George.

Mountie laughed and stared at Willies T-shirt

"So, Is that the only fruit you are labouring over?"

Willie and George looked at each other and then turned back and laughed.

"You noticed the plants growing out front then?" said Willie.

Mountie started smiling and nodded in agreement.

"It's not ours you know. We had a new zookeeper about two years ago. One morning we noticed that he had planted something behind the gingerbread people. It wasn't till they started sprouting that we immediately knew what he had planted there."

"I guess he thought it was a safe place. After all who would think to look for cannabis plants in a camel zoo enclosure" said George taking over.

Mountie and Charlton both nodded in agreement.

"We take some but still ensure we leave enough to make sure the zookeeper continues to keep growing his plants there. Thankfully he still does as you can see."

They all stopped to take another drink of the homebrew.

"Still, I don't expect you came here to discuss growing cannabis. I suspect you have come here as you want to discuss that evening's events." said George.

They nodded their heads and got their notebooks and pens out.

"So, tell us what happened then" said Mountie.

Willie looked at George and then started.

"Well Aussie was asked to run the bar at the fashion show. That Crocket is such a persuasive so and so. Aussie needed help and so he asked George and me."

"Didn't Crocket have concerns that the zoo's three leading boozers were going to be running the bar?" said Charlton.

George and Willie both laughed.

"To be honest he was so caught up with fashion side of the show that he didn't care much about the bar," said Willie.

Mountie wrote some more notes in his book.

"So, what happened then."

"We arrived at the show around 6.30 and started to set up the bar. Aussie then arrived later and helped us finish it off. We served drinks before the start and took interval drinks orders. We had a couple of beers whilst the first half of the show was on. We then got the interval drinks ready and manned the bar during the break," said George.

Willie nodding in agreement.

"At 9.00 just as the second half started Aussie

said we were running low on gin especially as the bar was staying open after the show. He said he needed some more fetching from the café," said George.

"Aussie mentioned Barnsley's event might still be going on and to be careful not to interrupt it. There were strict instructions not to persuade any attendees to join us back at the bar." said Willie.

Aussie said all the drinks had been carefully locked away to avoid tempting any alcoholic attendees to grab a drink. None of us wanted to go as it meant losing valuable drinking time. So, we had a quick round of rock, paper, scissors, and I lost," said George.

"You know I always choose that because you always lose. Haven't you worked out yet that Aussie and I have a code" said Willie laughing.

George shook his head in disbelief.

"All this time and I never twigged it."

Everybody laughed and sat back drinking more of the beer.

"So what happened then" said Mountie looking up from his notebook.

"I was walking towards the café when a very distraught Jimi came running towards me. I calmed him down and he told me he had found Barnsley dead in the café," said George.

He started looking down into his empty beer glass.

"I told him to go straight back home, and I would

get his Dad to come home as quickly as he could. I ran to Oscar's enclosure and told him what had happened, and we both rushed over to the café. Oscar told me to wait outside."

Charlton leant forward.

"Whilst you were waiting outside did you see anything or anyone else at all."

"No all was quiet. Oscar came out and told me to go the show and get Poppy. Also to tell Crocket to make an announcement at 9.15 saying he wanted them all to go to the café immediately. He said he wanted to tell them all the reason why when they arrived" said George concentrating hard to recount what had happened.

He then took a deep breath.

"So, I ran back to the show. I found Lemming and told him what had happened, and he zoomed off. Then I met up with Crocket and passed the news onto him and he took it rather calmly. He said he would speak to Poppy and told me to go back to the café to see if Oscar needed any help. I then returned to the cafe"

Charlton cut in again.

"Did you see anything on your way back that looked suspicious."

George thought hard for a couple of minutes.

"No, I got back and met up with Oscar who was naturally really upset. I told him I had passed on his instructions. He took me inside and showed me Barnsley's dead body with the water bottle sticking out of his mouth, not a pretty sight I can tell you. Then Poppy rushed in and I left him comforting her whilst I went and stood outside the entrance to stand guard. Then everyone arrived, including you Mountie. Oscar then came out and made his announcement. Then after that I came back here"

With that George got up and made his way into the kitchen to top up his glass.

Willie got up and went to follow George.

"He's still really shaken up by the whole event. I better go and see how he is doing. Do you mind letting yourselves out?"

They got up and made ready to leave

"I fully understand it must have been a real shock. If there is anything else either of you can think of then please let us know," said Mountie.

"We will"

Willie carried on walking into the kitchen.

As they were leaving Mountie stopped in his tracks and smiled as his nose detected a new sweet smoky smell coming from the kitchen.

"Looks like George has taken it a bit hard," said Charlton.

"Well, it's not every day you see a murdered dead body of someone you knew. It will take him a while to get over it".

They reached the gate and Mountie looked at his watch.

"That's good we have enough time to get to the café before Crocket arrives. We can prepare what questions we need to ask him".

They both started walking in the direction of the café.

CHAPTER 15 - FRIDAY 5TH AUGUST (PM- LATER)

At 7.45 entered the café and looked around and saw it was empty.

Aussie was standing behind the bar wearing a black T-shirt with a silver Harley Davidson logo on the front.

"Hi there you two. How's the case going any closer to finding the killer yet?"

"Still going very slowly. Please can we have 2 pints of Parrot Ale," said Mountie.

Charlton looked surprised as he hadn't expected him to order any alcoholic drinks.

Aussie slowly poured the pints and passed them over to Mountie.

"They are on the house." said Aussie smiling.

"Thanks, we would appreciate some quiet as Crocket is meeting us here at 8.00" said Mountie looking around the café.

"It's been a really quiet night. I thought it would be packed after such a hot day but suspect everyone is too exhausted to come out. So, I don't mind closing early and going out for a blast on the Harley."

"Oh, and Crocket usually has a chilled Chardonnay wine. I will bring it over when he arrives. "

"Thanks, you're a star," said Mountie.

He looked around trying to decide on the best table to sit down at.

"Aussie can I ask you a quick question" said Charlton moving forward to pick up his pint.

"Sure, what is it?"

"When we saw Oscar, he said he had asked you lock away all the alcohol in case the event was a flop and didn't want Barnsley to hit the bottle again to get over it. You didn't mention this previously is there any reason why?"

"Err I didn't think it worth mentioning. He and I go back years and were surfing buddies at Sydney Zoo did you know about that?".

They nodded in agreement.

"Oscar is a very proud lion and comes from a very famous line of lions. I knew he was okay and had approved of Barnsley's WAAR activities. He was very nervous about the event being a disaster and having to deal with any repercussions. He dreaded things getting out of hand and didn't want alcohol to be involved."

Aussie paused.

"I admit I had concerns about the WAAR launch and it not meeting Barnsley's high expectations. So, I agreed to Oscar's request and made sure all the alcohol was safely locked away and all the optics were empty."

" I can understand that fully. Come on Charlton let's get ourselves settled over there".

Dead on 8.00 the door opened and in strode Crocket.

Crocket was looking very dashing in a pair of black Pranda jeans and a black Pranda polo neck shirt. On his feet were a pair of very shiny black Doctor Marten shoes.

He was beginning to age and had some very fetching specks of grey intermingling with his pink feathers.

Perched on his beak were some black wrap around punk style Dolphin and Gibbona sunglasses.

Dolphin was a Dolphin called Paul and Gibbona was a Gibbon called Mike who both lived at Milan Zoo.

Both had poor sight and been appalled by horrible clunky spectacles they had been prescribed.

They discussed what glasses they would like to wear and found they had similar ideas.

Their first range of spectacles had been met with universal approval.

Their spectacle business was very successful and they were worn by all the fashion-conscious animals.

Crocket looked around and saw Charlton and Mountie sitting at a table.

He went and sat at the table without removing his sunglasses.

"So, this is where it all happened. I haven't been in here since the murder."

Aussie came over and put a glass of chilled white

Cabernet Sauvignon wine in front of him.

"On the house. I will put the closed sign up outside. Help yourself to the bar as I'm going out for a blast on the Harley and will be back in about an hour."

"Thanks a lot "said Mountie and waived as Aussie went out the door.

"So, are you feeling better?"

"There was nothing wrong with me. My zookeeper said I had a temperature, not surprising considering the heat wave we are going through. Between you and me I suspect Doctor Mike drags one of us in every week just to justify his job here"

Mountie and Charlton both laughed and Crocket joined in

"Does Doctor Mike still get in at 8.30 every morning" said Charlton breaking off from the laughing.

Crocket looked curiously at Charlton.

"Yes, he does. Why do you want to know?"

"Just something we are mulling over at the moment as part of the investigation"

"Fine, if you need any more information on Doctor Mike's House of Music Hell let me know".

Doctor Mike's surgery was commonly known as the House of Music Hell.

He had a diverse taste of loud heavy rock music that he played constantly.

The walls of his surgery were currently vibrating

with his new love of Operatic and Viking heavy metal.

"Thanks. As a bit of background how did the fashion show come about" asked Mountie.

"I was approached by an agent. She was looking at running a fashion show around all the zoos. I had done one before for her which had gone well. The deal she offered me this time was good, so I agreed to do it again."

"Obviously Charlton and I didn't go to the show. So, what were you showing that night?"

Crocket smiled and he looked at Mountie's red Mountie tunic and Charlton's England football top.

"You surprise me. I thought you would have been heading up the queue for tickets, only joking."

Mountie and Charlton both laughed and picked up their pint glasses and had a drink.

"But seriously. It was an exhibition including clothes by Pranda and accessories from Sushi."

Pranda was a label set up by a panda called Yoko who lived in Paris Zoo.

She was fed up with attempts to get her pregnant by a stream of dull male panda's that various zoo's kept foisting on her.

She had always wanted to be a clothes designer and started designing upmarket black and white clothes that had taken the animal world by storm.

Whilst in New York Zoo she had become very

good friends with a killer whale whose stage name was Jaws, but her real name was Melanie.

Melanie was great fan of Pranda clothes.

She had noticed the dire selection of accessories that adorned not only the zoo visitors but her compatriot zoo animals as well.

She had, with the help of Yoko, set up the Sushi accessory range.

Melanie had hit upon the name Sushi as it drove her to ensure that she was never complacent enough to end up on a revolving plate in a sushi restaurant.

"Once I knew the date I started planning where to run the show. The seal house was an obvious location with all the seating as I have used it before. The end area makes a good walkway for the models. I spoke to the seals, and they were happy to assist. They offered to provide the interval entertainment as they were in training for the Olympics and wanted to show off their potential Olympic winning routine and get some crowd feedback."

Mountie and Charlton were busy taking notes.

Crocket paused again to take a sip of his wine.

"I then started to coerce various zoo animals to help me out on the evening. I got Lemming to do the stage, lights and sound. Aussie managed the bar and some of the others were models including the giraffes. They do make excellent models with their long necks which are great for hanging jewellery around. Also, their bodies are excellent for displaying outfits and long coats."

"As you know I did have trouble with Katrina. I really wanted her in the show but that good for nothing Edgar kept putting his boot in. It would have been my crowning glory to have had her in the show and the final outfit had her name written all over it."

"What did you do about it" said Mountie looking up from his notebook.

"I tried talking to her, obviously away from Edgar, but I think that just annoyed him even further and even more determined that she wouldn't appear. Still can't see why perhaps he will tell you when you speak to him"?

"We still have to speak to him, so it's something we will ask him" interrupted Charlton, only to be met with a stern glance from Mountie.

"Tell us about your dealings with Barnsley" said Mountie bringing Crocket's attention back to him

"Such a charming and very misunderstood young male lion. He used to be a real Jekyll and Hyde character before he sobered up."

"What happened between you two regarding the show."

Crocket took a sip from his glass of wine.

"I must admit when I first heard about his WAAR venture launch party being on the same night as my show I was livid. I am a perfectionist, and I didn't want anything to clash with my event at all. I went and saw him, and we had a blazing row here. I threatened to humiliate him if he came to the show. I recall there were quite a few animals around that witnessed the row."

Charlton and Mountie carried on making notes.

"A couple of days afterwards I had time to think about his launch night clash. I noticed that ticket sales were now going a lot faster because of the row. So, I was happy to forget about it."

Crocket took another sip of wine.

"A couple of days later I was in here at the same time as Barnsley. We got talking about his WAAR venture and he showed me his new website. I must admit it did look very impressive and I commented on how he had obviously put in a lot of hard work. I asked him again whether he had reconsidered moving his launch date. His mood then changed. He became unpleasant and made me wonder if he was secretly back drinking again. I got mad again and I had another row with him and then I stormed out. This was again unfortunately witnessed by quite a few animals."

"Were you angry enough to want to harm Barnsley?" said Mountie sternly looking at Crocket from over his notebook.

"Barnsley was harmless. He had the uncanny knack of rubbing you up the wrong way. Although never enough for anyone including me to want to kill him though."

"That's what everyone seems to say about you"

blurted out Charlton without thinking.

Mountie gave him a stern look.

Crocket laughed out loud.

"Ah you have been doing your homework and very observant Charlton. Yes, we were like birds of the feather, assuming a lion can be referred to as a bird."

All three of them smiled and took sips from their respective drinks.

"So, what happened on the night of the show?" said Mountie.

"Organised chaos. I'm not sure what I would have done without Heather. She is so well organised and has such a great memory. I don't know how she can remember what each model should be wearing in each display. I just follow what she says and make sure the models go on when they should. I just host the show telling the audience about each dress and accessory. Also, I make sure Jerry, who is in charge of the music, plays the right track at the right time."

"So, what happened on the night?"

"Well, the show started on time at 8.00 and the first half finished on time at 8.45. Everything stopped and we all had a breather in readiness for the second half."

Crocket started twirling his wine glass.

"The second half started at 9.00. Then just after 9.07, I knew this due to our strict timetable, George came to see me. He told me Barnsley might have been murdered at the café and gave me Oscar's instructions."

"We have been told you were very calm when George informed you."

"I always like to be the consummate professional. Although inwardly I was livid as hell. I knew though that the situation called for someone to be calm and in control. I sent George back to be with Oscar. I left Heather to carry on running the show and for the models to still be sent out. I found Poppy and quietly told her what had happened."

Crocket's hand was shaking, and some wine spilt from his glass onto his jeans, and he wiped it away.

"I really didn't look forward to telling Poppy. It was a very emotional experience and one I hope I will never have to go through again. She left very quickly. At 9.15 I made the announcement as per Oscar's instructions and like everyone else I went off to the café to see what was going on. I recall you were there Mountie as well."

Mountie nodded in agreement.

Charlton inwardly groaned as again his presence hadn't been mentioned. Especially as this time it was by someone who also always checks out the appearances of all the others around him. He was now seriously considering going on a course on how to raise his profile.

Suddenly there was the sound of a door opening and Aussie walked in ruffling up his hair.

They all turned to look at him.

"Sorry. Have you finished? if you haven't, I can always go away again."

Crocket turned to Mountie.

"I can't think of anything else that you might need to know."

"If you do think of anything else, no matter how irrelevant you think it might be, please let us know".

Crocket then walked out of the café.

"Do you mind if I open? I have just been asked and I said that I was about to open."

"No problems. Although can you quickly explain something technical for me" said Mountie taking a drink from his glass

"I will have a go."

"It's about the café's Wi-Fi."

Charlton looked blankly at him.

"Hey, has Mountie finally moved into the modern world!! Don't tell me you have bought a tablet and are now ready to become a silver surfer."

"Very funny" said Mountie visibly unamused.

"Only joking, you know that. Fire away as I installed it but it is in desperate need of an upgrade as I am constantly getting reminded."

"We have been speaking to Jimi and he said he was coming here to download a new song. Do all the animals do the same?"

"Jimi is always coming here and downloading songs and games. We get on really well. He is a very smart lad".

"And the other animals?"

"The Wi-Fi I installed is an old model. Unfortunately, you can't reach it from any of the enclosures yet. You get the best reception in the café itself. I have set it up with 24/7 access and access within a 30-foot radius of the café, even when it is shut."

"Hmm. So, you can't see everyone who connects to it."

"Yep, those chimps could be watching Attenborough programs outside now and I wouldn't have a clue."

Charlton was trying to understand where Mountie was heading with the questions and got his pen and pad ready.

"So hypothetically someone could be using their tablet in the bushes outside without anyone seeing them".

"Yes they could" replied Aussie still confused.

"Aussie please can you not repeat to anyone what I say next." said Mountie looking around.

Aussie nodded his head.

"Charlton how about this for an interesting thought. What if Barnsley's killer was hiding behind that bush watching the WAAR launch that night? They could have been monitoring the WAAR website activity during the event and they would also have had a great vantage point. Meaning they were able to strike at the best and safest time."

"WOW" said Aussie in shock.

"WOW. That is a brilliant suggestion, but I am

not sure how we could ever prove it?" said Charlton eagerly.

Mountie sat quietly.

"The problem I have with that suggestion is that it means the killer arrived knowing they were going to kill Barnsley at the launch."

"But surely if that is the case, wouldn't they have chosen a better murder weapon than a bottle of water," said Charlton.

He sat back pleased that he had even surprised himself with that comment.

"I agree that if they had arrived here to kill Barnsley then they would have brought a weapon with them. Perhaps something happened it and they had to resort to using the bottle instead."

"Alternatively, if we are looking at a spontaneous killing then the killer would have used whatever was close by which in this instance was a water bottle."

Mountie and Charlton sat in silence.

"I did mention to you that I gave the bottles of water and juice to Barnsley as a present for the launch because his order hadn't arrived. The killer wouldn't have known they were going to be there beforehand as I only decided to donate them when he arrived to set up." said Aussie.

"The killer might have been spying through the café window then saw the water bottles and decided to use one of them to kill Barnsley with. Or as Charlton suggested the water bottle was the closest object to use as it was a spontaneous murder."

Mountie was in deep thought.

"We must find out if the water bottle was the murder weapon or if it was used to hide how Barnsley was really murdered." said Charlton staring at Mountie.

"We do now need to find out if there is an autopsy as quickly as possible then."

They were then interrupted by some banging on the entrance door.

Aussie went to take the closed sign off the entrance door and walked behind the bar in readiness for the new customers.

Charlton and Mountie walked to the bar and placed their empty glasses on it.

"Did you have a good ride by the way?" asked Charlton.

"Perfect evening for a ride. Have you ever been on the back of a Harley?"

"No, I haven't but it's on my bucket list of 100 things I want to do before I die"

"Just give me a shout and I will take you out one night on the back of it. I have a spare crash helmet that should fit"

"Thanks, I'd love that."

The entrance door creaked open and in walked Alistair and Richard and saw Charlton and Mountie standing together.

"Sorry to interrupt you two love birds but we need to use the café for some serious drinking" said Richard jokingly.

Mountie looked embarrassed.

"Well looks like we need to leave Mountie as we can't stay here and play gooseberries can we" said Charlton as he walked towards the exit.

Alistair and Richard stopped in their tracks and saw there was no one else in the café.

They then turned around and gave Charlton a rude gesture each.

Charlton and Mountie both laughed as they left the café.

"I think I'll have an early night to go over the interviews we have just had. I would like to see if there are any clues to help us identify the killer. I need to think about the killer's activities outside the café before the murder. Were they waiting outside for the perfect time to attack. Did they come armed to kill Barnsley and if so, what went wrong to make them use a water bottle. Also was the killer outside drinking whisky to help build up their courage. Lots of questions. I'll see you in the morning," said Mountie.

He slowly started walking away and then turned around.

"We need to discuss in the morning the surgery visit as this is now top of our priority list."

Charlton nodded his agreement.

Suddenly the air was filled with the sound of loud female Geordie voices.

Charlton looked to see where they were coming from and turned to say good night to Mountie

who had magically disappeared into thin air.
Charlton laughed and walked home.
He knew it would be empty as the rest of them were boozing at the café.
He looked through his notes and gathered his thoughts before drifting off to sleep.

CHAPTER 16 - SATURDAY
6TH AUGUST (AM)

Charlton woke up and instantly knew it was going to be another hot day.

He got dressed in a pair of baggy black shorts and last night's short sleeved England football top.

He skipped breakfast and walked to Mountie's hut and was surprised that he wasn't sitting outside doing the crossword.

He then spotted a piece of paper flapping on the front door ..

"Charlton – See you down by the river".

He left the zoo and headed towards the riverbank.

It was a glorious morning; the air was full of small buzzing creatures and lots of birds were singing. There was still dew on some of the plants and a slight mist floating on top of the river.

He stopped to take in the wonder of the moment. Suddenly his attention was interrupted by a voice.

"Big Animal Issue."

He looked around.

"Morning Charlton, care for a copy of the Big Animal Issue," said Tiffany.

Tiffany was a large white female swan who lived on the riverbank.

She was dressed in green combat trousers and a red T-Shirt with the face of Che Guevara on the front.

She was a very charitable animal, and her heart was in the right place.

Over the years she had rattled collecting tins for most animal charities in front of all the animals that lived inside and outside the zoo.

She was an honorary member of Greenpeace after helping human protestors fend off security guards at a power station.

He laughed and looked at her T-Shirt.

"Che would have made you a General for being up this early fighting for your cause."

"I don't think I would have lasted long with Che. I hate cigars even Cuban ones and I can't grow a beard either."

"I'm sure you could have worn a false one."

"It would have been far too itchy . Also, it would have hidden my good looks."

They both laughed.

"So can I sell you a copy then?"

"Well Cuba's loss is our gain. I won't this morning as I have to see Mountie."

He spotted him sitting by the side of the river with his legs dangling in the water.

He started towards him and then turned and called back to her "See you later and up the revolution."

She laughed and waved him off.

Mountie saw him approaching and beckoned him over.

Mountie had a black and red checked picnic blanket and on it was a thermos flask and two mugs of which one was full of steaming coffee.

As he got nearer Mountie poured some coffee into the empty mug and passed it to him when he arrived.

He sat holding his mug and looking out over the river and spotted a trout jump out of the water.

"What a glorious morning. I must admit I don't often come down here and can now see what I am missing out on" said Charlton.

Suddenly the tranquility was broken .

They looked over to see a mother duck leading out her four baby ducklings.

"How can you drag us out now as CBBC has just started on television" said the first baby duckling in a loud disgruntled voice.

"Yes, and why now when our favourite television show Count Duckula is just about to start. I can't see why we need to be dragged out at this time. Why couldn't we wait for half hour until the show finished" said a second baby duckling who was equally disgruntled.

The mother, noticing Mountie and Charlton's startled looks on the other side of the riverbank turned to her ducklings.

"Please be quiet you two. Can't you see you are disturbing the other animals enjoying this glorious morning by the riverbank."

She waved at Charlton and Mountie and then floated off down the river with the two ducklings still squabbling loudly about missing their television program.

Charlton looked at Mountie and they both laughed.

He noticed Mountie had dunked his legs in the river and did the same and found it really relaxing as the water was cold.

Mountie picked up a packet of shortbread biscuits and gave one to Charlton who dunked it in his coffee and ate it.

"I often like to come down here to get away from things and to think" said Mountie picking up his coffee and taking a drink.

"This looks like a really good quiet time to come down here and what a great spot."

"Yes, it is usually nice and quiet. I can see why Oscar likes to come down here for a swim."

There was brief pause whilst they both drank some coffee.

"I have been here since 5 O'clock this morning," said Mountie.

Suddenly Charlton pointed out a dragonfly flying past them singing something.

Charlton started listening to the song and then burst out laughing.

Mountie looked confused.

"You'll never guess what that dragonfly was just singing?"

Mountie, knowing Charlton's eclectic tastes in

music shook his head.

"He was singing "Watching the Detectives" by Elvis Costello. How funny and apt." said Charlton still laughing.

Mountie knew the song and started to laugh.

"Obviously word of our investigation has spread fast and wide."

They continued sitting on the riverbank with their feet dangling in the water.

After a couple of minutes Mountie broke the silence.

"I can't sleep properly thinking about this case. Whilst we have some ideas of what might have happened that night and where the animals were, we still seem no nearer finding out who our killer is."

"I agree with you, but we still haven't finished all our interviews yet."

"You are right we haven't. I would like to finish them all before we hit the surgery."

Mountie then spotted a kingfisher swoop and caught a fish in its mouth.

"I suggest we visit the surgery on Monday morning. I know it will be a struggle getting the lads up early, especially after their usual Sunday night drinking session watching live football matches."

Charlton spotted two salmon with their heads on the surface of the river quietly having a conversation.

"That's a good idea and I like the suggestion of

Monday morning. Also, it's the school holidays so the zoo is always busy from the word go. I think you are going to struggle getting support from the lads for the exact reason you mentioned. When are you planning on telling them your plan?"

"I'll look for an appropriate time. Also, I don't want them to blow it by telling everyone about it after a few drinks."

"That sounds like a good idea."

Mountie lifted his feet out of the water and started drying them on the grass.

"I think tonight we need to see as many of the other animals as possible. I would especially like to see Edgar and Katrina."

Just then a rowing skull came into view, and they instantly dived for the cover of some reeds as it flew past them.

"Looks like the river is beginning to get busy," said Mountie.

He packed everything away in his picnic basket and then folded the blanket.

He passed Charlton the picnic blanket and they walked back with Charlton dropping off the rug before he continued back home.

CHAPTER 17 – SATURDAY
6 AUGUST (PM)

It had been another scorcher and the animals, especially the hairier ones, had been struggling to keep cool during the day. .

The zoo had been very busy day with lots of families visiting and everyone making the most of the glorious weather.

Charlton put on a short sleeved red Manchester AFC football top with the name of one of his favorite wingers PUGSY emblazoned on the back and some bright yellow knee length shorts.

He was also sporting a bright rainbow coloured Mohican as he was feeling upset at no one noticing him, so he wanted to bring in the changes.

He arrived at Mountie's and was surprised to find him dressed in a pair of blue tailored shorts and a white t-shirt with a large red Canadian maple leaf on its front.

"Are we not going out interviewing tonight?"

"Looking at who we still have left to interview I thought I would dress down a bit tonight."

"I hope mum doesn't see you as she has a thing about men in uniforms."

Mountie went as red as the football top Charlton was wearing.

"Who are we aiming to see tonight then?" said Charlton.
"I would like to see Edgar and Katrina, preferably together. Then any of the other animals that we come across. I wouldn't mind starting with the rhinos as I don't recall seeing any of them at the café that night of the murder."
They headed towards the rhino house.

The 3rd year children of Hearts River Upper School had been allocated its design.
As they were studying pharaohs at the time they had designed a large Egyptian pyramid for the rhinos to live in.
Roy Lunnon was a budding art student and had designed a statue to be positioned outside the pyramid. It was a life size statue featuring a grey rhino balancing a roofless Land Rover Mark 1 on its horns. There was a plaque saying it had been designed by Roy.
Roy. This was before he became a professional artist and was famous for making statues out of various animal products mixed with various animal dungs.
He had been nominated for the Turner Prize and he hated anyone referencing his zoo statue and had tried for years to disown it.

When they got to the front door of the pyramid there was an intercom button to press because the rhinos lived at the bottom of the pyramid.
To reach them you either walked down some

stairs whilst looking at rhino information on the walls or you used the lift located at the side of the pyramid.

The lift had a television screen that showed a short film about rhinos living in the wild.

Mountie pressed the button.

Charlton looked at the statue, mainly staring at where the Land Rover joined the rhino. He was sure that it was about to fall off and land on him. He then spotted some "Jesus Loves You" and "Jesus Saves" fish shaped stickers on both the Land Rover and the rhino statue.

"I bet Joel and Elspeth put those stickers there" said Charlton pointing at the statue.

Mountie nodded in agreement and said nothing.

"Who is it" said a male voice with a broad Texan accent over the intercom.

"It's Charlton and Mountie" said Mountie into the intercom.

"Oh, I suppose it's about Barnsley so you all better come down. We are in the middle of our tea though" said the Texan voice gruffly over the intercom.

"It's ok we won't keep you too long" said Mountie into the intercom.

A buzzer went off and Mountie pushed open the door.

They walked down the steps and through a door at the bottom and found themselves walking straight into a dining room.

Sitting at large table were Joel, Elspeth, and their

son Carl.

Carl was sitting at the table with a pair of headphones stuck in his ears. He was holding a gaming tablet and playing with it. He was wearing a black Slipknot T-shirt featuring all the band members with their head masks on.

The animal world had its own collection of famous singers, musicians, and bands.

There were some human bands, that unbeknown to them ,were also extremely popular in the animal world.

Slipknot were famous in the animal world because of their song "People= Shit".

This track had been used extensively in a very vivid Channel Roar documentary that covered humans killing innocent animals such as seals.

The song became an anthem for the animals.

It was regularly covered by various animal rock bands and often played as the closing song at various animal rock festivals.

The animals loved Slipknot as they could attend their concerts by wearing one of their trademark masks to disguise themselves. As such the mosh pit was regularly filled with masked humans, gorillas, and orangutans without any of them, including the band, being any the wiser.

Joel got up from his seat and showed them to the two spare seats at the end of the table.

"Sorry to interrupt your mealtime but we are talking to all the animals to find out what they were doing last Sunday night" said Mountie putting his notebook on the table and opening it up.

Charlton started looking around the room and noticed it was very sparsely decorated. There was an old portable television set and a large radio.

He noticed there were various religious statues and crucifixes and a bookcase filled with religious titled books.

Elspeth had been watching him staring around the room.

"All we brought from Oklahoma Zoo was our faith" she said in a Texan voice as well.

"We try and live a simple life. We survive quite well on the state payments we all get each week".

Many years ago, there were some real fat cats who lived in London and were called Adrian, Freddie, and Jay.

They took offence when their human owners ridiculed them about being fat.

They regularly met for lunch and had started talking about human fat cats.

They knew they were very powerful people and what interested them most was their ability to make loads of money.

In revenge they began to hatch their own money-making plan.

They got a list of the richest people in Britain and then identified those who owned cats.

They then enlisted and trained these cats to spy on their rich owners and to pass onto them any useful financial, investment and tax avoidance information they overheard.

This insider information enabled Adrian, Freddie, and Jay to start making a fortune.

They utilized internet anonymity and the information supplied by the cats to set about amassing a massive fortune with most of it disappearing into offshore accounts .

Unfortunately, they discovered some of the owner's made money in ways that sickened them. To get their revenge they siphoned money out of their accounts thanks to their cats' spying activities that enabled bank accounts and login password details to be passed onto them.

They needed to decide what to do with all the money they had amassed. After all there is only so much a cat can do with a fortune.

They set up a business and named it after themselves- The Cat Services Party.

They agreed that they wanted to somehow help all the animals in Britain.

With the fortune they had amassed and with more to come they calculated they could give every animal in Britain some money each week to help them live on.

They set up a bank called Cats Best to help distribute the money.

Every animal had to set up a bank account and each week a sum of money was paid into their accounts for them to do what they wanted with. Adrian, Freddie, and Jay carried on their money-making activities and recruited the cats of any new rich owners they became aware of or owners they wanted to target.

Fortunately for the animals, they continued to be very successful and more importantly undetected by the human world.

"Would you all like a fresh glass of homemade lemonade?" said Elspeth.

"As you know we don't drink the demon alcohol down here" she continued aiming her comment squarely at Charlton.

Charlton moved uncomfortably in his chair as he was being reprimanded for the bad reputation the zebras had because of their drinking.

"That would be fine" said Mountie trying to diffuse the situation.

Joel got two glasses from the kitchen and filled them up with the homemade lemonade and some ice.

Mountie and Charlton both tasted the lemonade and smiled as it tasted good.

"Great lemonade isn't it, special recipe from our time back in Texas" said Joel sitting down proudly.

"That is the best lemonade I have ever tasted". said Charlton, trying desperately to get back into Elspeth's good books.

This was true as he didn't usually drink it neat

and usually had it mixed it with something alcoholic.

"Glad you both like it" replied Elspeth.

Charlton watched Carl still glued to the tablet.

Carl grabbed his glass of lemonade and drank some without losing where he was in whatever game he was playing.

"So, I suppose you wanna talk to us about Barnsley's murder then?"drawled Joel in Mountie's direction.

Mountie nodded.

"You know what, we were really pleased when we heard about his new WAAR venture. He was going to tackle the demon alcohol problems the animals around here have." said Elspeth again directing her reply squarely at Charlton.

"As you know we have on several occasions stood outside the café trying to preach about the dangers of alcohol" she continued "But does anyone listen?"

"Just them religious nutter's is all we always hear back" drawled Joel solemnly.

"Which is why we were pleased to hear Barnsley wanted to tackle it as well" said Elspeth taking a drink of her lemonade.

"We invited him here to see if we could help him" she continued.

"I was so surprised he came as he has made some very un-Christian comments to us in the past. I decided to let those slide so I could help him with this new venture." drawled Joel taking a drink of his lemonade.

"He came over and spent an hour with us. He was very pleasant and forthcoming about his new project. He politely declined our help with the launch night and said we may be able to help him afterwards. He thanked us for our time and our offer of support. We both wished him lots of success with his WAAR venture" " said Elspeth smiling.

"We had some leaflets about alcohol and its dangers. He gratefully took them and said they would be useful on his launch night. That was the last time we spoke to him" drawled Joel emptying his glass.

Joel stood up and topped up all the glasses of lemonade.

"That is all very helpful information," said Charlton still trying to get back into their good books.

"Thanks a lot as well. Going back to that evening what you were all doing" said Mountie with his pen poised over his notebook.

"After we had tea, we turned on the television at 7.00.Channel Roar has been doing a repeat of the most popular editions of Changing Rooms," said Elspeth.

Carl stopped playing his computer game and removed one of his headphones.

"Oh yeah, it was the episode where Laurence Tawny Owlen was doing a makeover of a blood-stained lions enclosure in Leeds Zoo."

"Everyone knew trouble was in store when Laurence ignored their Leopard friend's advice of what color scheme to adopt. He then muttered those immortal lines," said Elspeth.

Joel, Elspeth, and Carl in unison burst out loud.

"Now a lot of you ditched chintz several years ago. But you will be pleased to know it is now making a very fashionable come back".

The three of them laughed as did Charlton.

Mountie smiled too. Although he didn't have a television, he had read all about the episode in the Animal Times

Elspeth carried on enthusiastically.

"Everybody apart from poor old Laurence knew that chintz rose wallpaper for an enclosure with 3 male Lion's in it was never going to be a match made in heaven. Give him his dues though he still carried on regardless."

Joel cut in again, determined to deliver the finale.

"Well Laurence carried on to the finish. Then finally the 3 male lions were brought in blindfolded, and he then proudly unveiled the design to them. To say they were not pleased is an understatement. The screen was then filled with parts of Laurence's innards hitting the rose chintz wallpaper. I must admit they did blend in very nicely though."

"It is probably the way he would have wanted to have been remembered anyway" said Elspeth laughing.

Everyone else was laughing as well.

"Anyway, being a Sunday at 8.00 we left as usual to go to the abandoned chapel in the field just outside Tapton Cannon village. It is a 10-minute walk from here and it is conveniently out of the sight of any passersby." said Elspeth.

"Every Sunday from 8.30 till 10.00 there is a full gospel service held by the Reverend Drake. There is a full house every week. We all give our thanks to the great Lord" drawled Joel.

"After the service we usually have tea and cakes and get back here around 11.00" said Elspeth passing around a plate of cupcakes.

"We only found out about Barnsley when we turned on the Channel Roar news on Monday morning. We were all totally shocked by it" said Joel finishing his cupcake in one.

"We felt so upset for Oscar and Poppy and have been saying prayers for them since that night."

The room then fell silent.

Mountie finished his cupcake.

"So, you were all at the service and so wouldn't have seen or heard anything odd as you weren't here?"

He then started to get out of seat.

"No, it was only Joel and me that go" corrected Elspeth.

"Yeah. Despite Carl being born in Gods own country he still hasn't seen God's light yet. Although we live in hope," said Joel.

Carl was trying to ignore them and carried on playing on his tablet.

"So, you left Carl here doing what?" said Mountie.
"Probably playing Wild Craft on that Tablet that I bought him last Christmas with my TESCOW vouchers" said Elspeth looking at the tablet disdainfully.
"Create wonderful new worlds with new animals to live in them" Charlton couldn't stop himself from muttering the Wild Craft motto.
"Exactly God took 7 days to create this world. Carl can now create one in 7 minutes on his tablet. I have complained to the game designers though as I saw you could include any building you want in these new worlds apart from a church. Carl showed me the very rude emoji that they replied with" drawled Joel.
"Hey Carl," said Joel.
"What " said Carl taking out a headphone.
"I was telling Mountie that you didn't join at church last week."
"Course not its boring"
"Mountie wants to know what you did after we left for church last week?"
"What?"
"Last week when we were at church".
Charlton and Mountie looked at each other and smiled.
"How would I know? I was probably doing stuff."
"Was it playing on the tablet stuff or watching Top Deer stuff as it was 8.00 and a Sunday" interjected Charlton trying to speed up this line of questioning.

"Don't like Top Deer more boring than church. I reckon I would have been playing on my tablet instead."

Carl put the headphone back in his ear indicating that the conversation was over.

Mountie got out of his chair.

"As I said we are sorry to have interrupted your meal. If you do think of anything else especially around Barnsley's visit, please let us know."

They exited and entered the lift.

"So, Mountie what stuff are we going to do next" said Charlton putting on a very bad Texan accent.

Both were laughing as they exited the lift.

"I think we should go and visit the Jackals."

"Shame we didn't get anything useful from that interview."

"Well, we now know there were two animals off site at the church. Although we do now have another animal whose whereabouts on the evening is unknown."

"We do though, he was doing stuff somewhere, most probably in the enclosure"

"Very funny"

They started walking to the Jackal enclosure.

CHAPTER 18 – SATURDAY 6TH AUGUST (PM- LATER)

As they approached the Jackals' enclosure the sound of live rock music got louder and louder.

They entered and walked toward a replica of a large silver and gold articulated American Mack lorry that was towing a similar coloured large trailer.

Its design had been passed to Year 5 at Hearts River Lower School.

They had been really upset at not being allocated the lions or elephants enclosures and none of them liked Jackals.

As the deadline approached and with no design appearing forthcoming a note was sent out by the Headmaster to all the parents of pupils in the class.

One enterprising parent, who owned a local haulage company, suggested a life-sized replica American Mack lorry towing a large trailer.

He cheekily asked if it could be painted in his company's distinctive silver and gold livery. He would provide the paint and painters from his company to decorate it for free. In the end this was the only suggestion put forward.

The lorry and trailer had been built and as agreed had been painted in silver and gold for free.

The lorry was the Jackals living and sleeping quarters.
The trailer had been converted into a high-tech recording studio and jamming area.
Most of the top animal rock bands had spent time at the trailer either recording tracks or rehearsing for concerts.

They went to the back of the trailer and knocked on the door even though they could hear music blasting music from inside.
They waited a couple of minutes out of politeness and then walked in.
Inside were three of the four Jackals that lived there.
They were part of the infamous Day of the Jackals rock band.
The band was made up of four jackals. Edgar on vocals, Mikey on drums, Dan on lead guitar and Suzi on bass.
Inside were Mikey, Dan, Suzi and joining them was Billy playing a Gibson Les Paul Standard electric guitar.

Billy was a very hairy bearded gibbon.
He was wearing denim jeans cut off just below the knees and a Sex Pythons T-shirt with the arms cut off.
He had been the lead guitarist with the Antarctic Monkeys and was outraged at being kicked out just before they got famous. He had been sacked as he didn't fit in with their new clean-cut image.

When they saw Mountie and Charlton they stopped playing.

This was a great relief to Mountie as the noise had started to play havoc with his hearing.

Charlton though was upset as he loved Day of the Jackals and had seen them play live the previous year.

"Sorry, we will be doing autographs later" said Dan laughing.

He was dressed in a Day of the Jackals Tour T-shirt with the arms cut off and long pair of baggy black shorts.

Dan's comment was followed by a boom, boom, boom, ting from Mikey on his drum kit.

"Hey, Mountie, I didn't realise you were a fan of ours as well," said a smiling Suzi.

She was dressed in a bright pink vest top and a very short tartan mini skirt.

Her comment was followed again by a boom, boom, boom, ting from Mikey on his drums and cymbal.

Charlton and Mountie smiled.

"Very funny Mikey" shouted out Charlton.

"We are in the middle of practising. Is there anything we can do for you or are you just here to see Edgar" said Dan tightening the strings on his blood red flying V shaped Gibson electric guitar.

"Well, we did really want to speak to Edgar about Sunday night." said Mountie

"Sorry, he was here about 10 minutes ago and

has gone off somewhere with Katrina" said Dan still fiddling with guitar.

Charlton turned to Billy with a surprised look on his face.

"I didn't realise you played with Day of the Jackals."

" Well, I do like to keep my hand in playing with a proper band. I do keep asking them to let me join them."

"But your just too hairy man" chortled Mikey from behind the drums.

"Well as we do have you all here where were you were on Sunday night." said Charlton.

Suzi took off her white bass guitar and replaced it with a six stringed black one, shaped like a skull.

"On Sunday night we were all here practising. We are headlining at Glastonbury Zoo next month ".

Glastonbury Zoo is in the middle of nowhere about five miles outside of the town of Glastonbury.

Every year the zoo's animals drug their security guards on a Friday and Saturday night.

Then lots of animal rock bands arrive and safely perform.

The shows usually start in the evening at 9.00 and carry on till 3.00 in the morning.

At this time most of the animals then need to get back to their respective zoos, game parks or loving owners before their absence was spotted.

Also, the local zoo and domestic animals need

time to clear up before any humans start arriving.

"Were you all here all evening?" said Mountie.

He started looking at the large mixing desk he was standing next to and was intrigued by the number of knobs and buttons on it.

"We practiced some key songs and then Edgar left. I don't know what time that was as we don't wear watches," said Dan.

He then started strumming a few bars of Pink Floyd's "Time" on his guitar.

"I was here as well as I managed to get a pass out from the ape house," said Billy.

"Next thing we know Edgar came back looking shocked and told us what had happened at the café," said Suzi.

"Edgar being a great song writer then sat down trying to write a song about it. He came up with some great lyrics which we just need to put some music to it" said Dan.

"I still think my made-up blues song version fits the bill perfectly," said Billy.

He started strumming a few blues chords on his guitar and then started singing in a deep voice.

"Woke up this morning dur dur dur dur. The television news told me Barnsley had been killed, dur dur dur dur and this news, I said this news, just gave me the blues, dum dum dum dum. I got those water bottle blues".

Suzi turned to Billy.

"Billy, do you mind this is deadly serious."

"Sorry I know it's in terrible bad taste, but I just couldn't resist it"

Mountie looked at them in horror and disbelief as to what he had just heard.

Dan noticed Mountie's shocked expression.

"Don't worry. Any song about Barnsley's death would need Oscar's approval first, we're not the completely senseless bastards the press purports us to be."

Suzi, Billy and Mikey nodded in agreement.

"Although Oscar is a sucker for a good guitar riff, and it would definitely sway any decision" said Billy strumming his guitar.

Mountie breathed a visible sigh of relief.

"We know Edgar and Crocket were arguing about Katrina being in the show are you able to elaborate at all?"

Suzi shook her head.

"You best speak to Edgar. What went on between him and Crocket is his business. It didn't affect the band, so we kept our noses out."

"Thanks, we will do. Well, I think that's about it although if do think of anything that may help with our investigation, please let us know."

All the band members nodded their heads in agreement.

Mountie and Charlton turned and started to walk out of the trailer.

They were stopped in their track by Mikey announcing over the microphone.

"And this number is especially for Charlton".
Mountie and Charlton both turned around.
They burst into the Day of the Jackals very fast punk version of "Fog on the Tyne" which they had retitled to "Fooked on the Tyne".
Their version regaled the events of a very promiscuous post gig celebration they had enjoyed aboard the Tuxedo Princess floating nightclub in Newcastle upon Tyne.
This brought a wide smile to Charlton's face as it was one of his favourite Day of the Jackals tracks.
They finished 2 minutes later, and a still smiling Charlton clapped.
"Thanks, you lot that was brilliant."
The band all bowed.
"That's what we always like to see our audience leaving with smiles on their faces" called Mikey's voice over the microphone.
They waved, and then left the building.
Charlton still had a broad smile on his face.
He had never heard a better version of the song and vowed to dig out his copy when he got back home.
Mountie started looking in the direction of the reptile house.
"I still fancy seeing Katrina and Edgar tonight so let's go and see if they are in the reptile house."
They started walking with Charlton singing the lyrics out loud much to Mountie's annoyance.

CHAPTER 19- SATURDAY 6TH AUGUST (PM –EVEN LATER)

They started to make their way towards the reptile house.

Its design had been chosen by Class 1 of Hearts River Upper School.
They had been studying the birth of Jesus at the time and had thought a star would make an ideal shape for the building.
A ten-sided star shape was built to hold the ten different reptiles the zoo had when it opened.
One pupil was very artistic, and she had designed in the middle of the star a large fountain that looked like a waterfall. It was a twenty-foot rock construction with water cascading down either side of it.
During opening hours, a disc of jungle birds and animals was played. It was meant to bring a soothing calm to the building but had the complete opposite effect on the occupants. No matter how often they hid the disc their zookeeper always had a spare copy to hand.

They entered and were upset as the place looked deserted and then visited Katrina's enclosure only to find it empty.
They were about to leave when Mountie heard a noise coming from Jerry the cobra's enclosure.

They entered her enclosure and stopped rigidly in their tracks.

Jerry was standing with her back to them, and she was swaying her head menacingly from side to side. It looked like she was getting ready to kill something.

She then turned around.

They both breathed a huge sigh of relief when they saw she was wearing a large pair of headphones and was swaying in time to the music she was listening to.

She pulled the headphone jack from her micro hi-fi system and classical music filled the enclosure. It was Mountie's turn this time to smile and for Charlton to have the puzzled expression.

"I see you are both surprised" said Jerry in a broad Yorkshire accent.

She turned around and turned the music volume down from level 8 to 2.

"I know what you are thinking, why is a cobra listening to classical music and not the rock band Cobrahead? I must admit I do find Cobrahead's music so uncouth".

Mountie smiled broadly and eagerly nodded his agreement.

"You see I was raised in a council flat in one of less than salubrious parts of Sheffield. A place that always features in those depressing real-life television documentaries that always seem to be set in Sheffield." continued Jerry in her broad Yorkshire accent.

"My owner during the day was known as Mary Smith. But at night she performed in all the local working man's clubs and pubs. She had the exotic stage name of Bare'N' Sly. You see Mary thought it was a clever word play on her beloved hometown of Barnsley".

Charlton started to say, "The same as."

"Mary's stage name was Bare both in name and artistic nature and mine was Sly. Unfortunately, I was not sly enough to stop her from appearing in some very low-down seedy dives. Even I was scared to go to some parts of Sheffield that we performed in and I'm a cobra."

"It was in one such dive that Bare collapsed and died of a heart attack on stage. I recall the bouncers were called in to repel some members of a necrophiliacs society that happened to be in the audience that night."

"The rest of dive's occupants were scared as to what to do with little old me. A zookeeper from here who was at the club night agreed to look after me. I think he had been a big fan of Bare's and hoped I would help remind him of her".

"Naturally I was really upset by these events, as we both enjoyed a good lifestyle. Despite appearances though, Mary was a great lover of classical music. This rubbed off on me and I fell in love with classical music too".

Charlton started again to say, "The same as."

Jerry cut in again much to the amusement of Mountie.

"When I arrived here, I was sad. I then bumped into Barnsley one evening. As soon as he told me his name, we talked about how he had got it. I then told him about my life and about Bare "N" Sly. After that we became good friends. He called me Sly, and I called him Bare, but we never told anyone why. I must admit I really miss him. He was a shoulder to cry on, a friend to talk to and someone who would listen to me."

Jerry began to cry.

Mountie went to comfort her.

"I bet he was good listener" said Charlton trying to lighten the atmosphere.

"I do let people talk as well as me you know."

They all started smiling again.

"I don't suppose you are here to listen to me rabbiting away. I suppose you want to speak to Katrina and that infamous boyfriend of hers. It's not right a snake dating a jackal. Then there is her only eating one dormouse a day. "I need to keep my Size 0 figure" I ask you" said Jerry still not letting Mountie or Charlton get a word in edgeways.

"If it hadn't been for Edgar, she would have appeared in the show you know. Crocket was very upset, and he came around here a few times to get her to change her mind. But Edgar had persuaded her not to do it and that was that."

Again, not pausing for breath and with her head moving side to side in classic cobra attack style mode she continued.

"I heard him making derogatory comments about Crocket to her. He persuaded her to not do the show to teach him a lesson. They had no thoughts for the rest of us that were going to the show."

"Also, he told her the show was beneath someone with her attributes and talents. Please! Not that I am a great fan of Crocket, in fact I do find him a bit creepy to be honest, but he is very persuasive. He does generally get his way but not this time, He had met his match with Edgar."

Jerry then stopped talking, closed her eyes and swayed in rhythm to a new track of classical music that had started on the micro hi-fi.

"Ah that Beetlehoven knew how to write great music, I had this track lined up for the fashion show finale, shame I never got round to playing it."

"As you know I was doing the music for the show. After Crocket's first visit to Katrina, he was so impressed with the music coming from my room that he popped his head round the door. He then asked me about doing the music for the fashion show. I have done some DJ work before, something I picked up from working in the clubs. and I gratefully accepted. Any chance to add some much-needed culture around here."

Jerry, noticing that the track was finishing, picked up the remote control and pressed a couple of buttons and the track replayed.

Mountie nodded in agreement and saw an

opportunity to say something said "So."

Mountie's words were cut short by Jerry launching off again.

"So, Bruce the scorpion helped me carry what I was going to use over to the show, and we arrived at 7.00. I assume he then came back here. I then did a sound check with Lemming. I went through my music list with Crocket, and he agreed with all the tracks. Although he was so preoccupied I could have shown him a list of Cobrahead greatest hits, and he would still have said the list was fine."

They both had wry smiles on their faces as they both thought Crocket wouldn't have been able to get a word in edgeways to object or make any comments anyway.

"The first half of the show was 8 while 8.45. At 8.45 the first half finished, and I then started to play some interval music. At 8.50 I was then asked to put on some sort of rap music track. It was dreadful and by someone called Diddy Dolphin. He kept mentioning things about bitches and guns. It was what the seals had decided to perform their routine too, so I had no choice. Then at 9.00 the show started again with normal musical services resumed. Then everything stopped at 9. 15 when Crocket made his announcement."

Charlton this time tried to get an opportunity to speak "Did."

"Did I see anything? No, I didn't as I was busy

doing the music. I had my headphones on most of the time to help me line up the next music track .So sorry I can't vouch for who was at the show. I know the reptile WAGs were all there passing the IQ between them as the evening progressed."

Mountie looked confused.

Seeing his confusion Jerry burst into a fit of laughter.

"WAG is a term used to describe wives and girlfriends usually of famous footballers. Their only function in life seems to be to look glamourous whilst spending enough money to keep certain clothes designers and fashion shops solvent. They are not usually renowned for their intellect!"

"Outside sunbathing you will now find the following. Sarah, an alligator, girlfriend to Bobby Zebra the West Ham AFC player, Nikki, a crocodile, who is girlfriend of Steven Gorilla of Liverpool AFC and lastly Emma a rattlesnake who is dating Ashley Mole of Chelsea AFC. Now a snake and a mole that is a very interesting combination."

They exchanged doomed looks.

Jerry picked up on this exchange and burst out laughing.

"You do know that you are going to have to interview them at some point. I do wish you luck. I hope you get more sense out them than I ever have."

They made motions to leave.

"Oh, and to make your evening really complete you should also speak to the male reprobates of this reptile house. They are also outside playing cards. If you are lucky DG will not have lost all his money and picked a fight with one of the others"

They both in unison pulled "Oh no" expressions on their faces.

"Although all is not lost. I reckon you will find Katrina and Edgar down by the river."

Jerry then moved to the other side of her enclosure where a large rock resided with a duvet drying on it.

They looked at each other curiously as to what was going on.

"Do you want me to remove the duvet?

They again looked at each other curiously.

"So, you can check under the stone and truthfully say to everyone that you did leave no stone unturned in your investigation"

They both started to laugh and before they could say anything.

"Well, if you need to ask me anything else you know where I am. I will let Katrina know that you called in case you don't catch up with her."

She then moved back to the micro hi-fi and plugged in the headphones, indicating that the interview was over.

They exited and heard a shrill laugh coming from behind one of the star's prongs.

"That was very interesting," said Mountie.

Charlton stopped with a puzzled look on his face. "Jerry said that she and Barnsley had secret names for each other. I wonder if he had secrets with some of the other animals. Perhaps secrets that are not as pleasant as having friendly nicknames. Perhaps a secret that was worth murdering him for."

"With such a small close community everyone usually knows everyone else's business It is definitely something we need to consider."

"Anyway, let's get this next set of interviews over and done with," said Mountie.

As they moved around a prong, they saw three white sun loungers.

On the first one was Sarah in a dark blue bikini.

In the middle was Nikki in a dark green bikini that so blended in with the colour of her skin that to a casual observer you might have thought she was sunbathing in the nude.

On the last sun lounger dressed in a bright yellow bikini was Emma.

All three of them were looking at Nikki's edition of Marie Bear magazine.

It was Ellie magazine's main rival.

It had been started by a polar bear named Marie, a previous editor of Ellie magazine.

She had a bust up with Ellie over an article she wanted to put in the magazine, and Marie stopped it going in. Marie had leaked the disagreement to the press and as a result Ellie had sacked her.

Marie had decided to seek revenge and had started Marie Bear magazine in competition.

Suddenly all three of them started laughing.

Emma had a particularly annoying loud shrill laugh.

"I definitely couldn't see Bobby wearing a short Jean-Paul Giraffe red tartan leather micro skirt., I'm not sure I would even let him try it on," said Sarah.

Jean-Paul lived at Paris Zoo and had been a former catwalk model.

He had taken up clothes design after being frustrated at the awful clothes he was being asked to model on the catwalks.

His designs intentionally challenged normality.

His new collection for male animals featured a large range of differently styled skirts including the micro skirt.

The micro skirt though had been withdrawn following an obscene accident by a male animal modelling it at its fashion show launch.

Unfortunately, it had been withdrawn too late to stop it appearing in the fashion magazines where it had been met with much amusement.

Mountie didn't really know what to make of the wags as he had never had any dealings with them. He had seen them around, but he had never had the need or desire to speak to them.

He nudged a shocked looking Charlton indicating that he wanted him to lead with the interviewing of them.

Charlton had seen them around and likewise had never had the need to speak to them.

All he knew about them was comments made by the females at home. They regularly ridiculed them and expressed very low opinions of their dress sense and their complete lack of intellect.

Charlton coughed to get their attention.

They all stopped looking at the magazine and turned to face Charlton.

"Good evening, ladies, I'm Charlton."

Sarah looked at the other two.

"What a strange accent you have where are you from?"

She had a strong London accent after growing up in London Zoo.

Charlton was startled that she had never heard a Geordie accent before.

"I'm from Newcastle" Charlton proudly replied.

Although technically he had been born in Manchester it was easier to say he came from Newcastle as it matched his accent.

Sarah sat looking puzzled for a minute.

"Isn't that up North somewhere?"

Nikki then joined in

"I was going to say Liverpool due to his red football top. But you don't sound like Steven, so I thought it best not to answer for you ".

Sarah nodded her appreciation to a smiling

Nikki.

Charlton shook his head in horror and refrained from making a sarcastic comment.

Emma, who also spoke with a London accent, turned to Mountie.

"And who are you then?"

Emma had also been raised at London Zoo and knew Sarah very well whilst living there. Both had been moved to the zoo at the same time much to the relief of all the other London Zoo animal occupants.

"I'm Mountie" he said exaggerating his Canadian accent.

"Ah another strange accent if I'm not mistaken. Let's see if we can guess where you come from."

The three girls sat looking at each other and made various strange facial expressions but didn't say anything.

Mountie stood there waiting for them to inevitably issue the ultimate insult a Canadian can be given and be called American but to his surprise they all shook their heads.

"Sorry we give up where are you from" they all said in unison.

Mountie breathed a sigh of relief and pointed to the maple leaf on his T-shirt.

"I'm from Canada" He proudly said again with his exaggerated his Canadian accent.

"Yes. I know exactly where that is" said Nikki excitedly.

"Steven took me to the Lake District for the

weekend and we stayed there once. We stayed at an expensive 5-star hotel overlooking a lake there."

"How can you mix up Canada with Coniston! Give me strength" Mountie tried to whisper but it came out too loud .

He was at the point where he didn't much care anyway.

"Ooh really tell us about it. It sounds very romantic" said Sarah leaning forward. and getting excited.

"I didn't enjoy it much it as it rained. There was lots of water, hills and very few fashion shops," said Nikki.

The other 2 gave out shocked gasps.

Charlton and Mountie stood shaking their heads in disbelief.

"And would you believe it. Steven wanted me to go walking up one of these hills. He expected me to get my new Jimmy Gnu high heeled shoes dirty climbing it."

Jimmy was a Gnu and had set up making extremely expensive handmade fashionable female animal shoes from his enclosure at Penang Zoo .

They had become so successful that they now had their own fashion shows.

Again, the other two gasped in horror.

Charlton behind his back indicated to Mountie where he would have shoved one those Jimmy

Gnu shoes had he been Steven.

Mountie stifled a laugh.

"I soon put him in his place though."

Mountie coughed.

"Sorry to interrupt your trip down memory lane. But we are here to ask you all about Sunday night."

Sarah turned around abruptly to face Mountie.

"It's about time too! We were really upset when the show finished early. Especially as it finished before the grand finale. Everyone just got up and left. We waited ages for everyone to return but no one did. Crocket has been very funny with us since. All we want to do is to place orders for some of the clothes. I assume you are both here to apologise and to offer us our ticket money back?"

Mountie was taken aback by the response.

"But the show ended because Oscar's son Barnsley had just died."

Sarah was still on the attack.

"He wasn't the only one dying that evening darling. We had seen the finale dress in magazine pictures and were dying to see it on the catwalk. In the end we found the dress backstage we all tried it on, and it was gorgeous."

Nikki and Emma smiled and nodded in agreement.

"It looks great and even better it comes in three different colours. So, we can each order one and wear it at the same time in the safe knowledge that we won't clash," said Nikki.

"We just need to persuade Crocket to take our order" Sarah muttered under her breath.

"Now what was that famous quote that Steven's old football boss used to say?" said Emma.

Mountie and Charlton both knew the quote and waited in eager anticipation of what their version was going to be.

"I know what it was it was. He said some people believe that fashion is a matter of life and death but it's much more serious than that."

Sarah and Emma just sat there looking confused with mouths wide open as the quotation flew straight over their heads.

Charlton looked up to the skies.

"Bill, I hope you didn't hear that."

Mountie was trying in vain to hide a wide smile.

He remembered they had not been outside the café or the following night at the seal house but considered life was too short to ask them where they had been.

Charlton broke the silence and instantly regretted it.

"Whilst you were waiting did you see anything strange?"

Sarah smiled and quickly answered.

"Yes, we did. There was that electric blue tartan leather mini skirt in the show. It looked strange when we saw it hanging up. We just couldn't think who would want to wear something that hideous."

"Yes, I did consider it a very strange item to have in the show," said Emma.

Mountie and Charlton started walking slowly away with none of them noticing them going.

Charlton pretended to wipe sweat from his brow. "I can see what Jerry meant and why she wears those headphones all the time."

Mountie nodded in agreement.

"Well, we haven't finished yet. Let's go and find the gambling school."

They walked past two of the star prongs before coming across the gambling table.

Sitting at the table were Bruce the scorpion, Graham a praying mantis, Chris a tarantula, DG the chameleon and Eddie the fruit bat.

Chris was the most famous of the group.

He had just finished filming for Channel Roar the latest episodes of his live game show "Who wants to be "Wild" again" where zoo and game reserve animals are returned to the wild by correctly answering twelve progressively harder questions.

The show had hit problems in the previous series when a dingo had won his freedom. A Bald Eagle had made the authorities aware of another dingo in the audience who had been coughing when the correct answer from the list of answers was read out by Chris.

The authorities had investigated the claim and

didn't believe the dingo in the audience's excuse that they had been suffering from kennel cough. Dingoes were now banned from the show.

Eddie was famous as well.
His claim to fame dated back to when he was young and was regularly sick.
By sheer accident a vet specialising in food allergies had moved to his zoo and had started to wonder if he was suffering from some sort of food allergy.
Unfortunately for Eddie the results had made him headline news "Fruit Bat Allergic to fruit" .
The vet did narrow it down to certain fruits such as strawberries and kiwi fruit and his diet was changed to accommodate this.
Luckily, he was now very rarely sick and if he was it was usually because of a new zookeeper not being aware of his food allergies.

DG was famous at the zoo.
He had been given two very embarrassing names at birth and now called himself DG.
He successfully kept both names secret despite fervent attempts to uncover them from his mates in the enclosure.
The truth was that his mother after giving birth to three male chameleons had desperately wanted a girl chameleon.
When he had been born, she had gone into extreme post-natal depression, and everyone had pretended her new baby was a girl.

DG had been christened Doreen Grace.

Even after his mother found out she always called him Doreen, especially as a punishment at times when he had been naughty.

After his mother died, he had been moved to Hearts River Zoo and decided to now be called DG.

As Mountie and Charlton approached the gaming table, they all stopped, put down their cards and turned to face them.

"We have been expecting you Mr. Mountie." said Graham laughing and pretending to stroke a cat.

"I just went to the loo and I saw you were talking with nature's contradiction to Darwin's views on evolution".

All the animals around the table roared with laughter.

Mountie and Charlton smiled as well.

"I suppose you are here to ask us about Sunday night?" said Eddie.

He looked at his cards and put them back on the table.

"I'm not sure you will get much from us as we were all here playing cards till Jerry returned and told us what had happened," said DG .

He also looked at his cards and indicated that he was keen to get on.

"Well speak for yourself I went to the fashion show" said Chris with a big smile on his face.

He wriggled his body suggestively and mimicked

a London accent.

"Nikki told me in the fashion show that I would look great in that pink mini skirt and plunging yellow top."

Everyone burst into fits of laughter.

"Did you hear them when they got back at 10.15? They were moaning about the show being cancelled early. They were wondering whether they would be getting their money back! Talk about dense I ask you". said Bruce shaking his head.

Mountie looked at Charlton and they both turned to the players.

"OK well I don't think we need to take up any more of your time. If you do think of anything else, please let us know."

In unison they all said, "Yes we will".

They left making sure they avoided the wags on the sun loungers.

"I think we will head for the river next and see if we can catch up with Katrina and Edgar." said Mountie.

"It would be good to talk to some normal animals again, hopefully."

"I am in serious danger of losing the will to live after talking to that lot. "

"Perhaps we need to ask for some danger money from Oscar?"

"Let's say Charlton, I think our investigation can only go in one way now and that is up."

Charlton nodded his head in agreement.

They both carried on walking smiling.

CHAPTER 20 – SATURDAY 6TH AUGUST (PM – MUCH LATER)

They walked towards the river that was glinting in the distance.

"It's at times like this that you really appreciate being alive".

Charlton nodded in agreement.

The sun was still out, and the temperature was pleasantly warm.

They paused and looked up and down the river to see if there were any boats on the water, luckily there weren't any.

Mountie pointed out Oscar swimming in the water and waved and Oscar waved back.

Suddenly they were interrupted.

"Hello, you two I have one last copy of the Big Animal Issue to sell before I can go home for the day ".

They turned to see Tiffany walking towards them.

"It's my last copy."

Tiffany caught up with them and was dressed in combat trousers and a Greenpeace t-shirt.

"No thanks, Tiffany," said Charlton.

"Are you sure I can't tempt you? Even if you don't read it, you could pass it on to Alice as she would love it as it has loads of competitions in it for her to enter."

"I'm sure she will be very interested, but you will have to grab her next time she passes. I will let her know for you though".

Tiffany smiled and turned her attention to Mountie.

"How about you then? It has some crosswords in it which I know you love doing. Also, there is a giant crossword with a £1000.00 prize."

Mountie shook his head.

"No, I think I will leave it for now".

"Mountie it's my last copy. If you buy it then I can go home and put my feet up"

Mountie laughed, got some money out of his tunic pocket and handed it over.

"Okay alright I will take it then".

Tiffany smiled, took the money, passed her last copy of the Big Issue to Mountie.

"Thanks a lot, and both of you and have a good evening".

She then turned and left.

They carried on walking down towards the riverbank.

"When you have finished the giant crossword if you are not going to send it in could you pass it to me. I can pass it Alice for her to send it in and share any winnings."

Mountie nodded that he would.

Charlton spotted Edgar and Katrina lying flat in some long grass next to the river.

Edgar was always easy to spot.

He was a tall Snow Jackal and had amazing white

fur that always dazzled wherever he went. His strong jaws were a great asset for his role as the bands lead singer. His white body was ideal as it allowed the bands lighting technician to run a colour show off of it whilst he was on stage.

He pointed them out to Mountie.

He nodded and they started walking towards them.

Suddenly they both stopped.

Charlton pointed out the singing dragonfly that was coming towards and started to smile.

Mountie looked at him curiously as he initially didn't recognise the song it was singing as it flew past them.

"It's that dragonfly again. He's singing that old Joe Jackson song "Is she really going out with him" very apt".

Mountie smiled as he had heard the song before.

He had been given a CD of orchestral versions of popular songs that he had initially considered consigning straight into the dustbin. By accident he had played it and had been surprised how much he had enjoyed it. This song had been covered on the CD.

They arrived and found Katrina wrapped around Edgar with her head was facing his face.

If you didn't know better, it looked like Edgar was being crushed and about to be eaten by Katrina.

Whereas in fact it was the complete opposite as they had now been dating each other for the last 6 months.

Mountie coughed and they looked up.

Katrina uncoiled herself from Edgar and they both sat up.

They were wearing jeans, open toed sandals, and T-shirts from Katrina's "F" fashion range.

The T-shirts were a new part of her fashion range which she had called "FUCK!"

Edgar's white t-shirt was called "Off". All it had on the front was a large black "F" that was slightly off centre.

Katrina's white t-shirt was called "In Hell" and it featured a large burning F standing before a devil pictured in hell.

There were two other t-shirts in the range.

One was called "Ewe" where the F had been inverted and made to look like a shaggy Ewe.

The other one was called "In L" where a large red "L" had been filled with small yellow "F' letters".

"Mind if we sit down and join you" said Mountie addressing the question to Edgar.

"Sure, no problem. I was wondering when you two were going to come and talk to us," said a smiling Katrina.

Charlton and Mountie sat down.

All four of them started to stare out over the river.

Suddenly a Canadian goose started floating by chatting to a freshwater salmon and then they stopped abruptly

"John. Look I don't believe it but isn't that Edgar

the lead singer from Day of the Jackals" the goose said loudly to the salmon.

"Crikey it is Claire. And isn't that Katrina Fross with him as well?"

Edgar gave a very unpleasant scowl in their direction.

They saw this and hurriedly carried on their way down the river.

"I really love coming down here and spending hours just watching the river life floating by." said Mountie.

"Yes, it a nice place to chill out and watch the wildlife" said Katrina snuggling next to Edgar.

"Mores the point there are loads of bushes" said Edgar winking at Mountie and Charlton.

Mountie was surprised by Edgar's accent. He had seen him around the zoo, but they had never spoken before.

He had been expecting an aggressive yobbish voice as per his public persona.

Whereas in fact Edgar had a particularly well-spoken Scandinavian accent as he had grown up at Helsinki Safari Park.

Katrina went red and dug him in the ribs.

"Shhh you're embarrassing me".

"Sorry darling I didn't mean to embarrass you.".

Charlton was stunned as sitting in front of him was one of the country's wildest rock singers and yet he was being very polite, caring, and civilised.

Edgar saw Charlton's look and nodded.

"I know what you are thinking. There is a time to

be the wild man of rock and there is a time to just chill out and be the real me. Now is my chill out time".

Charlton smiled in acknowledgement.

"Just don't tell the press though as they wouldn't be interested in the real me as it doesn't sell papers."

Charlton nodded in agreement indicating that he wouldn't tell the press.

Mountie decided to change the subject abruptly.

"Please can you tell me where you both were on Sunday night?"

Edgar looked at Katrina who indicated that she wanted him to do the talking.

"Well, we planned to come down here and hide. Katrina didn't want any further harassment from Crocket about not appearing in his lousy fashion show".

Katrina nodded her agreement to Edgar's comment.

"So I rehearsed a bit with the band, you do know we are playing Glastonbury Zoo again next month"

They nodded to indicate that they did.

"I left the band around 7.45 and went straight to Katrina's. Seeing as the rest of the reptile house was empty, we decided to take advantage of the opportunity" said Edgar and then laughed loudly.

Katrina went bright red and gave Edgar a hefty nudge in the ribs.

"Too much information".

"It's a good job old Crocket did not appear then to harass Katrina as I'm not sure who would have been the more embarrassed".

There was a pause whilst everyone looked out over the river as the sun began slowly setting behind it.

They saw Oscar climb out of the water and dry himself and he waved when he saw them all looking at him.

"Then about 8.30 we both made our way down here, probably where we are now. We stayed here till around 9.15 when the sun began setting. It began to get cold, and Edgar suggested going for a drink at the cafe," said Katrina.

"When we arrived, we saw most of the other animals there. Oscar was just starting his speech. We saw you there too." said Edgar staring at Mountie who nodded in agreement.

Charlton inwardly fumed again as his presence outside the café had again not been acknowledged. This time it was worse because it was by his rock star idol.

"You said on the night of show you came down here to hide. Please can you expand on that?" said Mountie.

"I knew Crocket would come looking for Katrina as he just doesn't know when to give up. To avoid a further confrontation, we came down here to escape from him."

Katrina nodded in agreement.

"He was becoming a real pain in the butt towards the end, and I didn't want to be upset again. So as Edgar just said we both came and hid here".

"You see Crocket, is so obsessed with Katrina, not in a sexual way you understand although I could understand if he was. He became so persistent that in the end we decided to just keep saying "No". I must admit I wouldn't have stomached the sight of his smug little face smiling in victory if we had capitulated".

"It would have been intolerable".

"Still, I will be getting the last laugh though. I have tweaked the lyrics to a Tom Robinson Band song called "Don't Take No for an Answer". It is all about him and it will be on our next album".

"Did you see Crocket at all that night other than at the café with the rest of us?"

Edgar and Katrina looked at each other and shook their heads.

"No, we didn't. Although we did see Oscar going for a swim and looking deep in thought though."

"Did you have any dealings with Barnsley about his new WAAR venture" said Mountie changing the subject.

"As you know I have tried to give up the booze several times and always failed" replied Edgar awkwardly.

"I did bump into him a couple of times. I offered to help but said any help would have to be done privately as he didn't want any of my fans turning up and spoiling it. Also, we are back on the road with a new album shortly so being linked with WAAR wouldn't have been particularly good for my image if you get what I mean".

They both nodded in agreement.

"I said to him if WAAR was successful then I would record a rock version of that war song that everyone has been singing around here lately. I offered to hand over some of the proceeds from its sales to WAAR as well".

"We were wondering if you had any enemies outside the zoo. Anyone with a grudge who might have come here to teach you a lesson. They could have arrived and saw the word "alcoholic" on the event poster and assumed that you would be there. They then went to the cafe and killed Barnsley by mistake. We are wondering if Barnsley happened to be in the wrong place at the wrong time".

Edgar let out a loud whistle and looked stunned.

"You know that thought has never even crossed my mind. I know of a few mothers who might want to strangle me. I can't think of anyone who want to come here and harm me or even worse kill me!"

Edgar laughed nervously and gave Katrina a nudge.

She was not amused and moved away from him slightly.

"I must admit we do think Barnsley was the intended victim. We just needed to know though if someone has been seriously threatening you and if so determine if they came here and killed Barnsley by mistake. If there is someone, we would get Oscar involved and get you a bodyguard".

Edgar smiled and looked a bit more relaxed.

"I know I can upset a lot of people and especially Crocket in the run up to the fashion show. I really can't think of anyone that would want to murder me though. Although if I do think of anyone I will let you know. Thanks for the offer of getting Oscar involved although I suspect he has more than enough on his plate already".

All four of them sat looking out at the river as the sun slowly began to set.

Katrina gave Edgar a nudge.

"We are about to go off to the café you are both welcome to join us if you wish".

Mountie and Charlton could see they were being polite and didn't really want to be lumbered with them. They both got up to leave.

Charlton smiled.

"Good luck for the Glastonbury gig. We have just seen the band rehearsing and they looked good. They played my favourite track "Fook on the Tyne". You know you really ought to sign up Billy for the band before someone else signs him."

Edgar let out a loud laugh.

"Sorry but the guy's just too hairy for our band. If you are interested though I can get you a free Glastonbury ticket if you want to go. In fact, I'll give you Billy's ticket".

"Wow. I would love to go thanks a lot for the offer".

They both started walking back.

Charlton started humming "Fook on the Tyne" again.

Mountie turned back briefly to see that Katrina and Edgar were back lying down.

He also looked out across the river and noticed that Oscar had gone back as well.

Charlton stopped humming as he noticed the singing dragonfly approaching them again and was wondering what he would be singing this time.

Charlton smiled as it flew past then.

Mountie stopped and looked at Charlton.

"Well, what was it this time then?"

"He certainly is being perceptive as he was singing the U2 song "I still haven't found what I'm looking for" which I feel is about where we are now".

"Well Charlton, I have certainly enjoyed witnessing the wide spectrum of the lives of our fellow animals this evening. I agree we are still haven't found out who the killer is. We do need to see if there is an autopsy in the surgery as it may hold some clues for us".

"Well, that's on Monday morning and will brief the troops tomorrow night in readiness for it".

"Fine"

Mountie started to walk off in the direction of his

home.

"I think I will have an early night and see you in the morning".

"See you in the morning then".

Charlton headed home as well.

On his way, back he looked over at the reptile house and he longed to tell the others about his encounter with the wags and how they had got Canada and Coniston mixed up.

Alas though he knew he would have to keep it a secret but did wonder if he might be able to tell them all about it after the investigation was over.

CHAPTER 21 - SUNDAY 7 AUGUST (AM)

Charlton woke up and still had a smile on his face from the memories of the previous night's interviews.

He had loved seeing Day of the Jackals rehearsing and reminisced about the wags interview.

He went into the kitchen, and it looked like a bomb had hit it with bottles and glasses spread all over the place. It was always worse on Saturday and Sunday morning as the gang would have been at the café till the very early hours and then returned to carry on drinking.

He skipped making himself a coffee as he knew Mountie would have a proper one waiting for him.

Before leaving he sat down as he needed some time to plan what he was going to say to the others that evening to get their support with his diversion plan for Deidre and him on Monday morning.

He couldn't see why they wouldn't agree to help but they could be a very funny bunch.

He had to choose the right moment and appeal to their better nature and if that failed then hit them with the bribery of the free beer.

It was yet another sunny morning and the temperature was already beginning to build up as started to make his way to see Montie.

As he approached, he stopped in tracks as sitting in his usual deckchair was Oscar.

Oscar spotted him, smiled, and beckoned him to come and join them.

Charlton noticed that a third mug was on the table between Mountie's and Oscar's and as he got nearer Mountie filled it with coffee from a cafeteria and passed it to him.

He sat down on the grass in front of the two deckchairs.

"Good morning. I know both of you have been working hard on this murder case. I thought it was a good time to have a catch up with you both."

"I have just been giving Oscar an update as to where we are with the case. I couldn't resist telling him about the WAGs interview last night. We both laughed over them not knowing where either Newcastle or Canada were."

"Stories had come my way about how thick they were. It's good to see my concerted effort to avoid them has been fully justified and worth continuing," said Oscar.

He let out a loud laugh and was looking relaxed.

"Perhaps next time a troublemaker gets sent to me to be dealt with I will sentence them to three nights in the reptile house. I will make sure they have to share an enclosure each night with one of them."

Charlton and Mountie both laughed.

"I must admit though I reckon I would even

prefer chintz wallpaper at home than share with them, although... perhaps not."

All three of them picked up their mugs of coffee. Mountie and Oscar sat back in their deckchairs taking in the sun.

"So, what are you planning to do next?" said Oscar.

"We want to see if there is a report or autopsy in the surgery. If there is it might give us some information as to what happened to Barnsley. We want to find out whether he was choked to death with the water bottle or whether he was killed another way, and the bottle was used to hide it".

"That sounds very interesting. I just thought he had been choked to death and not some other way. "

"We are want to determine if someone had been planning beforehand to kill him at the WAAR event and if so then we need to find a motive. Currently we are finding the water bottle a strange murder weapon unless as I said it was used to cover up the real cause."

"Hmm I see. That is interesting. I will see if I can come up with any reasons why someone might have wanted to kill Barnsley. I must admit nothing has springs to mind so far. I will ask Poppy as well."

"So, tomorrow morning we are planning to visit the surgery just before the zoo opens at 9.00. The plan is for Charlton and Deidre to shimmy over

the fence. Deidre will then wreak havoc in the car park. At the same time Charlton will make a dash for the main road. Hopefully all the zookeepers and Doctor Mike will leave the zoo to capture them both. Hopefully I will then have enough time to look around the surgery whilst empty."
Oscar was quiet.
He sat contemplating the plan and trying to spot any flaws in it.
"Would it be more helpful if I escaped?"
Mountie turned to Charlton and then back to Oscar.
"Thanks for the offer but I think we can manage this ourselves. Although if it fails, then we may take you up on the offer for a second attempt."
Oscar nodded and again went into deep thought.
"So, will you and your mum be okay escaping? I didn't think any of your lot, present company excluded, surfaced before 10.30 each day?"
"I am having a rallying the troops meeting tonight to get their help. Whilst I don't see any reason why they won't help they might need bribing with drinks and a dinner date" said Charlton and he laughed.
Oscar also joined in the laughter whilst Mountie went bright red.
"Charlton, I heard that Deidre loves a man in a uniform. Didn't she have to be hauled away when that fire crew arrived after that fire alarm went off accidently, now where was it, ah yes the fire alarm near the zebra enclosure."

Charlton burst out laughing as he remembered the incident vividly.

Oscar also burst out laughing.

Mountie slid back uncomfortably into his deckchair and drank his coffee.

"But seriously. If they do give you any problems tell them that they will have to answer me. Or better still tell them I will personally strap them into the reptile house for a week".

Charlton and Oscar laughed and eventually Mountie joined in as well.

Oscar looked at his watch.

"Last time we met you mentioned that you wanted to see Barnsley's room. Poppy will still be asleep as she is not a morning person. I wondered if you both wanted to have a quick look around it now?"

Mountie looked at Charlton who nodded.

"Thanks a lot that would be great."

Oscar led them to the entrance of his Tent.

"I will just check that Poppy is asleep as she might find it upsetting seeing you two poking around in his room."

Charlton and Mountie nodded.

Oscar disappeared into the tent and reappeared a minute later beckoning them in.

He then led them to the entrance of Barnsley's room and stopped outside.

"We haven't been in the room since and if you don't mind, I will leave you both to look around it"

They nodded their heads.
He turned and walked back into the main tent area.
Charlton started to look around the room.
"So, what are we looking for?"
"I am not sure. Try looking out for any papers or letters to see if anyone was either threatening him over his WAAR venture or alternatively blackmailing him about something that we didn't know about."
The bedroom was small and contained a bed, a wardrobe, a small table and a chest of drawers with a small television on it.
Also, there was a Sony WalkAn docking station with speakers attached but no sign of the Sony WalkAN.

The Sony WalkAN was like the human Sony Walkman but built especially for use by a range of animals instead.
Sony were one of the few companies that knew of the animal world's double lives and had been able to tap into this massive animal market as well as the human market.
They had an ultra-secret division specially tasked with transforming their human products to be usable by a wide variety of animals.

"Wonder where his Sony WalkAN is? I wonder if he took it with him to the launch to use for background music," said Charlton.
"I don't recall seeing it . Hmmm . Perhaps the

killer took it and if so, it will help us prove it was them."

The room had two shelves that Mountie noted contained various DVD's and he made a note of some of the titles in case they proved relevant.

The table had some new WAAR t-shirts still in their wrappers on it.

On the floor were some magazine cuttings about alcoholism and treatments centres for alcoholism.

Mountie finished going through the chest of drawers.

Charlton finished going through the wardrobe.

Mountie looked under the bed and found a pile of leaflets advertising the WAAR launch night and he took a couple to keep.

Just as they were finishing, they heard a cough from outside.

Mountie went to the entrance and found Oscar waiting.

"Have you nearly finished as Poppy is beginning to wake up?"

They nodded to show he had finished.

"Thanks a lot, I think we have finished but I suppose we can come back if need be?"

Suddenly they heard Poppy's voice saying "Oscar, Oscar where are you?"

"Just coming dear. Do you mind seeing yourselves out. Please be as quiet as possible."

They nodded that they would.

"If I don't speak to you before I hope all goes to

plan tomorrow morning. Please keep me posted as to what you find."

They nodded in agreement.

"Oscar are you there? Is anybody with you?".

"It's just me. I am getting you a coffee. I will be there in a minute."

They followed Oscar into the main tent area and then left by the front door.

Oscar went to the kitchen to make Poppy a coffee. As they got to the edge of the lion enclosure the zookeeper's arrival alarm went off.

Mountie started to walk towards his enclosure, but Charlton stopped him.

"Tonight, as soon as the zoo closes, I am going to go through my plan for tomorrow morning with the gang."

"I hope it goes well. When you have finished, I will meet you in the café for an update. We do still have a few more animals to see tonight though."

Charlton looked a bit confused.

"Well, we still need to see the apes, giraffes, and the seals. I think that's about everyone left that I think we need to see for now."

"Of course, sorry I forgot about them".

Charlton started to wander back and was mentally going over what he was going to say to that evening. He was hoping that it would all go smoothly.

CHAPTER 22 - SUNDAY 7 AUGUST (PM)

The weather had decided to play its usual summer Sunday afternoon trick on the British public. It pretended it had another scorching hot day lined up only to change its mind at lunchtime with black clouds and heavy rain appearing.
All the visitors and coach parties got drenched and then after most of them had left the scorching sun returned.

Mountie was sitting outside going through the plans for the mornings raid on the surgery. He wanted to be sure that nothing had been overlooked in their plans.
Suddenly Postie Stevie arrived carrying a note and passed it over.
"Delivery for you Mountie".
He didn't instantly read the note up as he wasn't in a hurry.
Instead, he decided to take the opportunity to have a chat with him.
"Getting hot again".
"I'm hopefully going for a swim in the river later to cool off".
Looking at the note and then up at Mountie he continued "So how's the investigation going?"
"I think we are making some slow progress."

"Sorry I couldn't be of more help".

Mountie had already interviewed him when he had dropped off Crocket's note about meeting them in the café.

Postie Stevie was fortunate enough to have a nest in a tree with a spectacular view of the river.

Unfortunately, though for Mountie it was too far away for him to see the zoo from it.

He was also a car buff and said he had been watching Top Deer that evening.

He and some of his car mad pigeon friends were considered car snobs and they had recreated Top Deer's uncool car chart in his nest.

They had a competition to see who could be the first to land their droppings on each of the cars that were on it. Extra points were had by hitting cool cars that had been horrendously modified by their owners, especially pink vinyl wrapped ones.

They loved targeting cars they considered should never have built in the first place. As such the local Toyota garage had been designated as a points free zone although it was still regularly used by the pigeons for shooting practice.

He had taken great pleasure and gained 5 points for crapping on a bright pink Land Rover Discovery he had seen on his way to give Mountie his note.

"Well, I can't stay here all day as I have a river to cool down in and you have your note to read."

With that he flapped his wings and took off in the direction of the river.

Mountie picked up the note, carried it into his hut and unfolded it.

The note read.
> Dear Mountie
> We know you still need to speak to us about Sunday night. We would like to invite you over for afternoon tea this evening. Feel free to bring Charlton.
> Thanks
> Miss Michelle and Miss Amber.

Mountie read the note again and thought it was very good timing.

He didn't think Charlton would mind him going alone as he seemed to recall that he had not enjoyed his time at the dance classes that they ran.

They still had to see the giraffes and he had some spare time to kill.

He decided to dress up for afternoon tea and put on his red tunic and black trousers.

He left his hut and started to walk over to the giraffe enclosure.

The giraffe enclosure or at least the top of it could be seen from all over the zoo.

The children in 3rd Year Hearts River Lower School had been doing a project on rockets. They decided that three large rockets would be perfect for the giraffes, especially with their long necks.

There were three thirty-foot-tall rockets, a red one, a blue one and a silver one attached to each other.

On top of each of the rockets' nose cones were Hearts River Zoo flags.

Lemming had decided the insides of the nose cones were a perfect location to install things like the animals' satellite dish and mobile telephone transmitters.

Mountie opened the gate and walked in and found Michelle and Amber sitting on the grass.

In front of them was a red and yellow checkered picnic rug and on it was a silver tea pot, three white bone China teacups and saucers. There was a white plate with some scones, a small dish of jam and a larger dish full of clotted cream.

Michelle spotted him and beckoned him to join them.

"Do sit down and join us for afternoon tea. I assume Charlton will not be joining us" said Michelle with a light French accent.

"He has some other work on the investigation that he needs to follow up on now."

Michelle had originally been born in Le Mans Zoo in France, then she moved to Paris Zoo before her move to Hearts River Zoo.

Michelle poured him a cup of tea.

Amber put a scone on a plate with some jam and some clotted cream and passed it to him.

He looked at Michelle and Amber and tried to put an age on them.

He noticed that both were showing the first signs of aging with a few wrinkles appearing and some grey hairs but other than that he considered physically they both looked fit and slim.

Michelle was wearing a lightweight white cotton knee length dress that was covered in lots of multi coloured embroidered daisies.

Amber was wearing a bright green all in one swimsuit and a very colorful green and turquoise sarong hanging from her waist.

Both wore straw hats.

"A very civilised way to end the day" said Amber with a Welsh accent taking a bite from her scone.

Amber was born and grew up at Cardiff Zoo.

Mountie spread some jam and cream on his scone and took a bite out of it.

"I hope you don't mind us asking to see you?" said Michelle.

Mountie shook his head to indicate that he didn't mind.

"We knew you would want to speak to us at some point and so doing it over afternoon tea seemed like a good time."

"I'm not sure we are going to be of any help, but you never know."

"How well did you know Barnsley?"

"As you know we run our dance school here. Barnsley attended for a little while." said Amber.

"Amber and I met when she was transferred to

Paris Zoo where I was living at the time." said Michelle.

Amber nodded her acknowledgement.

She got up and moved and sat close to Michelle.

"I was living in Cardiff Zoo and next minute I was being moved to Paris Zoo. I was really looking forward to the move as I knew it was the home of the animals in the famous Froggies Bergere cabaret show. I must admit I secretly hoped that I might find an opportunity and be asked to join them."

The Froggies Bergere was a large stage musical extravaganza.

It had a world-renowned finale featuring twelve topless female giraffes high kicking their way through a Can-Can dance routine in perfect unison.

The show was the master mind of a French poison dart frog called Pierre.

An American bull frog called Arnie had started off as Pierre's minder and later became a joint partner in the running and management of the show.

They were not the sort of frogs to be messed about with.

There were several reports of Prima Donna animal stars disappearing after disagreements with them. Some of them turned up dead after being poisoned. Although none of these events were ever traceable back to Pierre or Arnie.

"I remember when you first arrived Amber. We hit it off right away and I took you under my proverbial wing."

"I remember it well. It was instant friendship. You encouraged me to take up dancing and got me ready to successfully audition for a vacancy that came up in the show's famous finale line up. Getting that part changed my life."

"It changed mine as well. We did have some great shows together. It was during that time we thought about setting up a dance school. When we both moved here, we decided to set one up. We have really enjoyed running the dance school."

Michelle and Amber turned to look at Mountie.

He had closed his eyes and looked like he had fallen asleep albeit with a large smile on his face. Michelle was a bit taken aback and tapped him on the should.

"Mountie, Mountie wake up."

Mountie opened his eyes and had a glow on his face.

"It's okay I did hear everything you said. It's just that I had ventured off down memory lane when you mentioned the Froggies Bergere. I had a spell at Calais Zoo years ago and had the pleasure of being in the audience at one of the shows. It was spectacular and I can still visualize the finale it was breathtaking."

Michelle and Amber both blushed.

"It is extremely likely that you would have been watching us at the time. I'm glad to see we left you with such a vivid lasting memory." said Michelle.

It was Mountie's turn to blush this time.

"Sill we are not all here for a trip down memory lane." said Michelle.

Amber sat and nodded in agreement.

"Anyway, back to Barnsley"

"Like all the parents around here, their children usually at some point pass through our dance school. Barnsley was no exception, and he joined our street dance class. "said Amber.

"He was great and seemed to have a natural ability" butted in Michelle.

"So why did he leave then?" asked the Mountie.

He secretly knew what the answer was going to be.

"He and the rest of the street dancers were great, and so we decided to include them in our annual summer dance production." replied Amber.

"Shortly afterwards Oscar came by to say that Barnsley had taken up climbing and it clashed with his dance lessons. So, he would not be coming anymore. Shame as I said he had real talent." Said Michelle.

Mountie tried to hide his amusement at the replies he had just heard.

The words "summer dance production" instilled fear into the hearts and wallets of the parents of

the animals who were destined to take part.
You could feel the mood around the zoo changing overnight as the invite letters were sent out and read in dread by the parents as they reached the costs section as all the costumes, and even the socks, had to be new.
Last year's production had been most expensive yet with costumes being flown in from America. Aussie joked that he could identify when each year's summer dance production tell date letters were sent out by the huge drop in the cafes sales on the day and subsequent days.

"Please can you tell me where you were on that evening?"
"We were both models in the show and we really enjoyed it. We never turn down any opportunities to be back on stage in front of an audience, it's in the blood you know" Micheel replied.
"So, what happened?"
" We arrived at the seal house around 6.30. We went through all the costumes and accessories that we would be wearing. Then we went through the running order." said Michelle.
Amber nodded in agreement.
"The show started at 8.00. with us strutting up and down the runway till 8.45. We then had some fruit juices backstage and got ready for the second half that started at 9.00. Unfortunately, Crocket then interrupted the show with his very

sad announcement."

Amber wiped a tear from her eye and Michelle moved closer to comfort her.

"We both stopped what we were doing and changed out of our costumes and then rushed to the café to find out what was going on."

Michelle also started to look a upset.

"We saw you and Charlton outside and then listened to Oscar. We were both so upset that we dashed back home and had a couple of stiff drinks and then went to bed"

Mountie tried hard not to laugh.

He found it extremely amusing that Charlton had missed the only time he had been name checked as being outside the café for the announcement.

Michelle gave him a strange look.

"Sorry I just remembered something I needed to tell Charlton afterwards."

There was a silence as Michelle and Amber comforted each other.

Mountie picked up his teacup and finished his tea.

Then he got up and picked up his notebook.

"If you do think of anything that might be useful then please let me know".

With that he started walking towards the exit gate.

He was now planning on how to wind Charlton up for missing out on finally being name checked as being outside the café.

CHAPTER 23 - SUNDAY 7 AUGUST
(PM – AT THE SAME TIME)

After the zoo shut the zebras cooled down under the only two trees they had in the enclosure.

To assist in the cooling down process each of them was holding a cold bottle of lager.

Charlton saw his opportunity to discuss his plans with them and rushed to his room to pick up his speech notes and the Top Deer magazine he had borrowed.

He returned and sat down in front of them.

"There is something I need to discuss with you all".

They all turned to face him.

Richard then spotted the car magazine.

"Oh no Charlton is about to buy a car?"

"I bet it's a Fiat Panda" said Alistair with a big smile on his face.

"Or A Ford Puma or a Jaguar." said Mark.

Charlton sat there shaking his head.

"OK, very funny. Whilst you are all here, there is something I need to discuss with you all. As part of our investigation there is something we need your help with"

The others stopped laughing and looked at Charlton with stern faces.

"As it is to do with your investigation, I am sure we will all help. WONT WE?" said Deidre.

Charlton saw from the body language that they were all not sharing Deidre's enthusiasm for helping him.

"As you know we are investigating the murder and we have interviewed nearly everyone in the zoo."

All nodded their heads in agreement.

"We must find out if Doctor Mike performed an autopsy or wrote up any notes about Barnsley's death. We have to know if he was choked to death or whether he died some other way."

There was some scratching of heads at this last comment as they had all assumed that Barnsley had been choked to death and so this was something new for them to take in.

"So, you are going to ask Doctor Mike to hand everything over to you then. Not sure we can help with that.?" Richard finally piped up.

"Well, that's why I am about to ask a big favour from you all."

There were loud intakes of breath from Richard, Mark, and Alistair.

Alice, Laura, and Gail just sat still with stern looks on their faces.

"Ignore them Charlton. Please tell us how we can help you." said Deidre.

"Well, I have a plan that should hopefully mean that the vet's surgery will be empty long enough for Mountie to nip in and have a look around."

The others had gone quiet and were all looking at him.

They were all mentally trying to pre-guess what it was he was going to ask them to do.

"So, the plan is going to take place at 8.50 tomorrow morning."

"8.50 on a Monday morning you have got to be joking." shouted Mark, Alistair, and Richard in loud unison.

"You know we never get up before 10.30 on any morning," said Alistair.

"I can't remember the last time I was up before 10.30," said Mark.

"I can it was last summer when the football world cup was on in South Korea. You always managed to be up at 5.00 in the morning for the live England games." said Alice.

Mark went bright red and decided it was best not to respond.

"The plan is at 8.50 tomorrow morning Mark, Alistair and Richard will help Deidre and me over the perimeter fence."

"But I have a bad back" said Mark rubbing his back with a feigned pained expression on his face.

"It didn't stop you yesterday carrying those crates of Newcastle Brown Ale that TESCOW delivered, did it?" said Gail laughing loudly.

Mark's face changed and a smile started to appear, and he was just about to say something when he was cut short by Deidre staring sternly at him.

"And if you are thinking about making any

comparisons between me and some crates of Newcastle Brown Ale I would think very, very, carefully about it".

Everyone including Charlton laughed at Deidre's threat.

"I would love to help you tomorrow morning so what do you want me to do when I'm over the fence?"

"That's our Deidre she'll do anything for a man in a uniform." said Laura.

Deidre went red and the rest of them laughed.

"Do you remember that incident with the fire brigade when..."

"If I may continue. When you are over the fence you will run towards the car park and position yourself near any expensive cars . This means the zookeepers will have to be extra careful when capturing you as they won't want you damaging any expensive car especially as they will then have to pay to get it repaired."

"That's a good idea but I know absolutely nothing about cars" said Deidre with a vacant expression on her face.

"That's why I borrowed this car magazine. I was going to show some cars that you could look to head towards." said Charlton.

He showed her Top Deer magazine.

"Charlton, I won't remember any cars from that car magazine as I have a memory like a sieve. When I go over the fence just point out one or two cars that I need to aim for and I will head towards them and cause as much chaos as I can for you"

Charlton nodded his head in agreement and wrote a note of it.

Richard started to show an interest.

"So, whilst Deidre is running around causing mayhem what are you going to be doing?"

"I will be running as fast as I can and hopefully reach the main road. If I can it means Doctor Mike and the rest of the zookeepers will take ages to catch me and haul me back. Hopefully Mountie should then have more than enough time to search of the surgery."

They all looked thoughtful and nodded in agreement that they thought the plan might work.

"One thing. Is someone keeping a look out and on hand to tell Mountie when to leave as I'm sure he won't want to be caught in the surgery with anything he finds." said Richard.

"I must admit I hadn't thought of that."

"I reckon you need some aerial reconnaissance. I am sure Postie Stevie would help you if you asked him." said Mark smiling.

"What a great idea, I will have a word with him." Charlton made a mental note.

"We obviously need you to keep all this a secret and not tell anyone till it is over. We don't want the killer tipped off and for them to put a spanner in the works?"

They all nodded silently.

They were looking a bit shocked as the full impact of this last statement hit them.

Deidre's face changed and she started smiling.

"I'm glad we can all be of help finally. I'm sure if we have any more suggestions, we will let you know. We will all meet at 8.40 in the morning to put your plan into action."

Gail, Alice, and Laura groaned out loud.

"I thought we would still get a lie in and just the boys would be up," said Alice.

Deidre shook her head.

"This is to be a team exercise and we might still need your help so best to be on standby."

Mark looked Deidre up and down and then turned to Laura.

"Don't stretch your muscles tonight as it looks like they might be needed with some heavy lifting in the morning."

Deidre spotted a small branch on the floor next to her and picked it up and threw it perfectly hitting Mark squarely on the nose.

"I would last of all like to say that Oscar, Mountie, and me really appreciate all your help with this exercise. We are hoping it will bring us a large step closer to finding out Barnsley's killer."

The mention of Oscar stopped them all dead in their tracks and reminded them how important their help with the plan was. They all fell silent again.

Charlton looked up and spotted Postie Stevie

flying over and waived to beckon him down,
He walked to a quiet corner and motioned to join him there.
Charlton found a suitable spot and he landed next to him.
"You are looking a bit stressed" said Postie Stevie.
Charlton started taking a few deep breaths and slowly calmed down.
He had been really stressed and was pleased that it was all over and had gone well.
"Anyway, how can I be of help to you?"
"I need to ask you a favour regarding the investigation and you must agree not repeat what I am about to tell you."
He nodded his head in agreement.
"We are planning tomorrow morning that Deidre and I are going to escape over the perimeter fence. We will be acting as decoys to get the attention of Doctor Mile and the zookeepers. The real reason is to get the vet's surgery left empty long enough for Mountie to have a rummage around and hopefully find an autopsy or any other important information relating to Barnsley's murder."
He nodded his understanding and read the situation perfectly.
"I guess you will be needing an aerial look out then."
Charlton smiled and nodded in agreement.
He got out a rather weather-beaten diary and looked at it.

"Hmm yes I think I'm free".

He showed Charlton that his diary was completely empty.

"At 8.50 tomorrow morning Deidre and I will go over the fence. As soon as Doctor Mike leaves to capture us you will need to give Mountie the go ahead to explore the surgery."

"Tell Mountie I will fly over the surgery and as soon as the coast is clear I let him know. He needs to leave the surgery doors open so I can fly in and tell him when he needs to get out. Also, if he wants, I can carry out any papers he finds and drop them off to him later whenever he is ready."

"Thanks a lot that sounds like a great plan. I am meeting Mountie a bit later and will update him. I'm sure he will agree, and he will tell you if needs you to do anything else"

"I will fly past his hut in the morning and if he needs anything he just needs to beckon me to come down."

"Will do"

"Right well I'm glad I can be of help. I do need to dash now though." He took off and headed towards Hearts River town.

Charlton finished writing up his notes.

He was pleased with how the evening had gone, especially the part about now having some aerial reconnaissance.

He looked at his watch and went and changed into a black Manchester United away football top with the defender "PIGBAA" emblazoned on the back and some long black shorts.

Lions and tigers made great defenders in the AFL although they were often sent off for eating any opponents who upset them.

He made his way towards the café and was feeling really pleased with himself. He couldn't wait to tell Mountie about his meetings with Postie Stevie and the zebras.

CHAPTER 24 - SUNDAY 7TH AUGUST (PM –LATER)

Around 7.15 Charlton arrived at the café and walked in and instantly appreciated the cool air that the fan inside was generating around the café and saw that it had five occupants.

Sitting by one of the computer screens was Victor and Paul looking at some pictures of a new Ferrari. They both turned around as he entered and waved to him.

On the other computer was Carl with his nose glued to the screen and he was so engrossed with the game he was playing that he didn't notice him entering.

As he was still carrying Paul's Top Deer magazine, he went over to hand it back.

"Thanks a lot for lending me this".

"Hope you found it useful." said Paul turning back to the computer screen.

"Wow is that the new Ferrari Icona. Now is that a great looking car or is that a great looking car!"

Victor nodded in agreement.

Charlton looked over Paul's shoulder at the car on the computer screen and nodded his agreement as well.

He looked over to the other computer screen.

Carl spotted him looking and removed one of his headphones.

"What?"

"I was just wondering what game you were playing."

"It has only just come out. Call of Nature- Black Panthers. You are part of a black panther's pack wreaking havoc and death across villages in Africa. These graphics are the best yet. I must play it here because my parents would confiscate my tablet if they caught me playing it at home."

Charlton burst out laughing.

He recalled Joel's comment that Carl had yet to see God's light and couldn't see this happening soon if this game was anything to go by.

Carl put his headphone back in and turned back to playing the game.

He saw Aussie behind the bar cleaning a glass and then spotted Mountie sitting by himself at a table in the far corner of the café and walked towards him.

Aussie looked up from cleaning the glass "I'll bring you over a beer".

"Thanks that would be great."

He sat down on a chair facing him.

"How did it go then?" said Mountie picking up his glass of beer up and taking a large mouthful.

"It was a bit tricky, but I finally bartered Deidre down to just one meal out with you" said Charlton laughing.

A mouthful of beer shot out of Mountie's mouth.

"Careful I am not having you two wasting good beer in here even if it is free" said Aussie putting

Charlton's glass of beer down in front of him.
Seeing they were there for meeting he turned around and went back to the bar.

"But seriously. There were some initial grumbles concerning the early start but the good news is they will all be helping us in the morning".

"That's great news."

"They did have one good suggestion though."

Mountie looked at him curiously.

"They suggested we needed some aerial reconnaissance and suggested Postie Stevie."

"What a good idea, I hadn't considered that."

"I thought so to and I had a chat with him earlier about our plan. Tomorrow morning, he has agreed to fly around monitoring what is going on. As soon as the coast is clear for you to enter the vet's surgery, he will come and tell you. You must leave the doors open so he can come and tell you when you need to leave. He has offered to carry any documents back to your hut later should the need arise."

"Well done Charlton that's a great plan. I'm not sure how we missed having a lookout. I'm glad we now have it covered and Postie Stevie's help will be priceless."

Charlton beamed and proudly took a large sip of his beer.

"I have had an interesting evening as well as I was invited by Miss Amber and Miss Michelle for afternoon tea with them. I didn't think you would mind missing it."

Charlton face broke into a relieved look.

"Mind of course I don't mind. I was going to ask whether I could skip our visit there as I still have nightmares and break into a sweat when I hear the words summer dance production".

Mountie had a big smile on his face.

"They both kept saying I had natural talent for street dancing. I am the first to admit that I have two left feet as far as dancing is concerned. To make matters worse they decided to link it with the London Olympics that were on at the same time. I ended up doing a street dancing routine in a bloody Chelsea AFC football kit. The lads still ridicule me whenever Chelsea AFC are on the television".

Mountie burst out laughing.

He had witnessed the production and Charlton's pained expressions. He remembered his totally uncoordinated dance steps which had been his highlight of the show.

Mountie sensing this was a good time to wind Charlton up further.

"You might be pleased to know that Miss Michelle specifically mentioned seeing you outside the café."

"Bloody typical, we finally find someone saying they remembered seeing me outside the café and I bloody missed it."

Mountie burst out laughing again.

"So, did I miss anything?"

"Apart from a delicious afternoon tea not a lot.

I think I am in the mood now to visit the apes what do you reckon?"

"Lead on then"

Charlton drained the dregs from his beer glass.

Mountie laughed and finished the dregs from his glass of beer and picked up Charlton's empty glass and took them over to Aussie and handed them over saying "Thanks a lot."

"That's Okay, how is it going."

"We are still making slow progress. If you can keep the zebras semi sober tonight it would be really appreciated as they are helping us in the morning. Unfortunately, I can't tell you anymore and please do not tell anyone."

"Mums the word. Although I can't hold out much hope with your request concerning the zebras. We all know they drink like fishes, although I will try my best."

"Any help to stop them from getting plastered would be very much appreciated as they are key for our work in the morning."

Aussie nodded his agreement.

"I will try my best for you."

"I didn't realise Carl frequented the café, I am surprised Joel and Elspeth have let him set foot over the threshold." said Charlton.

"Actually, he is excellent at computer games. He takes part in some on-line gaming competitions and gets a faster signal in here. He asked me a while ago to persuade his parents to let him come here and play on the computers. Now that was one spiritually enlightening meeting!" said Aussie with a smile on his face.

"Actually, it is good to see him back in here. I bumped into him a short while before Barnsley's launch night. He told me in private that his parents fully supported Barnsley's WAAR campaign and were really impressed with his visit to discuss it with them. Unfortunately, they decided to ban him from here until after the event. They didn't want Carl being inadvertently caught up in any alcoholic related problems Barnsley might encounter because of their previous ineffectual campaigns."

"They did mention Barnsley's visit to us. What did you make of Carl's ban though?" asked Charlton.

"It sounded like a good idea. Barnsley could easily handle any stick and dish it out as well. Carl is more reserved and doesn't like confrontations. Although we all know it's not a good idea to wind up a rhino. I haven't mentioned this to anyone until now."

"Thanks for letting us know." said Charlton.

They then left the cafe

CHAPTER 25 - SUNDAY 7TH AUGUST (PM – EVEN LATER)

The monkey enclosure was the brainchild of some twins in Year 3 of Hearts River Lower School who were big fans of the "Pirates of the Caribbean" film series.

As soon as the class was asked for ideas, they instantly came up with a pirate theme.

The enclosure housed two replica old Spanish galleon ships.

One was a normal Spanish Navy galleon, and the other was decked out as a pirate ship complete with a jolly roger.

They had big masts, crow's nests, replica cannons and rigging between the big masts.

The ships were strategically positioned to look like a battle was taking place.

The Spanish Navy ship was the bigger of the two and it housed the chimpanzees, gibbon, and baboon. They had arrived first and had all moved into this ship. It was the main meeting place for them all.

When Aussie arrived a week later, he was surprised to find that the pirate ship was empty and so he set up home in it and absolutely loved it.

They entered and made their way to the Spanish

Navy ship, and up the gang plank.

As they reached the main deck, they heard voices coming from the direction of the captain's quarters.

They opened a large red wooden door and walked in without knocking.

Standing at the front next to a big chart was Langley.

He was a large chimpanzee and was head of the ape enclosure.

Sitting on the floor in front him were four other chimpanzee's Zena, Stacy Declan, and the youngest member Rory.

Next to them was Sally, a baboon and Billy, the guitar playing gibbon.

Everyone turned to look at them as they walked in

"Welcome you two we are nearly at the end of our weekly awards ceremony. You are most welcome to wait if you want. It shouldn't be too much longer." said Langley.

Mountie looked at Charlton who nodded that he didn't mind.

They sat on the floor behind the rest of the apes.

Langley looked back at the chart.

Mountie noticed that all the ape's names were on it with various coloured stars by each of their names.

Langley coughed loudly facing the group.

"The Piss Take Award for urinating on the most zoo visitors goes to..."

The rest of the apes did a loud drum roll in unison.

Mountie couldn't believe his ears, whilst Charlton laughed out loud.

"The winner this week is Billy with 52 confirmed hits."

The rest of the apes clapped as Billy walked to the front to collect his award which was an old sample bottle attached to a plaque.

"This award means a lot to me. I know it's not very rock and roll, but my aim in life is to always leave my audiences with a little something to remind them of me."

All the apes and Charlton laughed whilst Mountie shook his head in disbelief.

Billy remained standing at the front.

"I have been asked to present the Star Pee of the Week Award."

Langley looked at Billy curiously and Billy carried on with a big smile on his face "The winner of this week's Star Pee of the Week Award is…. Langley"

All the apes including Charlton and Mountie cheered.

"The award is in recognition of Langley's excellent performance on Tuesday lunchtime. Whilst swinging between two masts he managed to urinate directly into an open lidded thermos flask. It belonged to two love-struck teenagers who had just unpacked their picnic on that grass patch opposite our enclosure."

All the monkey's burst out laughing and there were a couple of wolf whistles from Billy as well.

"This award shows there is still life in the old dog's bladder yet. I am upset though that the girl didn't drink from the flask due to that interfering old bag who tipped them off."

"I did try and hit her with a banana for you as I could see exactly what she was about to do" said Zena excitedly.

Her comment was greeted with a round of applause from everyone present.

"Now for the final award and this is the Star of the Week Award again as voted by you the audience."

They all did a loud drum roll including Charlton and Mountie who were enjoying themselves as well.

Langley picked up an award with a big star on it.

"This week the award goes to Rory."

This news was met with cheers and some more wolf whistles.

"This award recognises Rory's achievement of keeping four Catholic nuns mesmerised for a full five minutes with an energetic display of monkey spanking. That was until their shocked Mother Superior arrived and hurriedly moved them on."

Everyone in the room burst out laughing and Billy let off a couple more wolf whistles.

"That old Mother Superior did still hang around after she had moved the nuns on though, but

unfortunately my show was over." shouted Rory.
Rory collected his award from Langley.

"Hey Rory, you better not win the award every week by doing that. You know if you carry on doing that you will go blind." shouted a smiling Sally.

"Rory mate if you do go blind, I want first option on those adult magazines under your bed" shouted Billy quickly.

"Hell no. If I go blind, I will be trading them in for some braille versions."

"In that case I definitely want first refusal on any you get rid of." said Billy.

"That's if you can still open the pages" muttered Stacy.

She had been sitting quietly at the back and went bright red as she had only intended to mutter it quietly to herself.

Unfortunately, it was so loud everyone had heard, and they rolled around in fits of laughter.

Mountie then caught Langley's eye.

He stood at the front and clapped his hands to regain some order.

"Please can we have some order now you lot. We have some guests here on some more serious business, Mountie would you like to stand at the front?"

Mountie nodded and moved to stand at the front. Charlton stayed where he was and took his notebook and pen out.

Langley moved away and joined the rest of the

apes down sitting down.

"As you know we are investigating the murder of Barnsley".

He looked and saw all the apes nodding in agreement.

"As such we are interviewing all everyone to see where they were at the time and if they saw anything suspicious".

"I will start off whilst the other have time to think as I was not on site at the time." said Langley.

Mountie gave him a curious glance.

"Mountie you obviously don't know that most evenings after dark I drive a black cab earning money as a taxi driver in Hearts River Town. By the time I collect passengers they are usually so drunk or high that even if they suspected they were being driven by a chimpanzee they would never believe in questioning it"

Langley used to live at London Zoo where he had started his nocturnal stints as a black cab taxi driver.

His lack of English had not proved to be a handicap. Some more charitable customers had assumed he was an asylum seeker and given him larger tips.

He did boast that one night he had a member of the royal family in the back of his cab.

He had been very upset when told he was moving to Hearts River Zoo as he thought it would mean giving up his taxi driving work which he enjoyed.

When he arrived, he had discussed this problem with Aussie.

Aussie had hacked into the taxi driver licensing section of Hearts River Town Council records and added in Langley's details.

Langley had managed to find an empty garage nearby and had moved in his black cab.

"On Sunday night I left here around 8.00 as I needed to do some work on the engine before I took it out for the night."

"You didn't pick up Andy Cousins again, did you?" said Billy.

The rest of the apes all laughed.

Langley had twice picked up the zoo manager from his home and had chuckled how he hadn't noticed that he was being driven by one of his zoo's animals.

Langley shook his head.

"I then went out in the taxi starting around 10.30 until 5.00 on Monday morning. I got back here around 6.00. I only found out about Barnsley when I turned on the Channel Roar breakfast news. I was well shaken up."

Mountie waited a minute as he could see that Charlton was still writing.

"So, what were the rest of you doing?"

"As you know I met up with the jackals and I hung around playing with them all evening."

said Billy.

"Yes, I remember" and then looked at the others.

"The rest of us went to the fashion show. We left around 7.45 and got our seats and watched the first half of show. We stayed to watch the seal display which was excellent. We didn't leave our seats and sat through the start of second half of the show. Then Crocket made his announcement." said Zena.

The others nodded in agreement.

"Although I wish I hadn't gone though as there are only so many "I bet your bum would look big in that" comments you can take in one evening" Sally muttered out loudly.

Everyone burst out laughing.

Stacy in a bid to return order to the proceedings took over.

"We then went to the café to find out what was going on. We listened to Oscar and naturally we were all shocked. I remember seeing you there Mountie."

Mountie nodded his head in agreement trying not to smile.

Charlton sat at the back gritting his teeth as his presence had once again not been mentioned.

Mountie then turned to look at Rory.

"And what were you doing on the evening, surely you didn't go to the fashion show?"

"I did go. Although I didn't realise that I was going to be the only male in the audience"

"The only reason you went was because you

thought there might be some females prowling around in lingerie you old perv." said Billy.

"That's not true; there wasn't much else for me to do that night."

"If it wasn't for the WAAR event you would have been in the café looking at porn especially with Aussie out running the fashion show bar. You must have been gutted that Barnsley's event was in the café at the same time."

Everyone burst out laughing.

Rory looked crest fallen and turned to Mountie with his hand on his heart.

"Mountie don't believe all these malicious slurs on my character."

"Hmm I would have believed you, but Aussie has been enlightening me about your surfing escapades"

Rory went bright red.

Everyone else fell about in fits of laughter.

"That just leaves Declan. Did you go to the show as well" asked Mountie looking at Declan.

"Unfortunately, not. I was laid up in bed with a blinding migraine. I get one every so often and it usually knocks me out for two or three days. I took some sleeping tablets. I found out in the morning about Barnsley's murder via Channel Roar news when I woke up."

"Take it you are feeling much better now".

"Yes, I am a lot better. Although my migraine caused me major problems with TESCOW. As you know I do all their local deliveries and I had to tell them that I couldn't do their Saturday, Sunday and Monday deliveries. They said they were short of replacement staff and would let all my customers know about a delay in getting their deliveries and asking them to say if there was anything urgent that was needed. All my delivery information is stored on my tablet and linked to head office. Then everyone here chipped in on Tuesday to help with me with my delivery backlog as I was well again."

Declan clapped them all to show his appreciation.

"I remember that now. Deidre got an email on Saturday from TESCOW. She was concerned that we might run out of pizzas and the lads were worried about running out of beer during the live football game on Sunday evening. TESCOW not surprisingly replied saying they didn't see beer and pizza as fitting into their urgent category." said Charlton.

"More chance of Newcastle AFC winning a cup than your mates running out of beer" muttered Declan under his breath

Everyone heard his comment and roared with laughter including Charlton.

"Well, I can't think of anything else I need to ask. If you do think of anything that might help, please let us know."

"We will let you know if we think of anything important." said Langley.

They left and started walking down the gang

plank.

They stopped halfway down and turned around when they heard "Fog on the Tyne" being played on a penny whistle behind them.

"It's only courtesy that as you weren't piped on board it's the least that I can do is to pipe you off." said Billy.

They smiled and carried on walking down whilst Billy resumed playing "Fog on the Tyne" on his penny whistle.

CHAPTER 26 – SUNDAY 7TH AUGUST (PM – MUCH LATER)

"Well that just leaves the seals and dolphins to see before we hit the surgery in the morning. Although I doubt if we will get much from them as they were all tied up with the fashion show." said Charlton.

"I agree with you, but we do still need to see them as you never know they might have something useful."

They walked toward the seal house and went in the entrance.

The Year 4 of Hearts River Upper School had been covering Eskimos in Geography when they were approached for a design and had come up with an igloo design suggestion.

It was a large white igloo with a large glass door that divided the outside pool from the indoor water demonstration pool.

The door was lifted during show times to allow the seals and dolphins the extra space they needed as part of their demonstrations.

Around the outside pool were rows of raised seats

Inside the igloo was a large, raised seating area for visitors to watch the daily seal shows.

.

They walked in the entrance and saw that the seals were swimming around in the outside pool.
They were just about to call out when some very loud rap music started blasting out over the outside speakers.
Mountie covered his ears to muffle the noise as he hated rap music.
The seals started to perform one of their party pieces and they went and sat in the stands until they had finished.

In their display they transformed themselves into the objects being sung by the rapper.
They transformed themselves into cars, guns, and knives.
They finished the set by forming the shape of a shotgun with a curled-up dolphin looking like a bullet exploding out of its barrel and showering everyone with confetti.

When they had finished Mountie and Charlton clapped.
Mountie then quickly recovered his ears as the rap music carried on playing.
The seals and dolphins stopped as they spotted them sitting in the stands.
They all swam over to see them whilst Ant went to turn the music off.
The seal enclosure consisted of eight seals.
Four male seals called Owen, Ron, Ant, and Samuel.
Four female seals called Lisa, Angie, Fran, and

Sam.

Ron and Ant were twins.
They had stopped talking to their DIY loving parents after being ridiculed about the names they had given them.
They had heard most jokes about tins and filling in.
They had considered changing their names but found that they helped raise their profiles and had decided to keep them.

The enclosure was also home to four dolphins Otis, Prince, Charlie, and Jacob.
They all climbed out except the dolphins who all stuck their heads over the side.
Charlton nudged Mountie to indicate that the music had stopped.
"Rap music is great to work out to as you can hear the beat brilliantly underwater." Owen said catching his breath.
"They could probably have heard that beat in the Pacific Ocean as well" muttered Mountie to Charlton
Samuel ignored the comment.
"That's why P Dolphin's music is so great for us seals to perform to."
"And don't forget us dolphins either," shouted an eager Otis.
"Yeah, and dolphins as well. P Dolphin is one of us as he really knows the best beats for inside and outside the water" carried on Prince smiling and

continued

Mountie's face was looking completely vacant, and the discussion was going straight over his head.

"As does Snoop Doggfish" said Ant as he joined them after turning the music off.

P Dolphin was a dolphin called Philippe and one of the first aquatic rappers.

He had lived at New York Zoo at the golden time of the birth of aquatic rap music.

Whilst there he had teamed up with a marlin fish called Marlin Mathers.

He had also teamed up with an Amazonian Giant Centipede called Curtis who was brilliant at working the DJ decks.

A stingray fish calling himself Dr Stingdre had spotted them practising one afternoon and loved their music so much he offered to be their producer.

They were the first aquatic rap band and called themselves Swim DMC (Dolphin, Marlin, and Centipede).

They then proceeded to write their names in all the animal music history books.

Unfortunately, the New York Zoo had to be closed and all three of them were moved to different zoos.

All of them decided to go solo with Dr Stingdre still producing them.

Philippe Dolphin became a rapper called P

Dolphin. He also went on to design his own range of aquatic clothes and waterproof accessories.

Marlin changed his name and became a very successful solo rapper known as Emarlinem.

Curtis was really into jungle music. He broke the world record for playing the most DJ decks at same time. He managed to keep 50 decks going at the same time and became known as 50 Centipede.

Sam noticing Mountie's blank expressions coughed to catch the others attention.

"I don't think Mountie and Charlton have come here to discuss the virtues of rap music, have you?"

They both energetically nodded their heads in agreement.

"We are here to talk about last Sunday evening." said Mountie.

"That was so tragic. I still have nightmares about it" said Fran shuddering.

Ron moved to comfort her.

"I'm not sure what help we are going to be Mountie. We were all fully engaged that evening."

All of them nodded including the dolphins with their heads out the water.

Charlton was looking at dolphins nodding their heads above the water and couldn't stop the thought that he ought to be throwing them a fish each. He quickly decided it best to keep this thought firmly in his head.

"From 6.30 onwards we were either practising our display or generally helping out in any way we could." said Owen.

"We all watched the fashion show from the pool and then during the interval, we did our display, which was excellent." said Sam.

Everyone nodded in agreement.

"What did you think of our display you have just seen? We did it at the fashion show." said Fran proudly.

"It was fantastic." said Mountie.

"We are hoping it will help us retain our synchronised swimming gold medal at the forthcoming Olympics at Copenhagen Zoo." said Otis.

"I wish you all the best at the Olympics and winning the gold medal again." said Mountie.

All the seals and dolphins beamed with pride.

Otis dived into the water and did two large jumps before returning to the side of the pool.

Charlton again thought about rewarding him with a fish and instantly tried to blank this thought out of his brain.

Mountie noticed a funny facial expression on his face and thought it wise not to comment or bring attention to it.

"We had some soft drinks after our display. Then we went back in the arena for the rest of the show just before Crocket made his sad announcement." said Angie.

"Then everyone left to go the café as requested." said Ron solemnly.

"Not everyone left though. Don't you remember those three idiots from the reptile house. They stayed here as they were more concerned with looking at a specific outfit in the show rather than going to find out about Barnsley's death." said Lisa.

"They kept moaning about the show finishing early and then they all started swooning over some gaudy looking outfit. Please!!" said Angie.

"Please don't" said Charlton accidentally blurting it out loud.

Everyone laughed.

"We have interviewed them and that was a life changing experience."

"So, what happened then" said Mountie deliberately cutting Charlton short before he said something he shouldn't say.

"As we all couldn't go to the café, we waited for someone to return and update us. Jerry came back first to pick up her CD's and told us what had happened to Barnsley." said Lisa.

They all nodded their agreement.

"Well, if you do think of anything helpful then please let us know."

He then got up and started to walk out and Charlton followed him.

Outside Mountie looked at his watch.

"We both have an early start tomorrow. I suggest we rendezvous at my place at 6.15 in the morning and get ready to put Operation Autopsy in place".

With that Mountie wandered off in the direction of home.

"See you in the morning." shouted Charlton.

He started to make his way home and knew it would be empty.

He arrived home and was amazed to find everyone was still there either chatting in the kitchen or in the front room watching football on television.

Even more surprisingly he couldn't see any alcohol being consumed in either room.

He stood scratching his eyes and then his head for a minute wondering whether he was in the right house.

Alice came over and hugged him.

"It may not look like it, but we are all so proud of what you and Mountie are doing. We decided that if tomorrow morning is as important as you say it is then we will not let you down."

"We don't want to give the rest of the animals another reason to call us lazy bastards. So, we are all having a booze free evening and then going to bed early so as to be ready and raring to go in the morning." said Laura.

"I am totally gob smacked."

"It's only for one night though and you do realise we will need to drink twice as much tomorrow night to make up for it" Mark shouted from the living room.

"Hear, hear." shouted Alistair and Richard in unison.

"Thanks a lot everyone I really appreciate all of this support." said Charlton with tears coming down his face.

He left the room and went off to bed.

He couldn't wait to tell Mountie about this. He would wait till the morning in case he didn't believe him, thought he had gone barking mad and decide to call off the plan.

CHAPTER 27 - MONDAY 8TH AUGUST AM

Charlton woke up at 5.30. He had struggled to get to sleep and been tossing and turning in his bed all night.

He had been going over the plan over and over again and coming up with a different ending each time.

He put on a sleeveless red Manchester United football top with DE HARE, the name of Manchester United AFC goalkeeper, emblazoned on the back and some black shorts.

He wandered into the kitchen and was amazed to find it clear which was a first for a Monday morning or any morning come to that. He did consider taking some pictures as proof but resisted the temptation as he had more serious matters to contend with.

"So last night wasn't a mirage after all and they didn't break their promises after I went to bed either".

The kitchen door opened, and Deidre walked in.

Charlton looked in amazement.

Deidre was not an early riser and was not a morning person.

"Morning. I couldn't sleep much as I kept thinking about our escapade this morning."

"Fancy a coffee "

Charlton made them both a mug of coffee and

they sat down at the kitchen table.

"So let me get this straight. I go over the fence and then cause as much havoc as I can in the car park. I then carry on until I am caught by the zookeepers and Doctor Mike."

Charlton nodded in agreement.

"The key thing is to keep everyone occupied as long as possible as both of us need to give Mountie as much time as possible to search the surgery?"

"Do you really think your plan is going to work?"

"I am pretty sure it will mum. I really hope Mountie finds something useful. To be honest we are struggling to solve this case now we have interviewed everyone."

"I'm sure both of you will solve it. We all have a lot of faith and confidence in you both. Also, it will reflect positively for once on us zebras.'"

"Thanks a lot mum that means a lot to me. I'm sorry but I must go and see Mountie now to finalize everything.

Charlton finished his coffee.

He got up from the table and started walking towards the door.

"Don't worry I will have the rest of the gang up, breakfasted and ready for you."

"Thanks mum I knew I could count on you."

He walked over and noticed that the sky was cloudy, and it wasn't as hot as it had been recently.

He knew this cooler weather would help them

with their escape plans.

Mountie was sitting outside his hut as usual in a deckchair with a pot of coffee on the table next to him. He had even laid out the spare deckchair for Charlton.

He saw he had a frown on his face which turned to a smile as he wrote something on the back of the Animal Times newspaper he was holding.

He folded it over to show that he had just finished the crossword.

He sat down in the spare deck chair and poured himself a mug of coffee.

"Sorry I was a bit late. Deidre was up early and eager to go over the plan details again."

Mountie was so startled he spat out some of the coffee he was drinking.

"Please give me a warning before surprising me with comments like that."

"OK, warning number two. I can't believe it, when I got back home last night, I found them all at home. Not only that, but they had also not been drinking, not a single drop."

"Have you been secretly visiting the camels for some of those plants that I showed you? You do realise they can do strange things to your vision?"

"I was dumbstruck. They were all keen to make sure they would be in a fit state to help this morning. I felt so proud to be a zebra again this morning."

"Well, that is excellent news. Especially about

Deidre being up and raring to go."

"She wanted to go over the plan and is going to make everyone is up, breakfasted and ready to go by the time I get back."

"That is good news. How are you feeling about today's exercise?"

"I had a bad night with everything going around in my head. I now feel super ready to put my plan into place. And you?"

"I also had a bad night. I am worried that I won't find nothing in the surgery and then having to decide what our steps are going to be as we have now interviewed all the animals."

"I made a similar comment to Deirdre this morning. So, let's keep everything crossed that we have some good luck this morning. I think we are due some."

Mountie was surprised that Charlton had been discussing the case with Deidre.

Charlton picked up on this.

"I know but she is my mum and I know she will not tell anyone."

They both picked up their coffee mugs and sat staring across the enclosure.

Suddenly the silence was broken by a voice overhead.

"Is it okay if I join you two down there?"

They looked up and saw Postie Stevie flying overhead.

Mountie beckoned him to come down and join them.

He saw a space on the table and perched himself on the edge.

"Morning all"

"Morning".

"Well, is everything still on for this morning?"

They both nodded in agreement.

"So, the plan is around 8.50 Charlton and Deidre will go over the perimeter fence and they will then be chased by Doctor Mike and the zookeepers. As soon as the vet's surgery is empty, I will come here and tell you. You then visit it and have a search around inside."

They carried on nodding in agreement.

"And whilst Mountie is inside, I will be his eyes in the sky. As soon as I see any sign of danger I will fly and tell him to leave. If required I can take away any papers that you find and hand them over to you later. I also have a full stomach in case I need to help with any delaying tactics on any of the zookeepers."

Charlton and Mountie laughed.

"That's it in a nutshell" said Mountie with a large smile on his face.

"That's fine then. I have a couple of deliveries to make now but I will return and be ready to help you both later. Good luck with your endeavors this morning."

He then flew off,

Mountie looked at his watch.

"I think it's about time we went and got ready. Good luck to you and please pass it onto Deidre

for me as well."
Charlton got up from his chair.
"Good luck as well and I wish you happy hunting and find something useful for us."
He then made his way home.

CHAPTER 28 - MONDAY 8TH AUGUST (AM – A BIT LATER)

When he got back Deidre had been true to her word .

Everyone was up with a large plate of fried bacon, sausages, mushrooms, bread, and eggs sitting in the middle of the table.

Mark was rubbing his large stomach.

"You know I could get used to this. Are you sure you don't want our help every morning?"

"That's enough of your lip. Sit down and help yourself as you can't go to work on an empty stomach this morning." said Deidre.

Charlton ate his breakfast and went to his room to get changed and ready.

At 8.40 everyone convened outside.

Postie Stevie arrived to see if they were all ready and said Doctor Mike had arrived and was in the vet's surgery.

Charlton looked at his watch.

"Okay then it is time for action."

With that he started walking towards the perimeter fence and was closely followed by Alistair, Mark, Richard, and Deidre.

They reached the perimeter fence and all huddled by it.

And what a sight they all looked huddled there.

Alistair Mark and Richard were slouched with

cigarettes in their mouths and their Newcastle United AFC shirts hanging over their large beer bellies.

Deidre also had a cigarette in her mouth and was looking very nervous.

Charlton looked at his watch.

"OK are you ready to push Deidre over the fence?"

Deidre waddled over to the fence and turned to Alistair Mark and Richard

"You can put those fags out as well as I don't want burn marks on me bum."

Alistair Mark and Richard dropped their cigarettes.

They moved into position and started to lift Deidre up.

"Oi, be careful what you are touching. Don't forget I will be back later."

"Did you have double helpings of breakfast this morning" said Mark smiling.

His face was red with exhaustion as he wasn't used to lifting anything heavier than a Newcastle Brown Ale bottle or the television remote control.

"Of course I did, Chefs privilege. And if you are about to make any smart alec comments about me weight or size of me bum forget it"

"OK lads one two three push." said an exhausted Richard.

With one large push Deidre went flying over the fence.

A loud scream was heard on the other side of the

fence followed by a stream of expletives.

A couple of seconds later Deidre struck her head against the perimeter fence.

"That's a first I have never fallen over sober before "

"What's sober?" said Alistair.

All of them started laughing, which helped ease the atmosphere.

"Right, I'm next to come over "

He then scanned around the outside perimeter fence and back inside the zoo.

"I don't think we have been spotted yet."

Charlton, being more agile and fitter, just needed Mark's help to get over the top of the fence and land safely on the other side.

Looking through the fence, he handed his watch to Mark .

"Thanks for all your help this morning but you must get back now. We will hopefully see you all later."

They all got out new cigarettes and lit them before heading slowly back.

"Right stage one complete" said Charlton to Deidre.

"Now remember the plan is for you to head to the car park and cause as much havoc as you can. You need to try and keep yourself from getting caught as long as you can."

Deirdre nodded to show she understood.

Charlton scanned the car park looking for suitable expensive cars.

"When they do start closing in on you should head towards that blue expensive looking car or that silver sporty convertible car".

He pointed out two cars in the car park to Deidre. She nodded that she knew what cars he was pointing out.

"The zookeepers will definitely not want either of them getting damaged as they are very expensive cars, the silver one is a top of the range Porsche."

"Okay I understand but which way are you going to be going?"

Deidre was surveying the slowly filling car park.

"I will be running for the main road."

A thought then popped into head which he regretted mentioning instantly.

"If you get cornered a good piss or a large poo should get you some extra valuable minutes before capture. The zookeepers usually prefer to wait for aromas to pass."

Deidre looked indignant by the suggestion.

"I will do whatever I need to do. I know this is important to you, but a lady will only go so far. Just be grateful I have taken off my white stilettos for me running."

"You ready to go?"

Deidre nodded her head in agreement.

"Ok one two three go"

They both started running.

Deidre made a bee line for a group of school

children she had spotted departing from a school coach.

She had recognised one child who had been very rude about her previously and she decided it was payback time.

The children screamed when they saw her advancing and they all rapidly tried to get back on the coach.

There were loud shouts from the zoo staff as they spotted Deidre and then Charlton escaping.

Deidre spotted the silver Porsche convertible that Charlton had pointed out to her.

After she had finished "playing" with the school children that was her next port of call.

Charlton knew Mountie needed at least 20 minutes and Deidre was unlikely to last that length of time before getting caught.

He had decided in his plan that it would work best if he headed off site.

He ran through the car park and headed towards the zoo entrance and vaulted over a barrier just missing two old ladies in a Nissan Micra. The driver was so shocked that she crashed into the barrier.

He finally reached the main road and looking back he could see that the zookeepers were still a fair distance behind him. Although he could see that Deidre was already cornered.

At the main road, he looked left and right and then decided to go right as there was no traffic coming that way and he began running down the centre of the road.

Cars started coming towards him and were hooting their horns at him.

Undeterred he carried on running down the middle of the road causing cars to swerve off the road to miss him.

He was laughing to himself, imagining their owners phoning up their insurance companies and explaining how they had crashed their cars to avoid an escaped zebra running down the middle of the road.

Suddenly he felt a stinging pain in his hind leg .

He turned to see Doctor Mike in a Land Rover behind him holding a tranquilizer gun.

He then noticed the tranquilizer dart lodged in his back leg and instantly dropped down asleep in the middle of the road.

Postie Stevie decided it was time to fly back and tell Mountie that he should leave.

Flying back, he saw lots of zookeepers and staff mingling around outside.

Some of them were huddled around Deidre deciding on how to move her.

The others were talking to anxious looking visitors who were concerned at seeing the zebra's escape. Staff were trying to reassure them that everything was fine, especially now they had now been caught.

CHAPTER 29 - MONDAY 8TH AUGUST
(AM – AT THE SAME TIME)

At 8.45 Mountie was at his entrance in readiness. He started to do some stretching exercises and then some mental exercises to help him focus on what he had to do in the vet's surgery. He blocked everything else out of mind.
Postie Stevie arrived "The coast is clear and good hunting."
He then flew off to see what was going on. .
Mountie ran as fast as he could to the surgery.
He froze for a second outside as he had recently had an unpleasant experience in there. He thought he had forgotten about it, but it decided to make an untimely reappearance in his consciousness.
He opened the front door remembering to leave it open.
It felt strange being in the surgery room and not being confronted by Doctor Mike.
He found Doctor Mike a very imposing character.

Doctor Mike always wore a white lab coat that was always unbuttoned revealing an array of different T- shirts promoting some very obscure rock bands.
Even some of the more musically astute zoo animals had never heard of any of the bands on

his t-shirts.

Also, he usually wore a pair of black jeans, and a large pair of black Doctor Martin boots with rainbow-coloured laces.

He was momentarily struck by how tranquil and quiet the surgery was that morning.

There was a huge painting of a flamingo on the wall and under it was Doctor Mike's desk and a black leather swivel chair.

Suddenly he realised why it was tranquil it was because the room was not filled with Doctor Mike's thumping rock music.

The animals all agreed Doctor Mike's music was usually worse than the actual surgery itself. It was easier to quickly relent so as to help speed up getting the knockout anesthetics and thus having to endure as little as possible of his musical selections.

He quickly looked at his watch to see how he was doing for time.

He went to the desk and to his surprise he found Barnsley's autopsy report on top of some other papers.

He was tempted to have a quick read but decided speed was of the essence and that he would read it later.

He went over to the photocopier to make a copy.

He couldn't believe his luck as not only was it switched on, but it copied all the pages, first time, no paper jams, no paper running out, ink warning messages or any of the pages coming out scrunched up and unreadable.

Whilst he was waiting for the photocopier to finish an item in a clear bag lying on top of a cabinet caught his attention.

He couldn't believe his luck as he saw that the bag contained a bottle of water bottle and he hoped it was the one used to choke Barnsley.

He picked it up and it was labelled "Lion Death - Sunday 31 July".

He quietly cheered to himself as he hadn't expected to find the bottle still here.

He then wondered whether to take it or not and decided to take it.

He picked up his copy of the autopsy remembering to replace the original back on the desk where he had found it.

Just then Postie Stevie arrived "You must speed up, as they have just caught Charlton."

"Thanks, I had just finished anyway."

Postie Stevie looked at the papers and water bottle.

"Are you going to need a hand getting them back to your hut."

"Thanks for the offer but I should be okay getting them back home Thanks for all your help this morning."

Postie Stevie again looked at the papers "Looks like you had a successful visit then."

Mountie smiled and nodded his head.

"I'm going back to see what is going on." and flew

out of the surgery.

He started to leave and decided to quickly have a look at the flamingo painting. He didn't recognise the flamingo or its location in the painting. He saw it was titled "Flamingo Baby" by an artist whose initials were VF. Not an artist he was familiar with.

He had a quick look around to check everything was back in place and that he hadn't missed anything.

He then heard voices in the distance and ran back to his enclosure.

Postie Stevie then arrived and flew into his hut.

"Hope you found everything you needed. It looks like you were lucky in there."

Mountie nodded his head enthusiastically.

"Just to let you know. Charlton and Deidre were taken down by tranquilizer darts fired by Doctor Mike.

"Are they both Okay?"

"They are now. Although there is one very upset Porsche owner. When they captured Deidre, she decided to pee inside their Porsche. Unfortunately, the owner had made the mistake of upsetting Deidre by being extremely rude about her size. Not a good move. Still served them right as they still had the cars roof down."

Mountie burst out laughing.

"Good old Deidre perhaps I do owe her that dinner after all".

"That's not all. There are two old ladies in

the café being calmed down by staff as they nearly collided with Charlton as he vaulted over the main barrier. Not to mention the string of crashed cars on the main road that had to swerve to avoid hitting him as he was escaping."

Mountie laughed and glowed with pride.

"He deserves a medal for this. The plan was his idea you know, and it went brilliantly."

Postie Stevie looked at the papers "Well, I do hope it was all worthwhile."

Mountie looked at the papers "I hope so too".

"What do you want me to say to the others if they ask me what happened?"

Mountie stopped for a minute.

"Just say it was part of our ongoing investigation and leave it at that."

Postie Stevie nodded and flew off waving as he went.

Mountie suddenly remembered the zoo was now officially open and he rushed to hide the papers and water bottle in his bedroom for later inspection.

CHAPTER 30 - MONDAY
8TH AUGUST (PM)

Charlton and Deidre were placed in the back of a zoo Land Rover and transported to the recovery area in the back of vet's surgery.

Around 4.00 in the afternoon they both slowly woke up from the anesthetic they had been shot with earlier by Doctor Mike's rifle.

Although Charlton didn't feel too bad there was a loud banging noise mixed with Viking chanting that was giving him a real headache.

Suddenly they both looked at each other and they knew they were in the vet's recovery room because the awful banging and chanting noise was a Viking metal song that was blasting from Doctor Mike's stereo through an open window.

Charlton looked at clock on the wall and saw that the zoo was still open.

He hoped Doctor Mike would check them over soon and return them home after the zoo shut.

They sat with their ears covered mouthing comments about the awful racquet that they were being forced to listen to.

At 5.00 Doctor Mike visited them.

"It's good to see you two escapees are back in the land of living".

He got out his stethoscope and checked them both over.

"Looks like you two have not been harmed by your little escapade this morning. Although I wish I could say the same about the interior of that convertible Porsche you damaged. As soon as the zoo shuts, I'll get you both whisked back to your enclosure".

He walked off and returned a few minutes later with some apples and carrots.

"You'll probably need to eat these to help you build your strength back up".

With that he walked off again out of the recovery area.

Charlton lifted one of the carrots up and disdainfully looked at it.

He turned to Deidre.

"Carrots!! Why couldn't he have given us a large plate of chicken madras and an ice-cold pint of beer. Now that that would help me build my strength up again."

Deidre smiled and rubbed her tummy.

"Don't say things like that as you are making me feel really hungry."

Charlton still holding the carrot smiled.

"Well, if you are hungry, you can always eat one of these."

Deidre gave him a stern look.

"Say that again and you will be asking Doctor Mike to surgically remove it before you return later."

Charlton started to laugh, and Deidre joined in.

They sat down and recounted what had

happened that morning.

He was really pleased to hear about her peeing into the Porsche after the owner had been rude about her size.

Doctor Mike reappeared later with three zookeepers and a green golf buggy with a trailer.

They transported Deidre back first then followed by Charlton.

The zookeepers then left them and went off to finish closing up for the night.

The zebras all crowded around them and gave them a large round of applause.

Charlton was given a cold bottle of Newcastle Brown Ale by Mark.

"I think mate you have definitely earned this today".

Gail opened a cold bottle of Chardonnay and poured some into a glass and gave it to Deidre.

"You have definitely earned this as well".

"How are you both feeling?" said Alistair.

"We were alright until we woke up. Since then, we have been forced to listen to Doctor Mike's Viking rock music for hours." said Charlton.

"Not Doctor Mike's music" said Laura grimacing.

"That's like a fate worse than a fate worse than death." said Gail.

There was a knock on the back door and Mountie entered looking very concerned.

"How are you both doing?"

They both nodded to indicate that they were okay.

"That's good news. I heard from Postie Stevie all about your escapades this morning."

He then turned to Deidre.

"Especially about the weeing into that convertible Porsche. Well, done"

Deidre went a bright shade of red.

The rest of the zebras burst out laughing.

"Also, I hear two old people nearly had heart attacks when you leapt in front of their car whilst escaping."

"Their shocked looks will be imprinted on my memory forever".

Again, everyone laughed.

Charlton took a sip from his bottle of beer.

Well, you will be pleased to learn that I did find the autopsy and took a photocopy of it. I also unbelievably found the bottle of water that I think was used to killed Barnsley and took a chance by bringing it with me as well."

Charlton was stunned.

"WOW that is excellent news. I didn't expect the bottle of water to still be there. When do we get started on it?"

The zebras also appreciated that this was indeed excellent news.

Mountie shook his head.

"You two need to get some rest first and get over the effects of the drugs you were shot with."

"But I feel fine."

He stopped as he began to feel a bit tired and a bit queasy.

"Look you need to have a good rest tonight and a lie in tomorrow morning. I will look through everything tonight and tomorrow evening we will have a big catch-up session."

Charlton was about to complain when a pain shot across his head and reluctantly nodded in agreement.

"Once again thank you all for your help today we couldn't have done it without you all."

He gave Deidre and then Charlton a big hug.

"Get some rest and we will pick up again tomorrow".

With that he left and went back to his hut.

CHAPTER 31 - MONDAY 8TH AUGUST (PM- LATER)

When he arrived back, he cleared everything off his table.

He got out his notebook and pen and laid out the autopsy and the bottle.

He decided to look at the autopsy first.

On the front cover it said the autopsy had been undertaken by Doctor Mike at the vet's surgery on Monday morning at 10.30 AM.

The autopsy reported that a male lion had been chocked to death with a bottle of water. Doctor Mike thought the lion had been playing with a bottle of water and had somehow managed to get it jammed in its mouth. Unfortunately, he surmised the lion was then unable to dislodge the bottle and it had choked to death as a result.

He laughed to himself, if only Doctor Mike knew the real part of it.

He was glad that this proved that Barnsley's death had been caused by choking on the bottle of water.

It confirmed as he suspected that they were still looking for a murderer.

Mountie carried on reading.

Doctor Mike had written that he was unable to determine the time of death.

He thought it was a shame Doctor Mike hadn't

come and asked him as he would have told him that it was between 8.05 and just after 9.00. The times Oscar had last seen Barnsley alive and when he found him dead.

Mountie got up and got himself a glass and poured himself some Sortilège Canadian whisky liquer.

Sortilege Canadian whisky liquer is a mix of Canadian whisky and maple syrup and it was a particular favourite drink of his.

Mountie then spotted something else that caught him totally by surprise.

Doctor Mike had written that he found signs of freshly dried blood on the back of the lion's head and looking further he had found a large gash. It looked like the lion had somehow bashed his head before he died probably hit something whilst trying to remove the bottle of water.

He took a sip of his drink whilst taking in the relevance of this new information.

His attention was drawn to the bag with the bottle in it and began to wonder.

He got out a large piece of white paper to open the bag over.

Slowly he opened the bag and removed the water bottle.

He looked closely to see if it had any bumps in it or any dried blood still on it as he suspected it had been the cause of the gash.

He was disappointed as he couldn't find any evidence on the bottle.

His expression changed as just before he put the bottle back in the bag he saw some small fragments at the bottom of it.

He tipped the fragments out onto the white piece of paper.

He rubbed one of the fragments and it left a blood stain on the paper.

He knew this meant that Barnsley had been hit on the back of the head with the bottle before being choked with it.

He wondered if the bash had knocked Barnsley out or even killed him instantly depending on the force of the bash.

He had for a while been wondering about which animal could have tackled and choked a lion and been assuming that it would have to have been a large animal.

This new evidence had thrown this assumption up in the air.

He now realised that any sized animal could have whacked Barnsley on the back of the head when he wasn't looking. Then after he had fallen over it was easy for the killer to then choke the unconscious or semi-conscious Barnsley with the water bottle. It now meant that any size or sex of animal could be their killer.

He started writing further notes concerning his latest findings and thoughts.

He started looking back through his notes in the knowledge now that any of the animals they had interviewed could be their killer.

He spotted in his notes that during the zebra interviews they hadn't asked the girls what they had done during the fashion show interval.

He then realised that the football game had a half-time interval and that would have been during the murder time window as well and they hadn't asked the lads about that either.

He then began to wonder where all the other animals had been during the fashion show interval. Perhaps one of them had said they were going to the toilet and slipped off to kill Barnsley instead.

He made a note of this in his notebook to pick up with Charlton.

He re-read the autopsy and found nothing else relevant in it.

He refilled his glass and re-read his notes but nothing else caught his attention.

He locked the autopsy and water bottle in a chest under his bed for safekeeping.

He turned on some classical music to help him chill out and minutes later he fell asleep.

A very busy day had finally taken its toll.

CHAPTER 32 - TUESDAY 9 AUGUST (AM)

At 6.15 Mountie woke up and found he was still in his chair from the previous night.

As he knew Charlton was not going to join him, he decided to go for a stroll down to the riverbank taking his breakfast with him.

After he arrived, he spotted Oscar who was beckoning him to come over and join him.

So, he went over and put down his picnic rug, bag of warm croissants and a thermos flask full of coffee.

"It is such a glorious morning I decided to come down here for breakfast as I am not seeing Charlton this morning."

Oscar nodded in agreement.

Mountie poured himself a coffee and offered Oscar a cup as well which he accepted.

"Croissant as well?".

"It's okay I have eaten already this morning."

Oscar was looking out over the river and sipped his coffee.

"So how are Charlton and Deidre feeling after yesterday's little escapade?"

"I think they are all right. Although they are recovering more from an extended exposure to Doctor Mike's Viking rock music than the anaesthetic dart".

Oscar let out a big laugh.

"I know the feeling. I was in there recently for a 5-minute check-up and I had that noise buzzing around in my head for the rest of the day."
"I told him to get an early night, rest in this morning and resume the investigation this evening."
"So did you find much in the vet's surgery?"
Mountie took a drink of his coffee.
"Their escape gave me plenty of time to look around. I did find the autopsy that Doctor Mike had written and took a copy of it. An unexpected bonus was finding the bottle of water bagged on a shelf."
Oscar sat quietly looking out over the river.
"Oscar, the autopsy does confirm that as we expected Barnsley was choked to death."
Oscar just sat there quietly staring at the river and a tear swelled up in one of his eyes that he brushed away "Please continue."
Although they trusted Oscar, he still hadn't been ruled out as being the killer, or even being involved in some way. Although they agreed that this was very unlikely.
Mountie knew for the time being to be careful what he said and monitor Oscar's reactions.
"I need to speak to Charlton first and then we need to agree our next steps and actions."
Oscar nodded again and looked out to the river.
Mountie also looked out to the river.
"There is one thing that you might be able to help us clear up."

"Sure, what is it?"

Mountie refilled his coffee mug.

"It may be something or it may be nothing."

"Go on ask away."

"When we searched his bedroom, we saw a docking station for a Sony WalkAN. We couldn't see it anywhere. Do you know where it might be?"

"Yes, I recall seeing him take it to his launch night. Since he got it, he always had it with him. I assumed he took it for background music for the event."

"So later when you guarded inside the cafe did you to see it at all? and if you did, do you what happened to it?"

Oscar sat looking out over the river deep in thought.

"Later on, I must admit I did have a nose round myself to see if I could see any clues. Sorry I don't recall seeing his WalkAN. I'm sure I would have remembered if it had been there as I would have collected it and brought it home. We bought it as a Christmas present and it had a cool looking lion skin cover to it and he was so pleased it. So were we, as we finally got some peace and quiet as he was now listening to his music through his headphones rather than having it blasting out of his room".

Mountie smiled at the last comment.

"You think that is relevant, don't you? "

"This is just a guess. I think after you left him at

the café, he probably had two visitors before you arrived back and found him dead."

"Carry on I'm all ears" said Oscar looking full of interest.

"I think one of visitors was the killer and the other was Jimi who found him dead. So, if you didn't take the WalkAN that means it was either taken by Jimi or the killer."

Oscar's eyes lit up.

"Or it could be just one visitor. What if Jimi is the killer and he also took the WalkAN afterwards? He does like his music."

"That unfortunate thought has crossed my mind as well. We may need to investigate Jimi more thoroughly which I think could prove very tricky."

"I would be very careful there. It is in everyone's interest to keep Lemming sweet and happy."

Mountie took a sip of his coffee and picked up a croissant and took a bite from it.

"Don't you think I know that already."

"Good luck then. Suddenly I'm feeling a lot more positive about your investigation. I was expecting the worst. I am though very concerned by the possible name in the frame, and I am very worried by it."

"You must not discuss this with anyone, not even Poppy. I can't have Jimi finding out he is a prime suspect. We can't have anyone falsely accusing him of being the killer. It would be disaster for the investigation and our everyday lives."

Oscar smiled and handed Mountie back his coffee mug.

"You don't need to worry as this will not go any further than our four ears. You have my word on that. If I goof up, I promise to move into the reptile house permanently."

He started to laugh, and Oscar started laughing as well.

"I may hold you to that. That is great and I really appreciate it. This investigation is difficult enough and we must avoid having to deal with complaints about making wrongful accusations."

Oscar got up and looked at his watch.

"Please keep me posted and let me know as soon as find out who the killer is. I'm convinced you are very close to finding them."

He nodded and started to clear away his picnic stuff.

"Please give my regards to Charlton and Deidre and tell them that I have set up a free bar tab for the zebras. One night only though, I'm not made of money. I have also asked Aussie to arrange a special meal for you and Deidre, no expense spared."

Mountie looked shocked and was about to voice a complaint when he was overruled.

"It's the least you can do considering what she has done for you both."

He nodded his head and started to look a bit down.

"Don't look so down, you know you will enjoy it really."
Oscar started walking back towards the zoo.
He knew deep down it was the right thing to do and you never know it might even be fun, especially as Oscar was picking up the bill.
He started making his way back and thinking what meal he was going to ask.
Suddenly he stopped as he saw the singing dragonfly approaching him.
He heard what song he was singing and laughed out loud.
He was singing Billy Joel's "Italian Restaurant" song. Italian was now Australian, and the main characters were now Mountie and Deidre in the lyrics.
He carried on walking back and to his surprise was singing the song out loud.

CHAPTER 33 - TUESDAY
9TH AUGUST (PM)

Although Charlton had gone to bed early, he was woken up at 10.00 by an apple hitting him on the head. A child had wondered whether he was dead and had been upset to find out he had just been sleeping.

Sitting next to him were Mark, Alistair, and Richard.

"It is good to see those drugs have finally turned you into a proper zebra." said Mark.

Alistair and Richard started to laugh and Mark joined them.

"Do you reckon Doctor Mike has any drugs that will complete the process and turn him into a Newcastle United AFC fan as well?" said Richard.

"He does and it is called Valium. It is an anti-depressant, although it will have its work cut out with Newcastle football fans though." said Charlton.

All the zebra's burst out laughing.

Charlton then spent a lazy day recuperating.

Deidre was feeling the aftereffects of the drugs as well and spent a lazy day recuperating.

As soon as the zoo shut Charlton was chomping at the bit to go and see Mountie. He was desperate for an update on their efforts from yesterday.

He changed into his usual attire of black baggy shorts and put on a red Manchester United AFC football top with FELIONI on the back, she was their female central midfield playing lion.

In the AFL male and female animals played in the same teams.

As most of the animals spent their days naked in fields or in enclosures the after-match showers were mixed and not at all embarrassing.

Charlton ran over to see Mountie forgetting his notebook and pen and decided he would get them later.

Mountie beckoned him in and on the table was his notebook, the photocopied autopsy report, and the bottle of water.

"How are you feeling now?"

"I'm feeling miles better now, thanks a lot."

They sat down in the chairs positioned by the table.

Mountie passed him the copy of the autopsy and he started reading it and then stopped.

"So, this confirms that Barnsley was choked to death, and we do still have a killer to find."

Mountie nodded.

Charlton kept reading the autopsy through to the end.

"It says here that Barnsley was hit on the back of his head by an unidentified object."

Mountie nodded his head in agreement.

"You are right it says Barnsley was not only choked to death but received a knock to the back of his head."

Charlton was just about to say something when Mountie lifted the bag with the water bottle in it.

"I found the bottle that was used to choke Barnsley. I have examined it and alas there are no clues on it"

Charlton's face looked very disappointed with that news.

"I do have some good news though."

Charlton looked at him intently.

"I did notice some small particles in the bottom of the plastic bag that I have now identified as being dried blood. I believe Barnsley was hit on the back of the head with this bottle. As a result, he was powerless to stop someone choking him to death with it."

Charlton sat back absorbing the new information.

"Unfortunately, this is going to make our job a lot harder. I have been wondering which animal could take on a lion and choke it to death. I was swaying towards it being a large strong animal. This new evidence means that any size or sex of animal could have hit him over the head whilst he wasn't looking and then finished him off whilst he was lying either unconscious or semi-conscious or even dead on the floor".

Charlton sat back continuing to digest the news.

"I think it's time to recap where we are."

Mountie nodded in agreement and turned to a page in his notebook.

"I still believe someone was in the bush outside the café drinking whisky. They were either the killer or they witnessed everything and for some reason haven't told us yet."

Charlton nodded in agreement.

"We need to know if it was a premeditated murder or the result of something that happened during the killers visit to the café. The use of the water bottle suggests to me that it wasn't premeditated."

Charlton nodded in agreement again. He wished he hadn't left his notebook behind.

"If the killer had gone into the café and found Barnsley drinking, they may have seen it as a great opportunity to blackmail him. If the blackmail attempt had failed, they may have decided they had to kill Barnsley to stop him telling Oscar about their blackmailing attempt."

Charlton nodded and decided not to interrupt Mountie as he seemed on a roll.

"Lastly was someone in the bush spying on what was going on. They could have been interested in seeing who was attending the launch. Perhaps they were thinking of attending themselves. They may know who the killer is but are not telling us for whatever reason?"

"Or perhaps the killer saw them in the bush and threatened them to keep quiet or even threatened to kill them as well".

It was Mountie's turn to nod this time.

"Or perhaps the person in the bush was a lookout for the killer for example we have just used Postie Stevie to be our lookout. So, we could be looking for two animals that were involved instead of one."

Both sat back silently in their chairs, both deep in thought.

"Another thing Oscar confirmed Barnsley took his lion skinned Sony WalkAN to the café and it has now disappeared."

A broad smile came across Charlton's face as the penny dropped that they might now have some way to link the killer to the murder when they finally find them.

Mountie waited a minute for Charlton to think through what this meant.

"Now again this pure theory. I reckon two animals visited the cafe between Oscar visits."

Charlton looked at his empty lap and regretted not going to get his notebook and pen.

Mountie noticed Charlton had forgotten his notebook and pen went and found a spare notebook and pen and passed them to him.

"As I said I think there were two visitors to the cafe. One was the killer, and the other was Jimi, who found him dead. This means that one of them took the WalkAN."

Charlton started to write frantically in the spare notebook.

"I'm hoping it was the killer that took it as it will

be our link between them and the murder."
Charlton scratched his head thoughtfully.
"But what if the killer was Jimi. That t would mean only been one person visited him."
"I'm glad that the drugs haven't fully befuddled your brain. I have also considered that, and we need to prove whether it was him or not."
"That's going to be tricky as we can't upset Lemming at all. That would not go down well at all."
"Exactly my feelings as well. We must keep this secret as no one must know we suspect Jimi. If it gets out and he's innocent there will be merry hell for us to pay"
"So, what are we going to do next?"
"My plans for this evening were to be not too strenuous for you. I thought we would go to the café and go through our notes to see if we have missed anything, now we have some more information. I do want to see Jimi first though and I would like to see the text message that he told us about. Also, he does like his music and if he did take the WalkAN, then it may still be hidden in his room."
"I don't think we will be allowed to search his room or examine his phone. Lemming would go ape, excuse the pun."
Mountie got up from his chair and Charlton did as well.
"Sorry but I have to go back and pick up my notebook and pen."

Mountie locked everything away his chest.

He picked up his notebook and pen and said, "Ok then lead on."

They both walked over to the zebra enclosure and went in the back door and straight into the kitchen.

They were greeted by Alice, Laura, Mark, and Deidre

Mark put down his bottle of Newcastle Brown Ale on the kitchen table.

"Did you find anything useful yesterday in the vet's surgery?"

"Yes, we have had some good luck and now we have some more leads to follow up on." said Charlton.

"I'm glad to hear our endeavours yesterday proved fruitful." said Deidre.

Charlton left Mountie in the kitchen whilst he went to get his notebook.

"Sorry Mark I forgot to ask you what you all did during half time. Also, whether you had seen anything strange?"

"No. Newcastle United AFC were losing. Now if they had been winning."

Lots of laughter was heard in the main room and Richard and Alistair entered.

"What's that about Newcastle winning?" said Richard.

He walked to the fridge and got himself a can of lager.

"Mountie was just asking if we had seen

anything strange during the half time of the football match".

Richard decided to lighten the atmosphere with a broad smile on his face.

"The only odd thing I can recall was Graham Mole refereeing the game. I ask you a mole as a referee!"

"Aye they will be employing bats as referee's next" said Alistair jokingly.

Mark and Richard started laughing.

"Come on you lot please be sensible for a minute. Please answer whether you saw anything strange at half time." said Deidre.

Mark looked surprised at Deidre's intervention.

"Okay calm down. At half time we all went for a pee outside then stocked up on beer again. We went back to see the highlights or mainly the lowlights of the first half and to hear the television panel's usual drivel. So, no, we didn't see anything strange. Sorry"

Richard, Mark, and Alistair took the opportunity to go back into the front room.

Mountie turned to Deidre.

"So how are you feeling?"

"I still feel a little bit groggy, but I was pleased to be able help with your investigation. It was good fun, running around and keeping the zookeepers entertained. And when that stuck up Porsche owner made a rude comment about me, I felt more than justified in taking my revenge on their Porsche."

Laura and Alice laughed, and Mountie joined in.

"I was so pleased with your efforts and to show my appreciation I would like to take you out for a meal at Aussie's when you feel up for it."

Deidre went all red and was a loss for words.

Alice broke the silence and cuddled Deidre.

"Of course, she would love to have a nice romantic dinner with you. said Alice.

Charlton stifled a smile.

"But only if you wear your red uniform," said Laura.

It was Mountie's turn to go red this time.

"I have all my things now shall we make tracks?" said Charlton.

"I forgot to ask you last time what you did during the show's interval and did any of you see anything strange?"

"I must admit we all slipped out the back as the bar was not that heavily stocked and Aussie had been asked to bump up the prices. It was a good job we had packed our own supplies." said Alice.

Laura and Deidre both laughed.

"So did you see anything when you were out the back.?"

"We did look out for Crocket and anyone else from the bar as we didn't want to be spotted secretly drinking and be stopped from watching the rest of the show." said Alice.

"We should have been so lucky. Although that has just jogged my memory. I went to the loo, and I have just remembered that I did see Crocket making a beeline away from the show." said Laura.

Mountie and Charlton both looked at each other. Do you remember which way he was going?" interrupted Mountie.

"He was running back into the zoo. It looked like it was something very important or pressing that he had to sort out. I don't know perhaps he had left something behind."

"Thanks, and please don't mention this to anyone."

Alice, Deidre, and Laura all nodded in agreement. Mountie started leaving with Charlton following slowly behind.

"Very interesting" said Charlton as he finally caught up with Mountie.

"Yes. Very interesting indeed. It looks like we need to have another chat with Crocket urgently. Although let's see if Jimi is home and willing to answer some more questions"

Mountie finally felt they were making some real progress and was now confident they were getting closer to identifying the killer.

CHAPTER 34 - TUESDAY 9TH AUGUST (PM- A BIT LATER)

They reached the gate to the gorilla enclosure and entered.

They then heard a voice coming from the direction of the Ferrari saying, "Hi there, how's it going?"

They saw Lemming climb out of the Ferrari and he approached them wearing a Cobrahead T-shirt and a pair of bright pair of red shorts that had a Ferrari logo on them.

"I think we are making some real progress now." said Mountie.

Lemming then turned to face Charlton.

"So how are you feeling now mate? I heard about you and your mum's little jaunt yesterday morning. It's a good job it was a Porsche she peed in because if it had been a Ferrari I would have been round having serious words with her. "

"I'm still not 100%. I feel well enough to carry on with the investigation though. I will tell her to think twice before peeing in a Ferrari though."

Lemming turned to Mountie.

"I hear you went walk about as well and I hope it went well. Especially as no one voluntarily enters Doctor Mike's musical hell hole without a very good reason."

"You know it was eerie being in when it was all

quiet. I did contemplate wrecking the stereo but against my better nature refrained from doing so"
"Now if you had done that everyone would have been forever in your debt. I personally would keep you in drinks for months."
They all laughed.
"So, who do you want to speak to?" said Lemming, turning serious.
Mountie stopped laughing.
"Something has cropped up and we need Jimi to help clear something up for us."
Lemming scratched his head.
"Sure, he is probably inside playing on that damn computer of his."
Lemming went in and they followed.
Sitting on the table playing on the laptop computer was Jimi in an identical Cobrahead T-shirt and a pair of blue denim jeans.
He spotted them all coming in.
"So, why are those two back here? "said Jimi.
"Don't take that tone. They have been doing some further investigation and need you to clarify something."
Jimi sat bolt upright and started to nervously twiddle with the mouse of his computer.
"When you found Barnsley did you happen to see his lion skinned Sony WalkAN anywhere around the café?" said Mountie.
Jimi stared curiously at Mountie.
"A lion skinned Sony WalkAN?"

"Yes. We know Barnsley took it to the launch and it was missing when Oscar arrived later. We are trying to find out what has happened to it as it may be important."

"Oh, I see. You know I like music and you think I might have nicked it is that it?" " said Jimi testily standing up.

"No. We just need to know if it was there when you went in because if it wasn't then it could mean that the killer took it"

Jimi sat there with arms crossed and glared at Mountie.

"Ahh. I see. So, you not only do you think I might be a thief, but you also think I might be the killer. Is that it?"

Mountie was a bit taken aback.

"NO, it nots like that. Please understand we need to eliminate everyone from our enquiries. So we need to find the WalkAN as it may be key to helping us find the killer."

Jimi was still standing and turned to Lemming.

"Dad, are you going to just let them come in here and accuse me of killing Barnsley and then nicking his WalkAN?"

"I think that's about it for the evening Mountie."

Lemming looked at his watch and turned to Jimi.

"It's time for your bed as well. Go and get ready and I'll join you in a minute."

Jimi closed the lid on the laptop.

Then glaring at Mountie and Charlton he stormed off in the direction of his bedroom.

"I'm sorry about that outburst. You will understand though that I do need to show you both out though."
When they got outside Lemming stopped.
"I'm sorry about Jimi actions tonight. He is still having nightmares about that evening. I'm sorry he wouldn't answer your questions either. Leave it with me. I'll try and get you some answers, if there are any, but don't hold your breath."
They nodded their heads in agreement and then left.

CHAPTER 35 - TUESDAY 9TH AUGUST (PM- EVEN LATER)

Charlton was just about to open his mouth.
"We will talk in the café".
They then arrived at the café.
Sitting at one of the tables eating pizzas and drinking glasses of red wine were Miss Michelle and Miss Amber. They smiled and waved as they entered.
Sitting at one of the computers was Victor viewing a sports website and he turned and waved.
On the other computer was Carl wearing a headset and he looked like he was searching for something on the internet. He spotted them, waved as well, and returned to the computer screen.
They made their way to a table in the furthest corner of the café away from everybody.
"I will bring you over a couple of beers." said Aussie.
They went and sat at the table.
Aussie brought over the beers and returned to the bar as Victor was waiting to be served.
They both took large gulps of their beers and laid their notebooks on the table.
"Well, what did you make of that little display?" said Charlton.

"I don't rightly know. I appreciate he is still a bit shell shocked from his experience, but he was extremely nervous as soon as he laid eyes on us."

"He flew off the handle much too quickly for my liking. I reckon he is hiding something."

"I'm still not sure he is our killer though. I would be happier if we can eliminate him from our enquiries somehow."

"But how can we do that?"

"I have been thinking about that. We need to get someone to search his room when he is asleep. Also, I wouldn't mind having a look at his mobile phone for that text message."

"Who can we get to do that? As I said before Lemming will go ape if we get caught"

They both drank some beer.

"Luckily, I do know someone who can help. I just need to get a message to him to join us here late tomorrow night."

Mountie noticed that whilst talking the bar had emptied.

Aussie was standing behind the bar cleaning a glass.

Mountie beckoned Aussie over to the table.

"Aussie at your service and how may I be of help to you tonight?"

"We are planning something for tomorrow night. We would like sole use of the café from 9.30 onwards. Would you be able to shut early tomorrow night?"

Aussie looked around the empty café and it was

only 9.15 .

"It's usually quiet mid-week so I don't see why not."

"That would be great. Hopefully my friend can join us then as well."

Aussie looked at Charlton who shook his head to indicate that he didn't know who this friend was either.

"How are you feeling today? I heard about you attempted escape yesterday, my food and hospitality not worth staying around here for then?" said Aussie.

"I still have a few headaches but I'm nearly back to normal. Also, wild horses would have to drag me away from the services offered by this excellent establishment."

"That's good to hear" said Aussie turning to Mountie.

"It was a busy morning for you as well. I hear you entered the dragon's lair voluntarily and have lived to tell the tale."

"Yes, I did. I must admit it was a very fruitful exercise too."

"Good to hear that." said Aussie.

He began to return to the bar.

"There is one thing you might be able to help us with though." said Mountie.

Aussie stopped in his tracks.

"I'll try and help if I can fire away."

"Oscar told us that Barnsley brought his lion skinned Sony WalkAN here on the launch evening. It seems to have disappeared. I was wondering if you had seen it and disposed of it. You might have thought Oscar and Poppy might have been upset getting it back as it would have reminded them that it was the last Christmas present, they bought him."

"No, I don't know anything about it, why do you think it is important?"

"I'm not sure. It is missing and might have been taken by our killer. If it was then it gives us a connection between them and the murder"

"Wow I see what you mean now."

"Remember Aussie this is strictly for your information only. It must not to go any further than those present here."

"My lips are sealed. I will put a note up re the café being closed tomorrow night for you."

"That would be grea.t"

Aussie then went off and cleared away the dirty plates and glasses that were still left on the tables in the café.

"Do you want to let me in on this plan of yours for tomorrow night?" said Charlton.

"I'll let you know in the morning. We need to see Crocket tomorrow as well regarding him not saying he left the fashion show. I don't think he is our killer but again we do need to still question him again about where he went and if he saw anyone."

Mountie finished his beer and looked at his watch.

"I think we need an early night tonight. We may be having a late one tomorrow night and will need all the energy we can muster."

Mountie stood up, picked up his notebook and empty glass and walked over to the bar.

"Refill?"

"No thanks. I think it might be a late one tomorrow night, so an early night is in order."

Charlton joined Mountie at the bar and placed his empty glass on top of it.

Mountie then turned and walked towards the exit with Charlton following him.

"See you both tomorrow then." shouted Aussie.

They both waved back before disappearing out the door.

"I'll see you in the morning. I have a good feeling about tomorrow."

Charlton just shrugged his shoulders.

"I'll see you in the morning."

Chapter 36 Wednesday 10th August (AM)

Charlton woke up with a start and saw his clock showing 6.37 and knew he was going to be late meeting Mountie and quickly got up.

He put on his red England AFC football shirt with the name of their top scorer CRANE on the back in large letters and some blue track suit bottoms with the England 3 lion's football motif down one side.

He dashed out of the back door and over to Mountie's only to find a note.

"Charlton I'm down by the river. M"

He ran as fast as he could down to the river.

Mountie was seated a bit further down the riverbank and by the time he reached him he was hot and out of breath.

Mountie smiled as he sat down next to him, and he poured him a mug of coffee.

He started to drink it quickly but burnt his tongue as it was too hot. He put the mug down next to him to cool down.

"Sorry I'm late I overslept".

"I guessed as much. Probably still got some of those drugs circulating in your body"

Charlton spent another few more minutes catching his breath.

"Feeling better now." said Mountie and Charlton nodded.

Just then there was a fluttering overhead and Postie Stevie called out "Is it okay if I join you two?"

Mountie nodded and he landed on a grass patch in front of them.

"Not thinking of entering the Hearts River half marathon, are you? If you did you might get away with it as you could pretend to be a runner in a fancy dress zebra outfit" Postie Stevie said jokingly to Charlton.

Mountie and Charlton both laughed.

"Just a quick flying visit .Message from Crocket

he will meet at your hut tonight at 7.30 as you requested."

"Great news" said Mountie nodding his head.

"Also, your other guest said no problems as well. He has agreed to meet you in the café at 9.45 this evening".

"Even better news."

"Actually, between you and me he was rather pleased with my early morning wakeup call. I found him in some strange house with a female whose boyfriend was just arriving home at the same time. He managed to escape undetected just in the nick of time."

"I'll have to wind him up about that later."

Charlton was getting disgruntled by not knowing what was going on and being excluded from the conversation.

"Well, I must be off."

"So, what's going on? I'm getting fed up with all this cloak and dagger stuff. You said we wouldn't have any secrets between us on this case."

"I know I said that, but I need to make sure what I am planning to do is the correct course of action for us to take. I am very nervous about my plan, and I may still change my mind and not go ahead with it".

Charlton looked even more confused and finished off his coffee.

Mountie looked at his watch and finished his coffee.

"We need to be off soon; I'll need to see you

at my hut before 7.15 to get ready to interview Crocket again about his whereabouts during the interval."

Charlton nodded in agreement and wondered what excuse Crocket would use for not telling them previously that he had disappeared during the interval.

Mountie then packed everything away with a knowing smile on his face and started walking back home.

Charlton was annoyed as he still did not know what was going on but chose not to vent his frustration.

He trailed behind Mountie with a miserable expression on his face.

Just then they stopped as they heard a familiar noise closing in on them.

They turned and saw the singing dragonfly coming towards them.

As he got closer it was Mountie who let out a large laugh.

"That dragonfly is spot on again as he is singing "Help!" by The Beatles, very apt."

Charlton was even more miserable.

"I know. Bloody typical even the dragonfly knows more about what's going on tonight than I do."

Mountie laughed again and carried on his way back to his hut.

Charlton, who was still in a grump, carried on slowly back home.

CHAPTER 37 - WEDNESDAY
10TH AUGUST (PM)

After the zoo shut Charlton resisted the urge to rush and see Mountie even though he was curious about his planned activities for the evening.

Instead, he re-read all his notes in case there was anything else they might have missed. Unfortunately, no "eureka" moment struck him.

He looked at his bedside clock and it said 7.00.

He got up and changed into a black pair of jeans and a black sweatshirt with a small Manchester United AFC football club logo in the top right-hand corner.

He thought that as they might be working late that it might be worthwhile wearing camouflage in case the need arose.

He then had a brainwave that he must tell Mountie about and wrote it in his book.

He wondered if the killer had been wearing black clothes to hide themselves. It might be the reason no one had spotted them either leaving the café or returning to their enclosure.

He picked up his notebook and as he was leaving, he bumped into Richard.

"Going to a funeral, are we?" Richard said and laughed.

"Only yours if you don't get out my way.

He found Mountie sitting outside soaking up the last of the sun.

Next to him were two deckchairs and an earthenware jug full of sangria.

He poured Charlton a glass of sangria and gave it to him as he sat down.

Mountie then eyed up his black attire strangely, especially as it was still a hot sunny evening.

Charlton spotted his interest in his attire.

"I decided to dress in black in case I needed to go somewhere in camouflage later. It then struck me that the killer might have been dressed all in black and that is the reason why no one has seen them."

"A very good thought. I have been puzzled by the fact that that no one saw the killer and perhaps that is the answer. Well, done Charlton."

There was a loud noise of the gate to Mountie's enclosure opening.

They turned to see Crocket approaching them in his usual black Pranda jeans, black Pranda polo neck shirt and black sunglasses.

"See a suspect dressed all in black, eh?" said Charlton.

"We are over here."

Crocket came over and Mountie offered him a glass of sangria.

He looked suspiciously at it and accepted it.

He sat down in the spare deckchair and looked at Charlton with a big grin.

"I see my dress sense is rubbing off. Lose the

football logo and I might even agree to be seen out with you."

Charlton went red and Mountie smiled.

"Although I still need to get you out of that red tunic. I reckon a nice lightweight red cotton jacket; light brown chino trousers and a white polo shirt would suit you down to the ground."

He looked down at his outfit and had to admit the suggestion did sound like a good idea.

"That sounds like a good idea. Perhaps when the investigation is over you can come round and give me some fashion tips. I do have a date I need to look smart for."

Charlton looked stunned.

Crocket was taken aback and wasn't sure whether Mountie was winding him up or not.

"Sure, just let me know. Although I'm pretty sure you didn't invite me here to discuss my fashion tips."

He started drinking his sangria which he thought tasted good.

Mountie nodded his head and drank some of his sangria.

"Why didn't you tell us you left the show at the interval?"

"I didn't think it was relevant, why is it?"

He sat back in his deckchair totally unconcerned that his secret had been discovered.

"The interval was during the time window when the murder took place. Your disappearance leaves you without an alibi. So please tell us where you went."

Crocket took a large sip of his sangria.

"As soon as the first half ended, I did dash off. You both know I have been trying to get Katrina to appear in the show for ages."

"Yes, we know that."

"I really wanted her to be the model in the finale. I just couldn't bear not having her in the show. So, I decided to try and find her and persuade her to do the finale for me."

Mountie and Charlton nodded. .

"So, the finale was going to be that special?" said Charlton.

"Correct. The spectacular finale outfit had her name written all over it. It would have been brilliant and a great way to end the show. Unfortunately, due to the unforeseen circumstance it didn't take place anyway."

"So where did you look for Katrina then?" said Mountie.

"I went first to the reptile house, but she wasn't there. I skipped the Jackals because if she was there with Edgar, it would have been a complete waste of my time. I then tried down by the river, but she was not there either. So, I gave up and got back to the show around 8.55. Heather was in a bit of a flap as I wasn't around as it turned out a pair of shoes had gone missing, but we quickly found them."

"Did you see anybody else whilst you were rushing around?" said Charlton.

"Sorry Charlton I was running around so quickly I don't recall seeing anybody. I was only interested in finding Katrina and not looking out for anybody else."

"Did you look for her at the café or go near the café?" said Mountie.

"I did see the café on my travels. Part of me wanted to go in and see whether Barnsley's event was the flop I thought it was going to be, but in the end I didn't. If I had gone then I might have seen who the killer was for you. My god though, if I had seen the killer, they might have tried to kill me to stop me revealing their identity.".

Crocket started shaking and looked shocked.

They all sat there in silence and then emptied their glasses of sangria.

Crocket was still looking shocked as he started to get up.

"Is there anything else I can help you with?"

They both shook their heads.

"Well thanks for the sangria that's the best one I have had in ages. Good luck with the investigation and seriously do ask me for some fashion tips after it is all finished."

Mountie nodded his head.

Crocket walked out of the enclosure.

"You aren't really going to go and see him, are you?"

Mountie looked down at his red Mountie tunic.

"Perhaps my wardrobe is due an overhaul and who better to help me bring it up to date."

Charlton shook his head in astonishment.

Mountie looked at his watch and it was 8. 30 and he got up from his deckchair.

"I need to change and get ready for the rest of this evening's activities."

Charlton remained in his chair and went through his notebook again.

He returned dressed in a dark brown sweater and some dark brown cord trousers.

"I did have some black clothes, but I didn't want to clash with you."

"Or to be mistaken for Crocket either."

"Come on let's go to the café." said Mountie.

CHAPTER 38   WEDNESDAY 10TH AUGUST (PM- A BIT LATER)

Aussie had put a notice on the door saying the café would be shut from 9.30 that evening.
Mountie looked at his watch and saw it was nearly 9.20.
They walked in and the café was already empty.
"Good to see you both as it has been a very quiet night." said Aussie from behind the bar.
He was wearing a black T shirt with bright yellow writing "HOGS (Harley Davidson Owners) Hearts River Club Member".

Aussie had set the club up as an aside from his other Hells Angels memberships.
He had wanted to meet a different sort of biker from the Hells Angel gangs that he usually hung around with.
He had been extremely disappointed by the humans that had joined as most were over 60. There were some rich city bankers who were extremely obnoxious.
There was a vicar who he was sure was only coming to try and get a date with him.

"Sorry I didn't mean our request to have an adverse effect on your trade." said Mountie. They walked over to the bar.
"It's okay."

He automatically poured two pints of beer without asking them if they wanted one.

"I needed some time to sort out the kitchen area any way."

They picked up their glasses and went and sat at a table.

"My aim tonight is to determine whether Jimi is our killer or not." said Mountie.

"I agree so what's going on?"

" Jimi said he came here to download a new track from the Antarctic Monkeys. We need to see if he did get a text message at the time he said he did."

Charlton nodded in agreement.

"I am very keen to look at his phone and to see if the message is there and if there are any other clues. I would like to search his room to see if the WalkAN is hidden there."

"Jimi isn't going to hand over his phone or let us look around his room. We are too big to go quietly hunting around when he is asleep."

"Exactly why I have asked for help from my old friend Danger."

"Did you say Danger is coming here" shouted Aussie from behind the bar.

"I did say Danger."

"I thought he was banned after fighting with Willie after he knocked over his beer the last time he was in here."

"Yes. the one and only Danger "

Mountie laughed at the memory of a mouse picking a fight with a camel.

"It was just a misunderstanding though as too much drink had been consumed by both parties as I recall."

Charlton started to look concerned.

"You have recruited Danger to check out Jimi's room and to borrow his phone. Can he be trusted?"

"Of course I can" whispered a small voice in Charlton's ear.

A startled Charlton leapt from his seat.

He looked to see a small white mouse with an eye patch laughing at him.

Mountie and Aussie burst out laughing as well.

Danger was a rare albino Harvest mouse who was notorious for escaping from zoos.

He was currently living in a family house nearby.

He had met Mountie at a zoo where they had both lived and had built up a good friendship. Now that he lived nearby, he often came over to visit him.

He had acquired the eye patch after a fight with a cobra in another zoo who had returned from the pub drunk one night and felt a little hungry. He had decided Danger was going to be his midnight snack. In the fight that ensued Danger had lost an eye and the cobra had lost an eye and a fang. Danger took this as a victory for him.

It had been rumoured that the cobra had now turned vegan as a result.

"You could have warned me.as I nearly spilt my

beer". said a startled Charlton sitting back down.
"Waiter. Please can I have a pint of your finest snakebite." Danger called over to Aussie.

Danger drank snakebite as a reminder of his treasured victory over the cobra.

"I thought I had banned you" said a smiling Aussie from behind the bar.

"I did say please."

"OK then I'll bring one over to you."

He started making snakebite concoction and brought it over to the table.

"Glad you could make it Danger. I trust you got my message as well?"

"I'm pleased that I can be of assistance to your investigation."

Danger took a gulp of his snakebite drink.

"I have been watching the Gorilla enclosure. Jimi is in bed asleep. Lemming and Beth have just settled down to watch the film, King Kong. I'll finish off my pint and then go and have a look around Jimi's room. I will borrow his phone for you both to look at as requested and then return it."

Danger picked up his beer glass and downed the rest of the contents in one go.

"Waiter please set up another pint of snakebite for my return."

He then left the café.

Aussie had his back to him and pretended to ignore him.

After he had left, he started making him another

pint of snakebite and brought it over.

"I don't normally approve of breaking and entering but I will turn a blind eye this once. Also, you have my word that I will not tell anyone outside of these four walls what you are now doing."

"Thanks a lot. After much thought this looks to be our only option to answer our questions about Jimi's guilt."

Just then the entrance door swung open.

Danger strolled in looking furtively around him holding Jimi's phone.

"I had a look around his room but couldn't see the WalkAN anywhere. I reckon if he had taken it he wouldn't have hidden it in his room in case his parents stumbled across it by accident"

"It was a long shot anyway but thanks a lot for looking."

Danger put the phone on the table.

"So where do you want to start looking first on it".

Charlton turned to look at Mountie in anticipation of his reply.

"I suggest we look at his text entries first to find the text saying that there was a new Antarctic Monkey's track called "Meadowhell" that he could download from their website " replied Mountie staring at the phone.

Mountie then put down his pint and he picked up the phone.

"OK let's see what text he has stored on it."

Two minutes later Mountie was still looking at the phone.

They then simultaneously realized that Mountie was not only holding the phone upside down but obviously didn't have a clue how it worked.

Charlton and Danger then looked at each other, motioning to help him out.

Both shook their heads and looked embarrassingly down into their drinks.

A loud whopping laugh emanated from behind the bar, with the HOGS t-shirt riding up and down Aussies stomach.

"Look at you all, I didn't realize technophobes anonymous were meeting in here tonight."

Aussie walked over to join them.

"It's okay I won't tell anyone that the great detectives that orchestrated the theft of a mobile phone to check it over for evidence didn't have a clue how it worked".

He sat down and joined them at the table.

"Mind if I join you? of course you don't otherwise that phone will be a museum piece before the three of you work out how to use it".

"So, you want to know what's on it?" said Aussie.

He took hold of the phone and turned it the right way up and started flicking around lots of different screens.

"It's amazing what you can do with phones these days."

Mountie gave him a blank expression.

"We are looking for a text he said he received

on the Sunday evening. It should say that there was a new Antarctic Monkey's track called "Meadowhell" available to downloaded from their website" replied Mountie staring at the phone blankly.

"We want to try and eliminate Jimi from our enquiries." said Charlton.

"Okay. Well, that's lucky as he hasn't deleted it. It arrived at 8.32 on Sunday evening."

"Okay that matches what he said. Is "Meadowhell" on it and what other stuff is he listening to? "said Charlton staring at the phone.

"Okay. Right the last track he played was Day of the Jackals "Born to be Wild", I didn't think anyone could play that track that fast." said Aussie.

He began to sing the lyrics out loud and bang his head at the same time .

"What else is there?" said Mountie sternly trying to ignore the sound of Aussie's loud vocals and head banging antics.

"Well, Antarctic Monkeys singing "Meadowhell" as you mentioned is on it, not one of their better ones. Then Gorillarse's punk version of the Rolling Stones classic (I can't get no) Satisfaction" said Aussie scrolling down the list.

Aussie got up and started singing and swaggering around like Mick Jagger would have done, had he been a grossly overweight orangutan with a bright orange beard.

Mountie, Danger, and Charlton all burst out

laughing.

Aussie finally stopped his impersonation when Mountie made a loud cough and muttered that they had a murder to solve.

Aussie sat back down trying to get his breath back and continued scrolling through the screens on the phone.

"I can see why our young Jimi is a bit deaf as it's full of loud heavy rock tracks, even some human songs from Black Sabbath and Judas Priest."

"Please can you see if there are any messages on there that might help" said Mountie looking a bit downcast.

Aussie scrolled through some more screens and found Jimi's in box.

"Only a couple of messages "A special offer from a rock magazine and some messages from Cobrahead and Antarctic Monkeys telling him their forthcoming tour dates."

Mountie started making some notes in his notebook.

"Do you still need the phone as I do need to take it back before it gets spotted that it is missing" said Danger looking expectantly at the phone.

Aussie finished playing with it and passed it back to Danger.

"Looks like you can eliminate Jimi from your enquiries." said Danger.

Charlton, Mountie, and Aussie all nodded.

"Ok I will take it back now. I need shoot off as I need to see a young female whose boyfriend is working nights" said Danger winking and finishing his pint.

"See you all around some time and good luck with the case."

"Thanks a lot for all your help" said Mountie lifting his glass and taking a drink.

Danger held the phone carefully as he left to return it.

CHAPTER 39 - WEDNESDAY 10TH AUGUST (PM- LATER STILL.)

Aussie walked to the bar singing the Judas Priest song "Delivering the Goods" that he had just seen on the music list on Jimi's phone.
Charlton and Mountie smiled as they recognized the song from the radio.

TESCOW had employed a new marketing company and they had been experimenting with different songs for their radio adverts.
The Judas Priest track had proved a controversial choice with the religious animals, those that hated heavy metal and those animals that refused to listen to human music.

"I guess that rules Jimi out and looks like we are back to square one." said Charlton.
Both sat back and sipped their drinks.
Aussie was behind the bar and getting carried away singing the chorus to the Judas Priest "Delivering the Goods" song repeatedly whilst playing an air guitar.
Mountie stopped drinking and put his beer down and a smile slowly began to fill his face.
"Aussie can you join us again" said Mountie beckoning Aussie to come back to his seat.
Charlton had a curious glance over at Mountie.
Aussie stopped singing and came and sat down.

"What can I help you with?"

"You told us that you had given Barnsley the bottles of water for the WAAR event."

"Yes, I did. Although I wish I hadn't given him them as he might still be alive"

"So, he had no drinks then?"

"You can't really host a launch party with no drinks, especially soft drinks."

"Exactly" replied Mountie beginning to grin.

Charlton still looked confused.

"Am I right in saying the reason he didn't have any drinks was because Declan was ill and TESCOW hadn't delivered them "continued Mountie staring directly at Aussie.

"Yes, it was. I felt sorry for him as the bottles of water hadn't arrived in time because Declan was ill. He showed me the email from TESCOW, but the Tuesday delivery was going to be too late for his event. I suggested he email them back and cancel the order."

"Aye that was email I said Deidre received and how the lads were worried about running out of... beer" the penny finally dropped as Charlton finished the sentence.

"Exactly. Now this may be a long shot but what if our killer had run out of alcohol and couldn't wait till Tuesday either. What if they decided to go to the café where they knew alcohol was kept. They were expecting the café to be empty due to the fashion show and went to raid it and unexpectedly found Barnsley there. Something then happened inside the café between them, and it resulted in them deciding to murder Barnsley with whatever was close to hand. Perhaps he was killed to ensure they kept their alcoholism secret.".

"That is a bit of a long shot if you don't mind me saying." said Charlton as he paused and drank some more beer.

"And don't forget we discussed whether Barnsley could have been back on the booze and was killed by someone as part of an aborted blackmail attempt."

Aussie looked stunned and did not believe what he was hearing so interjected.

"Look Guys I worked with Barnsley on his WAAR venture, and he was totally committed to it. He would regularly meet here and I never once smelt alcohol on him. He was always sober. I have seen enough drunks in my time, and I would have known if he was back drinking or not and I sure he wasn't".

They nodded and made some notes.

"Do you know where Declan is now and whether he can join us here with his TESCOW tablet." said Mountie.

" I know he is working around the zoo tonight and I can go and fetch him . I will tell you both now that he won't divulge any customer information to you. He knows that if he did, he will get into serious trouble with TESCOW if they find out."

Aussie left and about 5 minutes later returned with Declan.

He sat down and placed his TESCOW tablet on the table.

Aussie refreshed all the beer glasses and came back and sat with them all.

Declan took a nervous sip from his beer glass.

"Thanks for coming so quickly. As you know we are investigating Barnsley's murder, and we hope you may be able to help us find his killer." Said Mountie.

"I will try and help you as much as I can. I would love to see his killer captured."

"Your TESCOW deliveries cover what area?"

"I cover the zoo and also any other animals living within a five-mile radius of the zoo."

"Do you know all the animals that you deliver to?"

"Some I do. Some of them I am their only contact each week and so I make sure I take the time to have a chat, cheer them up and do any odd jobs if needs be."

Declan paused to take a drink.

"Then there are the others who I never meet and just drop their orders off."

"Did you deliver to Barnsley at all? I was wondering whether you had been delivering any alcohol to him." asked Mountie with a stern look on his face.

"Look I shouldn't be discussing customer's details as it is strictly against TESCOW rules. As

Barnsley is dead, I feel it is okay though to say that I didn't have any regular alcohol deliveries for him."

Declan paused to take a drink.

"Why? He wasn't back on the booze again, was he?"

"That's what we are trying to establish" interjected Charlton.

"Ah I see do you reckon someone was blackmailing him then if he was?"

Declan then stopped abruptly.

"Hey. You don't think I was blackmailing and then killed him, do you? I was out cold that night after taking my special migraine tablets."

"I can vouch for that. We all went back and tried to wake Declan to tell him what had happened, but he was out like a light." said Aussie.

"So, you were definitely not delivering alcohol to Barnsley then?" said Mountie scratching his head.

"I can't say that for definite. As I said there are some deliveries where I just drop goods off at designated spots and I never see who collects them"

Declan started looking nervously at his tablet on the table.

"Also, since that Valentine's day fiasco earlier this year I have seen a large increase in fictious names being used on some of my deliveries."

Mountie looked confused.

Aussie and Charlton both started laughing.

Declan, seeing Mountie's confused look explained.

"In January this year that erotic bondage film 50 Shades of Grey Elephant was released. All the animals loved it and wanted on Valentine's Day to send their loved one's sets of hand cuffs and whips that featured in the film. The battery-operated elephant trunk was extremely popular, although bit bulky to deliver though."

Aussie and Charlton carried on laughing.

"Well. TESCOW customers all wanted to have these sex toys delivered secretly. So TESCOW secretly started allowing customers to set up accounts with fictious names and strange drop-off points to get around this and to not miss out on this new business spike. Suddenly this news went viral. TESCOW was going to put a stop to it but the increase in business it generated was so great they have let it carry on."

"Ahhh so Barnsley could have been having alcohol delivered somewhere under a fictious name and you wouldn't have known it was for him" commented Charlton.

"That is correct".

"You were ill on Saturday, Sunday, and Monday. Were all the customers emailed to say you were ill and that they would now get their orders on the Tuesday?" said Mountie.

"They were. They had a couple of urgent medical delivery requests that they managed to accommodate without me."

Declan had a feeling he knew what was going to come next.

Mountie looked at Charlton, then at Aussie and then at Declan.

"We think the killer is one of your regular deliveries on either Saturday Sunday or Monday. We think they ran out of alcohol as a result of you being off sick and took actions to get some more from the café that night."

Declan sat silent stunned by what he had just heard.

"From what you have just said I reckon it's a customer with a fictious name . They primarily order alcohol and have it delivered to a site outside the zoo" said Mountie staring this time at Charlton.

"I really shouldn't be telling you what I am about to tell you. You must promise that it wasn't me that told you as I will get sacked by TESCOW if they find out. I can't afford to lose such a well-paid job."

Declan was looking at the tablet on the table.

"We promise we won't say anything to TESCOW. If we are asked, then we will say that we received a mystery tip off. Agreed?"

Charlton and Aussie both nodded.

"Well, there is one order that instantly springs to mind that fits the criteria you just mentioned Mountie."

Declan picked up the tablet and started tapping away at it.

"You can't see the information, but I will read you the key points. There is account in the name of Mrs. Ginny Fox. It was set up in February this year when I started delivering her a regular weekly order."

"I wonder if she has any children called tonic, ice and lemon" said Aussie jokingly and stopped after seeing Mountie's stern face looking at him.

"Ginny has a weekly delivery of 6 bottles of spirits probably one a night. The order is usually 2 bottles of vodka, 2 bottles of gin and 2 bottles of that disgusting Glen Pig Ditch whisky that all the animals like so much" said Declan still looking at the screen.

Charlton looked at Mountie and gave him large glowing smile.

"The delivery is an evening delivery on the same day each weekend. It is delivered to the old disused Hearts River Rowing Club" said Declan looking up and turning off the tablet.

Declan then finished his beer.

"That is all I can tell you and I hope it will help you catch the killer. If it is not Ginny, then call me back and I will have another look at my deliveries. Unfortunately, I now must go back to work."

"We are truly indebted to you for that information. It sounds like exactly what we needed. It also fits in with some of our other clues. I promise we will keep your involvement out this trust me." said Mountie.

Declan got up and walked out.

Mountie and Charlton sat at the table deep in thought.

Aussie returned to the bar.

"Well, well, well. Looks like we might finally have a lead on who our killer is and where they reside." said Charlton, finally breaking the silence.

"That was very interesting , very interesting indeed. If Ginny Fox is our killer, then we need to find out whom she or he is. BUT and it's a big BUT if Ginny Fox was Barnsley, then we are right back to square one."

"I hadn't thought of that" replied Charlton looking a bit deflated.

"I must admit from tonight's discussions I now firmly believe that Ginny Fox is our killer. I believe they are one of the animals that live here. They walk to the rowing club each night after everyone is asleep to have something alcoholic to drink. It is dark and they know that they won't be spotted."

Charlton's mood changed and looked out the window.

"Looks like it is getting dark now. Should we go and visit the rowing club now? After all we are all dressed to go hunting around in the dark."

Mountie thought for a minute.

"We will go tomorrow night. I don't know the area around the rowing club, and we may need somewhere to hide and to observe from."

"Okay" said Charlton a bit deflated again.

"I will ask Postie Stevie to fly around it a few times tomorrow during the day. He can tell us if it is occupied by a fox or another non-zoo animal. Don't forget we might still have an unknown non- zoo animal killer on our hands."

Charlton nodded his head.

"I will ask him to do a reconnaissance of the area and to look for suitable hiding places for us. He might be able to give us a rough map of the area as well."

"That sounds like a great plan. Although I must admit I would love to just go out there now and see if our killer is there" replied Charlton

"So do I BUT we need to be patient and not scare Ginny away. We will go tomorrow night and hopefully find out who Ginny is and whether they are our killer or not."

Mountie finished his beer.

"I suggest we meet at my hut tomorrow night at 10.00. We should leave now and make sure we both get a good night's sleep. Tomorrow night looks like being a late one and we will both need to be awake and alert. Don't forget we may finally be coming face to face with the killer we have been hunting."

They both got up and started to leave.

"Are you going out to capture Ginny now?" said Aussie enthusiastically.

"No. We still have some final plans to put in place first. Both of us though will be out Ginny hunting tomorrow night."

"Well, if I don't see you both before good hunting tomorrow night. I'm glad Declan was able to help you. Don't forget he took a great risk giving you that information. He is a great lad so please respect his request for privacy about him giving you private TESCOW delivery information."
They both shook their heads.
"Goodnight then and happy hunting again"
Aussie gave them both a big hug.
They left and silently walked back home deep in thought of what lay ahead for them.

CHAPTER 40 - THURSDAY
11 AUGUST (PM)

The zoo had been packed again due to the school holidays.

Charlton's mind was so much on other things that he didn't spot a small boy calling him a lazy sodding zebra before being hit squarely on the nose with his apple.

Deidre decided to put her abilities with the Porsche to good use by weeing on the smiling boy who then ran off wailing to his mum.

"You alright Charlton. Have the drugs not fully worn off yet, mine have?"

"Please keep this a secret but we had a major breakthrough last night. We are following it up tonight, so please keep everything crossed. Unless of course you see any more small children about to throw something at me."

"Take special care of yourselves and good luck with tonight's investigation. You know everyone would love you both to solve this case. Everyone is so proud of what you both are doing."

Then she gave him a big hug

"Ah we ought to take a photo of this and send it to Mountie to see if he gets jealous" shouted Richard with a large smile on his face.

"Unless you want to see my hoof crushing your genitals on "You've been framed" tomorrow night I would keep thy gob shut" replied Deidre swiftly turning round.

Richard pulled a pained expression on his face.

The rest of the zebras burst out laughing.

He spotted Postie Stevie flying around, and he smiled down on him.

After the zoo shut, he had something to eat and a powernap in his room.

Deidre woke him as requested at 9.00.

He changed into the same black outfit as the previous night.

He picked up a couple of torches as well and put them in his pockets.

He was about to leave when he heard Alistair behind him.

"I thought you might need my black Newcastle United AFC cap."

Charlton started to look around for some hidden cameras.

" I thought it would help with your camouflage, it's me lucky one."

Charlton pulled a quizzical look on his face.

"Newcastle only lose by the odd goal when I am wearing it." laughed Alistair.

Charlton reluctantly put it on his head hoping the others wouldn't see him.

"I hope the cap can stand it as it may be witnessing its first win tonight."

"Hey good luck mate and all the best. Remember don't do anything silly. Also, me, Newcastle

United AFC and all its supporters need me wearing that lucky cap every week, so you must come back with it" said Alistair laughing.

Charlton stepped outside and saw it was getting dark and slowly walked over to Mountie's.

He went in and sat down and wondered why Mountie was looking at him strangely and then realized it must be the cap.

"Ah the cap, its Alistair's lucky one. He thought it needed to see a winning team in action, so he gave it to me for the evening."

"Well, I hope we don't disappoint it then" laughed Mountie sitting down.

"Ok so what are the plans for Operation Ginny tonight then?".

"Ok let me give some updates first."

"I saw Postie Stevie was busy."

"Indeed, he has been. He reported that the rowing club was empty which ties in with my thoughts that Ginny is either a zoo animal or was Barnsley."

"That is going to be one less obstacle assuming Ginny wasn't Barnsley."

"He said the rowing club door didn't appear locked at all. He has also identified a large clump of trees that he thinks we can hide behind. We are in luck as there is a full moon that should help us spot Ginny, but we must make sure not to get ourselves spotted at the same time."

"All good news then so far" said Charlton leaning

back in chair.

Mountie got up and put on a large, long black raincoat and a black Stetson style hat.

"Let's go as it is getting dark outside."

When they got outside Mountie stopped.

"I have been wondering why no one saw the killer that night."

"Me too which is why I mentioned the black attire."

"Follow me as I have a strong hunch about why no one saw them."

They walked over to the large perimeter gate located closest to the café and located between the camel and elephant enclosures.

Charlton was not sure what was going on but decided to keep quiet.

Mountie turned on his torch and then passed it to Charlton asking him to shine it on the padlock on the gate.

Mountie took hold of the large padlock and found it opened straight away.

Charlton gasped in amazement and couldn't believe how easy it was for Mountie to open the padlock.

Mountie opened the door slightly and asked him to shine the torch closer to the gate.

Suddenly the torch light hit some reflective foil that had been inserted part the way down the gate.

Mountie inspected the reflective foil and didn't remove it as he knew someone had put it there to stop a warning beam alarm from going off.

Lemming had fitted alarms to all the gates to alert everyone whenever a gate was opened out of zoo hours.

"The lock is broken as I suspected. Also, someone has put foil on the gate to prevent Lemming's alarm sensor from going off."

"Oscar will be furious when he discovers the outside gate alarms have been tampered with. Somebody has put everyone in the zoo in danger from outsiders again as a result."

Apart from the main entrance there were 10 perimeter gates around the zoo.

All the perimeter gates used to be open for the animals to use out of zoo hours.

This had worked fine until a couple of years ago when the zoo was targeted one night by external animal thieves. Lots of electrical equipment and money had been taken.

As a result, Oscar had got Lemming to install security equipment on all the gates except the one located near his enclosure.

The animals were free to leave by this designated gate, but they knew it automatically locked shut at midnight. If they were late the only way in was waking Oscar up which was not a good idea.

Some of the animals with night jobs had a special key for access during the night. This was carefully monitored through a computer program Aussie had built. Oscar reviewed usage on a weekly basis via a report produced by the computer

"That answers the question why no one saw the killer. They must have escaped through this gate then run around the outside perimeter fence and re-entered using the gate near Oscar's. They would have known that gate would have been open till midnight."

Charlton was still looking stunned by what he had just seen.

"Come on follow me and bring that torch. Let's see if we can find our way to the Rowing Club from here."

Mountie shut the gate and they walked around the fence until they came to the next perimeter gate.

Charlton pointed the torch at the gate.

Mountie once again found he could easily open the padlock.

He opened the gate slightly and they saw more reflective foil had been added again.

"Well, it looks like the killer has covered all their bases by tampering with another gate. They can come and go as they please without anyone knowing. We must tell Oscar and Lemming immediately." said Charlton.

"All in good time. Come on let's go and do some Ginny hunting shall we" whispered Mountie.

Mountie used his torch to look at the map Postie Stevie had drawn.

They started walking through the woods, reached the river and then stopped.

Suddenly the silence was broken by the unexpected arrival of the singing dragonfly.

Mountie and Charlton both started laughing quietly.

They both recognized that he was singing "I drink alone" by George Thorogood

"How is he always so spot on with his choice of songs" whispered Charlton.

Mountie just smiled and shook his head.

They carried on and then saw the old rundown disused hut a short distance away.

The hut had a faded sign hanging on one side of it and as they got closer, they saw by moonlight that it said, "Hearts River Rowing Club Established 1932".

Suddenly the sound of heavy rock music filled the air, and it was coming from inside the hut. There was a light inside as well.

Mountie grabbed Charlton and pointed out a clump of trees behind the hut where Postie Stevie had suggested they have their stakeout.

They both rushed and hid behind the trees.

Charlton was smiling as he recognised the song that was being played and had an idea who Ginny might be.

The song then reached its chorus line.

Mountie recognized it as well and started smiling as well.

Mountie looked at Charlton who indicated that

he thought he also knew who Ginny was.

"I think this will prove that Ginny wasn't Barnsley. Also, it looks like Declan's information is going to be invaluable in helping us solve this case."

"I think you are dead right with that. I think it also means that Ginny is…"

Suddenly the music stopped.
Charlton instantly stopped talking.
There was a sound of clinking of bottles.
The light went out.
They heard the door being opened and then shut.
They then heard footsteps.
They peered from behind and saw the person who was walking away.
It was who they thought it was going to be.
Charlton's heart was beginning to pound with all the excitement.
Mountie whispered to Charlton for them to wait 5 minutes in case Ginny came back.
After 5 minutes they went and stood by the river.
"Well that certainly explains everything" said Mountie still breathing heavily.
"It certainly does" replied Charlton also still breathing heavily.
"Let's go and search the hut to see if there is any evidence in there."
"I wonder if the music was coming from Barnsley's WalkAN and if so, I hope Ginny left it behind."

They got to the front door and noticed it had a a padlock on the front.

Mountie tried the padlock, and it opened straight away.

Mountie opened the door, and they walked in.

He flashed the torch around inside stopped when the beam illuminated a small black sports bag in one of the corners.

They moved to it and opened it up and then shone the torch inside.

Inside were some spirit bottles. Lying on top of them was a TESCOW delivery printout relating to a recent delivery of various bottles of spirit to a Ginny Fox at the rowing club.

Mountie lifted the delivery print out and shone the torch into the bag again.

They then spotted the lion skinned Sony WalkAN and a plug-in speaker.

"Wow now that is a fantastic sight. Finding that means we now have our proof that Ginny killed Barnsley" said Mountie loudly with a big smile on his face.

"I reckon we have them bang to rights now "said Charlton with a beaming smile.

"So, what do we do now?" said Charlton.

Mountie stopped and thought for a minute.

"We need to leave all the stuff here as we don't want Ginny to suspect that we have found out who they are and return and destroy the evidence. We need Oscar to hold a meeting tomorrow night so we can close the case and get everything back to normal."

Mountie put the black sports bag back in the same position he found it.

They walked out of the hut and put the lock back on.

They stood by the river with their hearts still beating fast.

"I was beginning to think we would never crack it "said Charlton trying to control his breathing.

"So, did I. Then last night it all seemed to fall into place. I will be voting for TESCOW to keep using "Delivering the goods" by Judas Priest as their theme tune even though I hate it. We were so lucky to identify Ginny so quickly and to wrap up the case. Oscar will be extremely pleased." said Mountie.

"Everyone will be so pleased and grateful back at the zoo."

"We need to be careful going back now as can't bump into Ginny if they are coming back for any reason."

Suddenly they stopped in their tracks as they heard a familiar sound.

"He can't be back again" whispered Charlton to Mountie.

The singing dragonfly arrived singing again.

Mountie looked at Charlton who was in fits of laughter and started laughing himself. "Spot on again as he is singing "We are the champions" by Queen." I suppose we are"

"I reckon we are just that." said Mountie carrying

on laughing.

They quietly headed back and through the perimeter gate between the camels and the elephants.

When they reached the point where they had to go different ways Mountie turned and took Charlton by surprise by giving him a big hug. He had tears rolling down his face.

"We did it Charlton, we bloody well did it".

Mountie then started to walk off home.

Charlton felt tears running down his face and couldn't believe they had solved the case.

"Mountie." shouted Charlton.

Mountie turned around slowly.

"You do realise you have successfully continued the Mountie tradition of always getting their killer. Due South's Fraser would have been very proud of you."

Mountie started to laugh.

"Yes, I'm sure Fraser would have been very proud of both me and you."

They both walked back very happy and a little bit tired by the strain of the day's events.

CHAPTER 41 - FRIDAY 12TH AUGUST (PM)

Early in the morning Mountie had summoned Oscar to his hut and told him about the events of the previous night.

They told him they knew who the killer was and had the evidence to prove it.

Oscar was stunned by the name of Barnsley's killer.

He couldn't argue with the evidence they presented before him.

They then agreed the best way to break the news to everyone.

Mountie said they needed time to visit the rowing club and pick up the evidence before any meeting started.

Also they did not want to tip off the killer that they knew who it was and give them time to rush and destroy all the evidence.

An emergency meeting would be called at very short notice for 6.45 that evening.

This would give them time to visit the rowing club and collect all their evidence.

They would then return and go straight to Oscar's tent around 6.30.

Oscar agreed that as soon as they returned, he would then get Aussie, George, and Willie to go out telling everyone of a big meeting he was about to hold in the seal house and that everyone had to attend.

This would mean that the killer wouldn't have time to get to the rowing club, see that they had been uncovered and to do a runner.

Then Poppy, Mountie, Charlton and Oscar would go to the seal house to make sure everything was going to be ready for their announcement to take place.

After the zoo shut, everything had gone to plan. Mountie and Charlton had collected the black sports bag that still contained the spirit bottles, delivery order and the lion skinned Sony WalkAN. It was still exactly where they had left it the previous night.

The seal house was buzzing with excitement.

Every animal had been told of the big meeting in the seal house.

They had been ordered to be there or else answer to Oscar. No one wanted that ordeal especially under the current circumstances.

Everyone hoped the meeting was because the killer had been found.

They were all discussing who they thought it might be.

Sarah, Nikki, and Emma were there and totally confused as to why they had been summoned. Nikki suggested it was because the last half of the fashion show was now going to be run. This perked all three of them up no end.

Lemming and Beth sitting behind them burst out laughing when they heard this ludicrous suggestion.
They were all oblivious to this as they were engrossed in talking about the finale dress, and which colour they each wanted.
Danger and Postie Stevie were there.
Mountie had got Postie Stevie to get a message to Danger telling him about the meeting.
Danger was surprised as all he had detected the previous night was doom and gloom and how they were still no nearer catching Barnsley's killer.
Danger whispered to Postie Stevie "Where are Mountie and Charlton?"
"I can't see them anywhere".
In the middle of the stage there were four chairs and at the front was a wooden lectern with a microphone.
Suddenly the seal house went quiet.
Oscar walked in wearing a smart black suit, a white shirt, and a black tie.
Behind him was Poppy in a dark black Pranda trouser suit.
They took up two of the chairs.
Then all the heads turned as Mountie walked in wearing black trousers and his signature red tunic top
Charlton then followed wearing a pair of dark blue chinos and a plain white polo shirt. Deidre had made him dress more smartly for the

occasion. He had still spiked his hair into a Mohican though but had left it a shiny black colour.

They went on stage and sat next to Oscar and Poppy.

Oscar looked at Mountie who indicated that he was ready.

Oscar walked to the lectern and tapped the microphone to make sure it was working.

He paused for a minute and did a quick scan to see if anyone was missing and decided everyone was present.

There was deadly quiet with everybody waiting in eager anticipation of what they thought was about to be announced.

"Thank you all for attending at such short notice but I have a very good reason for doing so. This morning Mountie and Charlton told me had identified who killed Barnsley that evening in the café."

The seal house suddenly erupted with all the animals talking following this news.

"Quiet everyone please"

Suddenly a deadly silence descended again.

Oscar looked back at Mountie who nodded again.

"I would like to hand over to Mountie to explain his investigation and his findings."

He went back to his seat and everyone started talking again.

Mountie walked over to the microphone and although he had seen it working for Oscar he tapped the microphone again. The noise from it caused all the animals to go quiet again.

He put the speech that he and Charlton had prepared earlier on the lectern.

"I would like to start off by thanking you all for the support and help that you have given us with our murder enquiry."

"I would like to thank Deidre for her endeavours on Monday morning. Although I don't think any more Porsche convertible owners will be visiting us in the very near future."

There was a loud round of applause and laughter re the Porsche owner remark.

There were some wolf whistles from Richard and Alistair.

Deidre went bright red in her seat.

"I can confirm that Barnsley was choked to death last Sunday evening at the launch of his WAAR venture in the cafe. He was killed between 8.05 when Oscar visited him and just after 9.00 when Jimi found him dead. This time slot unfortunately included both the fashion show interval and the half time of the live football game on television."

Mark, Alistair, and Richard looked nervously at each other as they were not expecting the football match interval to be mentioned.

"This investigation raised lots of questions that we were struggling to find answers to."

"Firstly, we needed to determine whether the murder was premeditated and executed by someone who saw the opportunity to do it whilst everyone was distracted at the show."

Mountie took a sip of water.

"Behind a bush near the café we found an empty bottle of Glen Pig Ditch whisky. We kept it in case it was evidence because it could have belonged to the killer, a look out for the killer or... Barnsley."

There was a loud chattering from the audience.

Mountie tapped the microphone to regain order.

"Yes. I did say Barnsley. We did wonder if he had started drinking again and been caught by someone who decided to try and blackmail him. We wondered if his murder was the result of an attempted blackmail that went wrong that night. Thankfully our investigations showed he hadn't started drinking again."

Oscar gave Mountie an appreciative nod for the last comment.

"The purpose of Charlton and Deidre's attempted escape on Monday morning was to lure Doctor Mike and all the zookeepers away from the zoo. In doing so it enabled me to search the surgery for an autopsy."

Mountie paused to take a sip of water,

"Thanks to their diversionary escapade I was able to visit an empty surgery. This was a much more pleasant experience as there was no Viking rock music playing at the time."

There was ripple of laughter that filled the seal house.

"Luckily, I did find an autopsy and it confirmed

to us that Barnsley had been murdered."

There was audible intake of breaths.

"I also found the water bottle in there lying around in a plastic bag".

Mountie looked back and saw Poppy was valiantly holding back the tears.

She waved for him to carry on.

"The autopsy was very informative. It revealed that before he was killed, he had been struck on back of the head with an object that we identified as being the water bottle."

Mountie looked up from his notes.

There were some loud gasps from the audience as some of them realised what this meant.

"This new evidence made our investigation even more complex as it now meant that any size or sex of animal could have wacked him on the back of his head when he wasn't looking and then killed him whilst he was either dazed or unconscious."

Mountie paused as he saw all the animals were looking around at each other suspiciously.

"The water bottle being the murder weapon has always been strange to us. We wondered if someone had entered the café and had been surprised to find Barnsley there. Something then happened between them meaning they had no choice but to kill Barnsley there and then. The water bottle was possibly the closest suitable weapon to hand."

Mountie paused again to take another sip of

water.

"We then had another conundrum to tackle. You see that evening Barnsley took his lion skinned Sony WalkAN to the café for background music, Oscar saw him take it. Since then, we have been unable to find it anywhere."

Mountie paused as a bead of sweat rolled down his head.

"So, between Oscar's visit and when he returned it had somehow disappeared".

Mountie again paused to take a sip of water.

"This this meant that it had either been taken by the killer or by Jimi who found Barnsley dead. We are very sorry Jimi for upsetting you previously. Luckily, we were able to prove you didn't take it and you were then eliminated from our investigation".

Mountie found Jimi's face in the audience and Jimi nodded to accept the apology.

Lemming looked confused as to how they had managed to do it so quickly.

Jimi then began to get confused also as to how they had done it, especially without his help.

"It has been puzzling us how the killer moved around without being spotted. Last night we checked the perimeter gate between the elephant and camel enclosures and discovered the lock had been tampered with. Also, we discovered the intruder warning sensor had been overridden using some reflective foil. The killer has been coming and going as they please without detection."

Mountie paused for the expected uproar.

As expected, this news was met with uproar. Everyone couldn't believe that someone had tampered with the security system that made them all feel safe at night.

Oscar shot Lemming a glance and mouthed "See you later."

He indicated that he needed him to urgently check and fix all the gates.

Lemming had a very worried look on his face as this was distressing news to him.

Mountie then tapped loudly on the microphone to bring back order and silence.

"We now come to the crux of solving this case. The key, believe it or not, was the 50 Shades of Grey Elephant film that featured, so I am told, handcuffs and battery-operated elephant trunks."

There was a mixture of confused faces, smiling faces and some rather red faces.

"Let me expand. TESCOW customers wanted them to secretly deliver these erotic presents on Valentine's Day this year. Due to customer pressure they decided to allow their customers to set up fictitious accounts and private delivery spots to enable these deliveries."

Again, there was a mixture of confused faces, smiling faces and some red faces.

"We did wonder if Barnsley had set up a fictitious TESCOW account and was having alcohol delivered to a secret address of his choosing. I can confirm that this was not the case as I have mentioned already."

Mountie paused again and then found Declan in the audience.

"Now this whole case happened because Declan became ill with his one of his migraine attacks. The killer we discovered was a secret drinker and every Sunday night they got a regular TESCOW delivery of 6 bottles of spirits to a hidden location where they would then secretly drink a bottle every night."

The noise levels started to increase again.

Mountie tapped loudly on the microphone for quiet again.

"So, on that Sunday night they were shocked to discover that no new bottles of spirits had been delivered. We guess all they had left was whatever remained in their whisky bottle. They took the whisky bottle with them when they went to the café to check their emails. There they found an email from TESCOW saying that due Declan being ill orders would now be delivered on Tuesday."

Mountie looked up and saw a lot of nodding faces.

"The killer though had run out of alcohol and knew they couldn't wait till Tuesday for their delivery. They then realised they were standing outside the one place that was filled with alcohol. They knew that it was going to be empty because of the noise coming from the fashion show direction. We believe they then went in the café to steal some spirit bottles to tide them over. Unfortunately, they forgot Barnsley was holding his WAAR launch there, which unluckily for him as no one had attended this left him alone with his killer."

Mountie again paused looked around the audience.

"We received a tip off suggesting we should speak to a Mrs Ginny Fox at the disused Hearts River Rowing Club. Aussie did wonder if she had any children called Tonic, Ice and Lemon."

A ripple of laughter crossed the seal house.

"Charlton and I were very fortunate in our travels late last night."

Mountie looked out again at all the animals.

They were all dying to find out who the killer was and were sitting on the edge of their seats in anticipation.

Mountie stood still and then took a sip of water.

"We visited the hut last night. Fortunately, Ginny was there and was playing a Slipknot song that we both recognised. Ginny then left and so we went inside. In a corner we found a black sports bag that contained spirit bottles and a delivery note for Ginny Fox. We had hoped that the killer had taken the Barnsley's WalkAN, and we found it lying in the bottom of the bag and so it tied everything up really nicely."

Mountie turned around to Charlton.

Everybody was now at fever pitch wanting to know who the killer was.

Mountie took a sip of water again and a deep breath.

"The evidence we accumulated pointed to the person we saw leaving the hut. We knew the killer had to have a tablet and liked Slipknot. They knew they were always going to be free on a Sunday night to pick up their weekly spirits delivery. They also knew they would be in deep trouble if Barnsley broadcasted it to everyone who he had caught trying to steal alcohol from the café. Not only would he have been in major trouble with Oscar but more importantly he would have brought shame on his religious teetotal parents who had previously done such sterling work in advising us all of the dangers of alcohol."

Mountie looked up to where Carl was sitting.

He had made a point of locating him when he saw him arriving earlier.

There was a loud gasp from everyone in the audience and they all turned to look at Carl.

He was shaking nervously in his chair and trying to hide his face.

Mountie returned to his seat.

Charlton gave him a pat on the back and whispered, "Well done mate."

Oscar walked to the front of the stage and bellowed.

"Carl, come down here this instant!"

WAARTER CATASTROPHE

Carl got up looking very shaken and nervous.

He ignored his parents as started moving down to the stage and finally arrived and stood in front of Oscar on stage.

"You need to explain yourself lad to all of us here."

Carl was now sobbing loudly.

"Oscar I'm so sorry that I killed Barnsley."

"Go on."

"It all started with visitors leaving bottles and cans of alcohol around the zoo and I unfortunately got a taste for it. I knew I had to hide my drinking from my parents and the rest of the animals here."

Carl looked up to his parents with tears in his eyes.

"The zoo was shut in February for repairs and so no visitors. I needed to find a way to get some alcohol and then the fictitious TESCOW accounts news came out. I had already started using the rowing club to escape and have some time by myself and a drink. I decided to do a trial drinks order with TESCOW using the name Ginny Fox and to my surprise it worked, and my order arrived with no one knowing that it was me that had ordered it. I have since then been putting in a regular order for Sunday nights for when my parents go to church. Each week like clockwork the alcohol arrives just as I had ordered it."

Carl paused and started to stare at the floor.

"It was all going well until Declan got ill and my

delivery didn't arrive. I dashed to the café and saw the TESCOW email and knew I couldn't wait till Tuesday."

Carl paused again.

"I saw lights on in the café and no one appeared to be inside. I then heard some loud music in the distance and remembered the fashion show was on. I walked in and was pleased to find it was empty. Fortunately, Aussie had talked my parents into letting me use the café and as such I knew where all the alcohol was in case an emergency ever arose such as this. I went to the bar and was stunned to see all the empty spirit bottles. I then noticed a cupboard with a chain on the door that I hadn't seen before. I was trying so hard to get into the cupboard that I didn't see Barnsley return. When I finally saw him and a WAAR poster I then knew why all the spirit bottles were empty and everything had been locked in the cupboard." said Carl with his head bowed.

"He said he could smell the whisky I had been drinking and he had seen me trying to break into the locked cupboard where all the alcohol was being held. He then said he smelt alcohol on me during his visit to my parents. He then joked that an alcoholic can always spot another one. He smiled and said he was off to tell Oscar and my parents about finding me drunk and trying to steal Aussie's booze. I was so mad I picked up the nearest object which was the water bottle and bashed him over the head with it. Although he was still semi-conscious, he was somehow still laughing at me. I was so angry and upset that I choked him with the bottle to shut him up for good."

This confession was met by a loud gasp from the audience.

"I grabbed his WalkAN as I needed one and thought I would make use it at the rowing club. I then dashed to the club and stashed it there. I then returned home via one of the gates I had tampered with, it's amazing what you can find on the internet these days." said Carl with his head held in shame.

Suddenly there was a loud sobbing noise from the audience, and everybody looked and saw that it had come from Elspeth.

Joel had a glazed expression on his face and couldn't believe what he was hearing.

He then started to comfort Elspeth who in a state of shock.

Carl was looking down at his feet.

"I am truly sorry for what I did in the heat of a moment. Oscar I am begging you for your forgiveness. I know I should have confessed at the time but I didn't want to have to put any strain or shame on my family."

Poppy was in floods of tears.

Oscar stood there for a minute standing rigid and shaking his head.

Carl just stood there head down tears falling

from his eyes and shaking as he didn't know what was going to happen to him next.

Oscar then walked to the lectern and tapped the microphone to get everyone's attention. "Poppy and I would like to extend our thanks to Mountie and Charlton for their speedy investigation and the uncovering of my son's killer. True to form the Mountie has once again got his man or animal in this case. In doing so we all owe them both our utmost gratitude in ensuring that we will all now sleep a lot safer in our beds tonight. Even more so once Lemming has sorted out all the gates later."

Oscar turned and started to give Mountie and Charlton a standing ovation.

Poppy and everyone else stood up and started clapping as well.

Then everyone else stood up and started clapping as well.

All the animals started hugging each other and some were in tears.

Even Sarah, Nikki and Emma stood up, but this was only because Nikki had said that the clapping must mean that the fashion show was starting. They had been getting bored with the all the "pre fashion show announcements" as Sarah had called them.

Charlton and Mountie hugged each other and then suddenly stopped as they heard a familiar sound and saw the singing dragonfly heading towards them.

He then landed on Mountie's head.
They both laughed out loud as he was singing Tina Turner's "Simply the Best" song.

CHAPTER 42 - SATURDAY
13 AUGUST (AM)

At 6.05AM on Channel Roar News across the screen came a message. saying "BREAKING NEWS, BEAKING NEWS BREAKING NEWS"

This disappeared and the camera moved to the face of a smiling Ariana.

"Breaking news this morning"

She was standing away from her desk and looking straight into the camera.

She was dressed in a bright red Zebra Rhodes trouser suit.

"Last night at Hearts River Zoo the animal that killed Barnsley at his WAAR launch venture was finally revealed. Let's go to Trevor McDromadary outside the zoo."

The screen changed to show Trevor McDromadary standing outside the entrance sign to Hearts River Zoo

He was a large camel with silver rimmed glasses, silvery hair, and a long dark green trench coat. It was raining and he was looking very wet.

Above the zoo sign viewers could see the heads of Miss Amber and Miss Michelle.

They had both got up early and made themselves look pretty so as to get their faces seen on television, despite the bad weather.

The dragonfly had made a brief appearance singing Nickelback's "Rockstar" song until he spotted a very hungry looking armadillo manning the television camera.

"Trevor this is marvelous news please tell us what has happened" said Ariana brushing her hair back from her face.

"Well Ariana, As you know Mountie and Charlton who live here offered to find out who killed Barnsley, the son of the famous lion couple Oscar and Poppy."

Pictures of Mountie and Charlton then appeared on the screen.

Only Charlton saw this as the rest of the zebras were all still asleep.

"As we reported previously Barnsley was murdered at the launch of his new WAAR venture that was going to help wild animals with alcohol problems."

Trevor paused to wipe some rain off his glasses.

"They have now finished their investigation and last night they announced that a young rhinoceros called Carl was guilty of the murder."

Trevor briefly wiped more water off his glasses.

"That is really good news" purred Ariana as the camera zoomed in on her smiling.

"So, what happened then?"

"Carl confessed to the murder. Ironically, he had an alcoholic drinks problem that WAAR would have been able to have helped him with. He apologised to Oscar and Poppy and asked for their forgiveness."

"So, what is going to happen to Carl now?"

"Well Ariana, late last night Carl was loaded into a zoo van and is now residing at Coventry Zoo awaiting his fate. I can report that no one was here to wave him off. His parents are still too shocked by the revelations to speak to anyone."

Trevor removed his glasses as he couldn't see anything out of them because of the rain.

"Oscar praised Mountie and Charlton for their thorough investigation and hard work in quickly finding his son's killer."

The television screen panned back to the studio and where Ariana who was now perched on the end of the news desk.

"Thank you, Trevor. Good to hear that as usual a Mountie got his man or in this case animal. Now we will move onto some financial news...... "

Printed in Great Britain
by Amazon